D0961867

ENGLISH

ENGLISH

WANG GANG

TRANSLATED FROM THE CHINESE BY

MARTIN MERZ AND

JANE WEIZHEN PAN

VIKING

VIKING
Published by the Penguin Group
Penguin Group (USA) Inc., 375 Hudson Street, New York, New York 10014, U.S.A.
Penguin Group (Canada), 90 Eglinton Avenue East, Suite 700, Toronto, Ontario,
Canada M4P 2Y3 (a division of Pearson Penguin Canada Inc.)
Penguin Books Ltd, 80 Strand, London WC2R 0RL, England
Penguin Ireland, 25 St. Stephen's Green, Dublin 2, Ireland (a division of Penguin Books Ltd)
Penguin Books Australia Ltd, 250 Camberwell Road, Camberwell, Victoria 3124, Australia
(a division of Pearson Australia Group Pty Ltd)
Penguin Books India Pvt Ltd, 11 Community Centre, Panchsheel Park,
New Delhi – 110 017, India
Penguin Group (NZ), 67 Apollo Drive, Rosedale, North Shore 0632, New Zealand
(a division of Pearson New Zealand Ltd)
Penguin Books (South Africa) (Pty) Ltd, 24 Sturdee Avenue, Rosebank,
Johannesburg 2196, South Africa

Penguin Books Ltd, Registered Offices: 80 Strand, London WC2R 0RL, England

First published in 2009 by Viking Penguin, a member of Penguin Group (USA) Inc.

10 9 8 7 6 5 4 3 2 1

Originally published in Chinese as *Ying Ge Li Shi* by People's Literature Publishing House, Beijing.

Grateful acknowledgment is made for permission to reprint excerpts from the following copyrighted works:
"The End of the World" by Arthur Kent and Sylvia Dee. Copyright © 1962 (renewed) by Music Sales Corporation (ASCAP) and Edward Proffitt Music. International copyright secured. All rights reserved. Reprinted by permission.
"Moon River," music by Henry Mancini, lyrics by Johnny Mercer. © 1961 Sony/ATV Music Publishing LLC. All rights administered by Sony/ATV Music Publishing LLC, 8 Music Square West, Nashville, Tenn. All rights reserved. Used by permission.

ISBN 978-0-670-02059-1

Printed in the United States of America

ENGLISH

ONE

I

Around May of that year, the city of Ürümchi was bathing happily in the sunlight cascading down from the Tianshan Mountains. Like a fluttering snowflake, I drifted into the classroom, then sat down and stared out at the snow and the sun. Ürümchi's often like that: Sunlight mingled with snowflakes splashes right onto your face. This was springtime in Ürümchi, when you know-it-alls from the other side of the pass have already begun to tire of looking at your peach blossoms and your open fields.

No one called out for us to stand when Ahjitai walked in. The classroom was like the wilds by a river, and we were buzzing little insects. Ahjitai walked forward a few steps. Garbage Li cried out, and our eyes all turned toward our teacher.

We hadn't expected Ahjitai would actually come.

I had put her chances at less than 50 percent.

Ahjitai stood on the podium, tears running down her face as she got ready to speak.

You should have figured out already that all the boys were sad that day because Ahjitai was leaving. She was beautiful, her skin snowy white—she was a "double turner." I should explain: "Double turner" is a term from Ürümchi that means the mother is Uyghur and the father Han Chinese, or the other way around.

We had stopped learning Russian the year before, and from that day we would not be learning Uyghur. We weren't really interested in languages. We were interested only in women like Ahjitai. She might have been a teacher, but the curve of her neck and her tears were things I yearned for at dawn much more than the sun.

Ahjitai was leaving. Can you imagine what that meant to us?

She scanned the classroom. At that moment all the boys held their breath as if awaiting a verdict. There had recently been rumors about Ahjitai. Someone even said she had boarded a truck and, sitting up front next to the driver, gone to Kashgar, where her mother is from. But rumors are just that. Here she was, standing on the podium, so Garbage Li was right—she would still teach the last class.

Ahjitai turned. Chalk in hand, she wrote five words on the blackboard: The Sayings of Chairman Mao.

She'd hardly finished writing when she turned to us and said, "I don't want to go. I don't want to leave you."

The boys whooped and began to fly about like sparrows. Ahjitai smiled. Whose smile could match hers? Whose lips could compare with hers? Suddenly Garbage Li cried out, "Long live Chairman Mao!"

The whole class laughed—even the girls. Then everybody shouted: "Long live, long live Chairman Mao!"

Ahjitai waited for the clamor to subside, then asked, "You really want to learn Uyghur that much? You want me to stay?"

The classroom fell silent. The boys were not interested in any language—not even Chinese, let alone Uyghur—and the girls had hankered for English classes for a long time. Like the first spring rains, English would soon drift over the Tianshan Mountains and fall on the riverbanks of Ürümchi and the swamps of the Seventeen Lakes beside the school.

Ahjitai suddenly locked her eyes on mine: "Love Liu, you're daydreaming. What are you thinking about?"

My face turned red. The whole class was looking at me. I stood up. This was the first time Ahjitai had questioned me like that.

"Nothing," I stammered.

She smiled and asked me to sit down.

I hesitated, then said, "Miss Ah, you—"

"I've told you many times," she interrupted, "don't call me Miss Ah. Call me Miss Ahjitai, and from now on just call me Ahjitai. Anyway, I'm not going to be a teacher anymore."

"You're not leaving, are you?" I asked.

"I am leaving," she said. "I'm going to work in commerce."

I sat down wondering what "work in commerce" meant. Did it mean she would work in a shop? Which one?

"I want to learn English with you," Ahjitai said. "I saw your English teacher yesterday. His name is Second Prize Wang."

The boys groaned.

Ahjitai smiled. "All right," she said, "class dismissed."

Our eyes followed her as she walked out. Again I stared at her fair hair as it swayed like lake grass.

It was quiet, very quiet. No one said a word.

Russian was gone. Uyghur was gone. English was coming.

II

Growing up, I would often stare blankly at the snowy peaks and the sky, wondering why we couldn't choose where to be born. Why was I born in Ürümchi, a place where snow still falls in May and even June, and then turns the ground into a muddy quagmire? In spring, everything is waterlogged from the melted snows. I would walk along roads glittering with reflected sunlight, and silvery objects would wink at me in the distance. On days when classes were canceled, I would look toward the horizon to see what was out there shimmering like water. I went once to Yamalike Hill, but there was only dirt and sand. I also went to the East Hill Graveyard, where people were often executed by firing squad.

Ever since I was a child I have felt Ürümchi to be a lonely place. Or maybe I was just lonely there.

When I was four I went to Nanking with my parents. The journey was long; I thought we'd never make it. When at last I saw before me this huge city, I felt giddy at the sight of the tall buildings and the crowds.

Mother said, "This is where Daddy and Mommy grew up and went to school. Look, these are plane trees from France."

It was the first time I had heard the word *France.*

"Where is France?"

"Where? In Europe."

"Where is Europe?"

"Across the sea."

"Where is the sea?"

"There are many seas."

"Then why haven't I seen one?"

"There are no seas in Xinjiang."

"Why are there no seas in Xinjiang?"

"There was a sea at one time, but it dried up."

"Why did you have me in a place where even the sea dried up?"

Hearing me fire off questions like this, Father took over: "There are no seas in Xinjiang, but we have the Tianshan Mountains."

Mother added, "Every spring, the snow on the Tianshan Mountains melts, and the water flows into the Ürümchi River. . . ."

"Why did you have me in Ürümchi? I don't want to be from there. I want to be from here."

What I really wanted to say that day on the streets of Nanking was this: "I want you to have me here. I want to be born in Nanking."

My parents looked at each other for a moment, slightly embarrassed. They were smiling. Love was in their smile.

Mother said, "Do you know why we gave you the name Love Liu?"

I didn't want to listen. Mother had told me before. "I'm dizzy," I said.

I immediately switched my mind to something else. Ever since I was a child, I could quickly divert my thoughts when I didn't want to hear something, directing them to the sky, the mountains, or the sea that I had not yet seen.

Really, there is nothing as tragic as being forced to be born somewhere, because once you come out, everything is already decided, and nothing can be changed.

Growing up in a bleak backwater, drinking water from the melted snows of the Tianshan Mountains, you discover that people from Nanking see you as different—your skin is rougher, your accent makes people laugh. And even when you tell them Ürümchi is a city, they still ask, "You ride horses to school, don't you?"

I was forced to be born in Ürümchi, but what about my parents? Were they forced to live there? And why did they give me an awful name like Love Liu? Love represents compassion, nobility. Doesn't that sound pretentious? Love Liu, Love Liu. It really is a pretentious name.

That day in Nanking, the air felt like it was on fire. After I put the last piece of duck in my mouth, Father took Mother and me to buy a phonograph. Carrying the phonograph out of the store, Father walked in front with Mother, and I followed. We walked along a path lined with plane trees. After turning a corner, we entered a small wooden building. Father knocked on the door of an old classmate's home, and we were let in. Father and his classmate sat for a while, contemplating each other. "Returning to Xinjiang tomorrow," Father finally said to his classmate. "Don't know when we'll be back again."

His classmate's eyes misted up. "Yesterday," he said, "I looked again at that photograph you sent me."

Father smiled modestly.

"I want to see the photograph," I demanded.

The classmate took it out of a drawer, passed it to me, and said, "Love Liu, you're going to be like your father."

The photograph was of a building, which I immediately recognized as the Nationalities Theater. I had been there to watch movies and Uyghur song-and-dance performances. Uyghurs play the dap drum, and their voices are more vibrant than those of Han Chinese. Did they ever wonder, as I did, why they were born in this place without seas?

In the graying photo I saw a dome and white columns. Father was an architect, and this was his work.

Father took the photograph from me. Looking at it with pride, he said, "I brought you another photograph today, a picture of our family taken in front of the Nationalities Theater."

Mother took out the photograph and passed it to the classmate. The three of us were at the entrance to the theater. Father was holding me, Mother's arm in his. Father's glasses were crooked. It was probably my fault.

The classmate examined the photograph and said, "Love Liu looks just like you."

"Never mind the people," Father replied. "Just look at the building."

The classmate retrieved a phonograph record from a cabinet. "This is for you," he said to my father. They uncovered the phonograph and put on the record. The music started.

I asked Mother, "Why can't I hear the Uyghur dap drum?"

"It's a violin and a piano," she said, "not a dap drum and a rawap."

"I don't like how it sounds," I declared.

What I really meant was that it sounded strange to me. It was a sound that didn't exist in Ürümchi, where I heard mostly Uyghurs playing dap drums and plucking rawaps. When I was small there was a popular song called "My Rawap." It's beautiful—I can assure you it's the most beautiful music in the world. It conveys the vast desolation of Xinjiang. But my parents wanted me to listen to this stuff—a violin, they said. Father's classmate kept on telling Father that the composer's name was Glazunov.

I listened for a short time, then fell asleep. I know I had a dream, and that parts of my dream were imagined, like Nanking and Glazunov, and parts were real, like Ürümchi and "My Rawap."

III

One sunny day that crisp cold May, I walked along a muddy road, lunch box in hand, to take food to my father. That morning he'd mentioned he wouldn't be home for lunch because he had to finish a painting.

A wall had been put up right in front of the theater. Father was standing on some scaffolding. He had just finished painting someone's head and was now painting the shoulders. Everyone was skinny in those days, except this guy. It was Chairman Mao.

I walked up and said, "Dad, time for lunch."

He ignored me, focusing on the portrait.

"Dad, lunch," I persisted.

Without turning around he asked, "Does it look like him?"

I glanced at the painting. "One ear is missing," I commented.

"What do you know?" Father snapped. "This is according to the laws of perspective."

"One ear *is* missing," I insisted.

Father became annoyed and stopped painting. He adjusted his glasses and started to climb down from the scaffolding as nimbly as a monkey at West Zoo. After a few swings between the steel pipes and the wooden boards, he jumped to the ground.

I saw sweat on his forehead. "Painting is hard work, right?" I asked.

"That depends on the subject," he replied.

"Look," I said, "can't you tell an ear is missing?"

"If you have the chance, you should also become an architect when you grow up. The basics of drawing . . ." As he spoke, he took a huge bite out of a maize cake and bit down on his finger. He checked his finger and saw only teeth marks; the skin wasn't broken. He grinned. "I'm just a glutton," he said. "It's been a while now. I haven't eaten meat since the Spring Festival. The taste of pigs' feet is a distant memory for me."

Father began to grind the maize cake with his teeth. The sound reminded me of a cement mixer. I stared at the portrait, engrossed by its missing ear.

Father probably noticed my fixation. "Let me explain the laws of perspective," he lectured. "Look at me. If I stand at this angle, you can see only half of my face, one ear, and the outline of my nose and lips, right? What if I turn a little?" While speaking, he put the last piece of the maize cake into his mouth and turned a bit.

"I can see that ear," I said cheerfully.

He was visibly irritated. "Can you?" he demanded. "You can't. You can see only my head and my face. If you really want to see my ears, I have to be like this." Just as he was about to turn again, he tensed up.

Two men approached from a nearby building, one tall and the other wearing glasses. The one wearing glasses was Director Fan.

Father looked nervous. "Go home now," he ordered. "Tell your mother I'll be back early today if I can finish."

"I don't have classes this afternoon," I responded. "I can watch you paint."

"Go home," Father insisted.

I did not move. I could see helplessness and even fear in Father's eyes. My presence was clearly making him more nervous. Looking at him, I started to hesitate, thinking I would leave if he asked me again. But it was too late. The men were standing right in front of us.

The tall man looked at the portrait and said, "Exactly the same, really. It looks exactly like the one I saw at Tiananmen Square." Suddenly he paused. "Why is there a left ear but no right ear?" he asked.

I was secretly pleased with myself—Father was wrong for sure. I was the first one who'd noticed. He just wouldn't admit it.

Father looked at the portrait and began to explain. "Director Fan, Commander Shen, this is according to the laws of perspective. Think about—"

"What damn laws!" Commander Shen snarled. He glared at Father. "Hurry up! Put the ear back."

Father didn't move. A huge smile appeared on his face. "It won't work if I add another ear," he insisted through his smile.

The tall man came up and grabbed Father's hand. Then he changed his mind and tweaked Father's ear. He tugged gently at first, then pulled roughly when he felt Father was not cooperating. "Now! Get up there and put the ear back."

Director Fan, the one wearing glasses, was smiling all the while. "He wants you to put it back. Just do it," he chimed in.

Father still hesitated. He turned to Director Fan, pleading with his eyes. He knew Director Fan was an educated man who understood more than just the laws of perspective.

I wanted to laugh with them, but when I saw the man pulling my father's ear like that, I couldn't. I wanted to tell them to let go of my father's ear, but I didn't dare speak. Somehow my ear hurt a bit, too.

Father nimbly climbed back up on the scaffolding. Looking up, I saw his hair quiver, his glasses glinting in the sunlight. He took up his brush and added an ear to the right side of the face. We were all stunned—the image looked weird. It did not resemble a normal person's head.

"You're messing around," the tall man rebuked. "You've painted the ear too big."

Father rubbed out the ear and painted it smaller. Chairman Mao's image looked even funnier.

"It won't work," Father pleaded again.

The tall man yelled, "You come down, then."

Director Fan joined in. "Hurry up."

Father climbed down and looked at the portrait with them. All of a sudden Director Fan slapped Father in the face. Father almost fell to the ground. "I know what's on your mind," Director Fan barked. Then he turned to the tall man for approval.

"Brush it all off. Start again!" Commander Shen ordered.

As they were about to leave, I jumped forward and grabbed Director Fan's leg. "Why did you hit my father?" I cried out.

Director Fan smiled. "You are still a child," he said. "You will have to make a clean break from him when you're a bit older."

I clung to his leg.

"Pull your son off, will you!" he yelled at Father.

"Come here!" Father shouted at me. "Let go of uncle."

I held on. Father came over to pry my hands away, but I still would not let go. He then kicked me hard on my butt. It hurt a lot, and I finally let go of Director Fan's leg.

The men left. Director Fan continued talking to Commander Shen as they walked away.

Father waited until they were gone, then asked, "Did that hurt?"

I shook my head.

Father sighed. "I'll start all over again in the afternoon. I'll paint a full frontal this time, so there will be two ears."

"He hit you. Why didn't you hit him back?"

"He's tall—I can't take him." Seeing my face contorted with rage, Father gently patted my head.

I looked at the ear Commander Shen had pulled. "Then why did you hit me?" I asked.

Father smiled. "Silly boy, who else could I hit?"

His words are burned into my memory. It is said there is always something that can make you cry. Let me say it again: There is always something that can make you cry—and it is seeing your father get beat up.

IV

I couldn't sleep that night. The smile on Father's face after he was slapped whipped about in my mind like washing left out on the line in a storm. Later, I heard Father weeping in another room. It was spooky, like the sound of wind howling through Wulabo Gorge.

I quietly got up, went to my parents' bedroom door, pushed it open a crack, and peeked in.

Father was indeed crying. He said to Mother, "They actually hit me. The left side of my face still hurts. They don't understand, they just don't understand. And there is no way you can explain anything to them."

Mother stroked his face and asked, "Is this where it hurts?"

"I really didn't expect it. They didn't criticize me or hit me during the struggle session last year. Why today?"

Mother tried to comfort him. "Maybe they were in a bad mood today," she said.

"Do I have more white hairs?" Father asked.

Mother smiled. "Come to me." Father then meekly lowered his head onto her belly and let her pluck his white hairs. Mother searched meticulously, pulling them out one by one. Father was at ease, like a dog enjoying his master's every stroke. He moaned after each hair was plucked and then moved his head closer to Mother.

Mother was also relaxed. "It's spring again." She sighed. "Another year has passed."

"Who needs a spring like this?" Father said.

Mother was tiring of plucking Father's white hairs. "Are you feeling better now?"

"Guess who killed Bai Wen?" Father asked.

Mother paused. "He killed himself," she said.

"No, his wife killed him."

Mother seemed puzzled.

Father continued: "He would not have died if his wife had been like you. Men who commit suicide are really killed by their wives."

"Last night I actually dreamed about that phonograph record he gave us," she said.

"Let's listen to some music," Father said.

"No," Mother countered, "we're lucky we haven't been kicked out of this apartment and sent packing to Iron Gate Pass, or even Karasahr. And you want to risk listening to that stuff?"

"I'll keep the volume down."

"I just said no," Mother protested.

Father ignored her. He gingerly retrieved the phonograph and the record from under the bed. "When I was studying in Moscow," he said, "I heard this Glazunov piece performed at a concert."

As the music started, Mother urged him to turn down the volume.

I listened to the music, and through the crack in the doorway I watched Father embrace Mother and take off her clothes.

"Is Love Liu asleep?" Mother asked.

Father didn't say anything. He just switched off the light.

In the dark, Mother's moaning blended with the sound of the violin. Glazunov was the first composer I had heard of, and I'll forever associate his ethereal music with my parents' forlorn love-making.

TWO

I

Our yellow school building, with its three-gabled roof, was also my father's work. I still have the colored architectural drawings he made of it all those years ago. The steep, Russian-style roof was covered in a green metal, making the building look like a man wearing a yellow overcoat and a green hat. In Chinese, "wearing a green hat" means to be cuckolded, and our school stood there proudly, seemingly unaware that its wife was sleeping with someone else, as the sound of our songs and laughter—and, of course, of students reciting—reverberated out of the windows where its eyes would be.

When luck was with him, Father exuded self-satisfaction. He was unable to restrain himself from boasting about his achievements. To a student of his named Song Yue, he said, "I have built myself a monument, and weeds will never grow on the path to it."

Song Yue always gaped, nodding incessantly in agreement. I often wondered how Mao Ze-dong possibly could have started the cult of the individual. Clearly my father had started it. He said the Nationalities Theater and the steeply gabled People's Liberation Army Memorial Day Middle School were his masterpieces. They would long outlive him. In Ürümchi, immortal architecture was not limited to Russian churches. There were also my father's theater and the school.

But when Father was boasting, he never realized that, even in those years when luck was on his side, some of his students did not like his aesthetic. Walk through the front door of a building with such an old-fashioned exterior, they said, and you find yourself on one end of a long corridor. If the doors at each end were closed, the narrow corridor would be as dark as a tomb, so lighting was a must, even in daytime. If you walked in from the sunlight, you felt dizzy, and the gloomy light made it difficult to breathe.

II

One day I was walking down just such a corridor, counting the lightbulbs above my head. I passed the men's and women's bathrooms, then went upstairs and walked toward the darkness. From one direction came the smell of cold cream, which I thought very strange. The corridors my father designed always smelled moldy because the floorboards—made of pine from deep in the Tianshan Mountains—had begun to rot. Where could this unfamiliar scent be coming from? Excitedly, I opened my mouth wide to suck in as much air as possible. A side door suddenly opened. Bright sunlight shot out at me from the room. A well-dressed man emerged. His shiny hair and the intense light behind him dazzled me. The door closed, and the lightbulbs lit the gloom enough for me to see his features. He was a tall man, clean-shaven, and he walked in a self-assured manner. Under his arm he carried a thick dictionary and the English textbook we had just been issued.

Come to think of it, that was the first time I saw the dictionary—the English dictionary. It was very thick, with a stiff blue cover. The man held it tightly under his arm, and it looked completely different from the ubiquitous *Sayings of Chairman Mao*. There was lots of red in those days, and a little black, but navy blue was rare. Years later I would realize this was the only English dictionary in the Ürümchi of my childhood.

Clearly this man was our English teacher—Second Prize Wang. His presence was a mystery because a school like ours had never before had English classes. We had lots of Uyghurs, and so we learned Uyghur. We lived in the closest place to the Soviet Union, so we learned Russian. But what use would English be? England and America were much too far away. So who would have decided out of the blue, in that era when even temples were being destroyed, to let us learn English? I still can't identify that great person, even though I've been through all the archives in the Capital Library.

Second Prize Wang's arrival caused great anticipation among the girls, and they began flipping through the red English textbook at least two days beforehand. The male teacher who knew English would replace Ahjitai on the podium, and his eyes would linger on them.

Second Prize Wang would not disappoint the girls. He had a noble manner. When he walked up to me, I should have given way, but I was nervous and momentarily did not know which way to step. So when he went to the left, I went left, and when he went right, so did I. Despite this, he never looked down—he just looked straight ahead. I was so embarrassed I almost laughed out loud. Finally I stood off to one side and let him pass, not daring to look at his face. And then I felt the urge to pee.

Maybe he glanced at me, or maybe not. He walked away in his self-assured manner without looking back.

I turned around and went into the bathroom, thinking: This Second Prize Wang is quite strange. I've never seen a man like him before.

Suddenly I heard footsteps and knew that Second Prize Wang was coming back to use the bathroom. He didn't seem to notice me when he walked in. He just stood at the urinal and flopped out his thing.

I couldn't help peering over. I cringed in shock—it was enormous. I'd never seen such a big one. When I was small I went with Father to the bathhouse, and I saw that every man had one. This world is amazing, I thought. The image of those comfortably warmed symbols of manhood flopping about in the misty bathhouse became deeply ingrained in my memory.

I didn't dare take another peek but was too nervous to pee until after he had finished. He began to wash his hands. I kept facing the wall.

"What's your name?" he suddenly asked.

I froze. Nervously turning around, I found he was looking at me.

"Love Liu," I replied.

He was a little taken aback. "Love Liu?" he asked. "Which 'love'?"

" 'Love,' as in 'I love Tiananmen Square,' " I explained.

He smiled to himself as he slowly walked out of the bathroom.

Finally I could relax.

His footsteps faded into the distance. A refined man like him needed to pee just like I did, and his thing was enormous. It was unbelievable, I thought.

I burst out laughing. I laughed uncontrollably as I peed. The more I thought about it, the harder I laughed, until my shoulders heaved.

Then all of a sudden someone rushed up from behind and gave me a hard kick in the backside, almost propelling me into the urinal. I turned to see Garbage Li.

"What are you laughing at?" He smirked.

His kick had hurt. I was angry and couldn't say anything.

I had a pact with Garbage Li, a common pact among boys in Ürümchi. The rule was that from the time we entered the school gate, and even on the playground, we had to pat our own behinds. If we didn't and it was spotted by the other party to the pact, he could kick as hard as he liked. Even if the pain was enough to make you pass out, it was your own fault.

I grimaced in agony. "Fuck! Do you have to kick so hard?"

"What were you laughing at?" he asked. "Your shoulders were shaking."

I began to laugh again. "The English teacher's thing is this long," I said, indicating the size with my hands. "I saw it."

"Liar," said Garbage Li, wide-eyed.

"If you don't believe me, follow him to the bathroom sometime and see for yourself. It's incredible." As I spoke, I kept a close eye on Garbage Li, hoping that while speaking to me or peeing he would forget about the pact and I'd get a chance to kick him back. But he used his left hand to pat his behind while he urinated, and I never got a chance.

"You're lying," he said. "Only a donkey's is that long."

"He has a scent, too," I continued, "of cold cream."

"I was going to say," Garbage Li responded, "the bathroom smells like face cream. It smells good."

III

Our principal stood on the podium, looking serious as usual. He explained he was substituting for our class teacher, Guo Pei-qing, because Guo's mother had just died. He asked who the monitor for the Chinese class was.

Sunrise Huang, the girl sitting next to me, stood up.

The principal asked, "Where are you up to in your Chinese class?"

"'In Memory of Norman Bethune,'" she answered. "We've already had five lessons on it."

The principal then wrote the three characters of Bethune's Chinese name—Bai Qiu En—on the blackboard and said to her, "Then you lead the class in reading it aloud."

"Bai, Bai, as in Bethune's Bai," Sunrise Huang recited loudly.

We followed her: "Bai, Bai, as in Bethune's Bai."

"Qiu, Qiu, as in Bethune's Qiu," Sunrise Huang continued.

"Qiu, Qiu, as in Bethune's Qiu," we repeated.

For some reason a grin flashed on the principal's face. But then he squelched it.

By the second round of recitation, Garbage Li burst out laughing—he realized that "Qiu" sounded the same as the word for ball in Chinese. "Qiu, Qiu, as in Bethune's balls," he chanted in an extra-loud voice.

The whole class guffawed.

The principal also laughed. It was the only time I can remember seeing such a relaxed look on his face.

Sunrise Huang's face went red. She cried out, "I don't want to be the monitor for the Chinese class anymore!"

IV

Long Live Chairman Mao.

Lonely-wolf-chai-mun-mao, I recited, using Chinese words as mnemonic devices.

Long Live Chairman Mao.

Lonely-wolf-chai-mun-mao.

I stood in front of my desk, earnestly reciting the phrase. I knew that my road to learning English started here, just as the sun rose in the east and illuminated the Tianshan Mountains.

Second Prize Wang said, "Your pronunciation is wrong. It should be 'Long Live Chairman Mao.' "

I tried to repeat it but still didn't get it right. I was nervous.

The whole class laughed.

Second Prize Wang asked me to sit down. He then led the class in a chant. We repeated after him with gusto.

For the phrase "Long Live Chairman Mao," English is just so different from Uyghur, and it is also very different from Russian. The girls went crazy over it. I had never seen them so excited about a language.

Second Prize Wang wore a dark gray tunic, similar to Mao's but with only one breast pocket. A silver pen was clipped to it. His collar was higher than usual, making his neck look long. He was holding the textbook with his left hand, and his right arm hung at his side. He read out English words and walked up and down the aisles between the desks. His refined posture met our expectations—English simply had to come from a man like him. The scent of cold cream was with him wherever he went. When he walked past me, I could sense a minty coolness from his breath.

Suddenly he stopped. He picked up my textbook and had a look. With a slightly supercilious smile he said, "Love Liu, read it again."

I stood up again, feeling ashamed.

"I can't do it," I confessed.

He gaped at me and said, "If you can't do it, you should try harder. Pronunciation is the foundation."

I didn't know what to do. My face turned red.

Apparently without sympathy he went on: "Don't transliterate English into Chinese characters anymore. We Shanghainese call that pidgin English. Other people won't understand you."

When he said "other people," he meant, of course, the British and the Americans.

The class went silent. All the girls were gazing at him.

Second Prize Wang glanced at Garbage Li sitting to my right and said, "The male student sitting to the right of Love Liu, stand up and read aloud."

Garbage Li's face went red. He slowly stood up and whispered to me, "Whoever sits next to you is jinxed."

Second Prize Wang asked, "What did you just say?"

"What?" Garbage Li asked back.

We laughed.

Second Prize Wang didn't get angry. He smiled and said, "You read it."

"Read what?" Garbage Li asked.

We laughed again.

"Read the text," said Second Prize Wang.

"I don't know how."

We didn't laugh this time. We were a bit tense and looked at Second Prize Wang, who didn't seem to notice Garbage Li's challenge. He just said: "Please sit down. Let's find someone who does know how to read it."

His eyes scanned the faces of the girls and settled on Sunrise Huang, who was sitting next to me. He had found his favorite. She was skinny and had a pale face. Second Prize Wang went to her desk and examined her textbook. It was then that he realized she was the only one in the class who did not use Chinese characters as phonetic symbols.

A smile appeared on his face. He returned to the podium and said, "The female student sitting next to Love Liu, stand up and read aloud."

Sunrise Huang's pale face turned red. She stood up and read the text in a loud voice.

The English teacher became excited. "Good," he said in English.

Girls are smart. Without exception, they can always tell what's happening around them, even when they're young.

Sunrise Huang blushed and looked up at the teacher. She then quickly lowered her head.

Second Prize Wang didn't say anything more. He had surely decided on his class monitor.

On the blackboard he wrote four large characters: The International Phonetic Alphabet. "In a month's time," he said, "you will start to learn the International Phonetic Alphabet."

We gawked at the four characters.

"Once you have learned these symbols," he explained, "you will be able to recite the most difficult English words by yourselves."

The whole class stirred with excitement. Those four characters filled us with hope. We felt we could ride away on the winds of the Gobi, fly over the Tarim Desert and the Erchis River by the Altay Mountains, go all the way to Britain, and finally land in the United States.

After the class was dismissed, I followed the teacher outside the classroom and tapped his arm to get his attention. "Sir, please don't ask me to stand up and read things aloud all the time," I implored. "There are so many of us in the class. Don't just pick me."

He smiled and said, "But in your class, I know only your name at the moment."

"You should get to know other people's names," I protested. "Don't keep calling for the student on Love Liu's left, or Love Liu's right, or sitting behind him—they're gonna hate me."

"Hate? Really?" He smiled. "Don't just think about hate. Remember, your name is Love, the opposite of hate."

Many years have passed, and I've forgotten most of the English words, but not these two: love and hate.

V

The second English class began like this.

Sunrise Huang didn't come into the classroom until after the bell had rung. She carried a small, flimsy-looking phonograph. After placing it on the table at the front, she returned to her desk. She appeared excited.

Second Prize Wang then rushed in and announced, *"Lights-bee-gun."*

Sunrise Huang loudly called out in English, "Arise."

We all stood up.

I still had to use Chinese characters to get the pronunciation of that stuff. Otherwise I wouldn't remember.

In class I could feel that Sunrise Huang sometimes stared at the English teacher, as if fantasizing about something.

Second Prize Wang breezily led our recitations.

When he sounded the letter *b* a second time, Garbage Li burst out laughing. He'd been restraining himself for quite a few days. He wanted to use the sound of that letter to make everybody laugh by reminding us that, in Chinese slang, it means that thing on women's bodies.

But no one laughed.

We had not yet lost our enthusiasm for English—none of us, that is, except Garbage Li. He had never liked any language—not Uyghur, not Russian, not English, not even the local dialect of Chinese we spoke in Ürümchi.

During the break, Sunrise Huang let me look at her English book. She really did use the phonetic symbols.

"You know them all?" I asked.

"I stayed up all night and memorized twenty symbols," she answered.

I didn't believe her. I never believed geniuses actually existed. Can they really teach themselves something as difficult as the International Phonetic Alphabet?

Then Sunrise Huang asked to see my textbook.

"There's nothing to see," I dodged. "I still use Chinese as a phonetic aid."

Sunrise Huang was surprised. "You're still doing that?" After thinking about it for a moment she said, "I'll teach you a trick. You can make some cards. Keep them in your pocket so you can take them out and memorize them wherever you go."

While listening to her I saw my chance: Garbage Li was standing on the podium, and his hands were not patting his buttocks.

I leaped over the desk and charged toward him.

Before Garbage Li realized he should be patting his bottom, I planted an almighty kick on his backside. Perhaps out of revenge, my kick was ferocious. When an astonished Garbage Li turned around to find out who had kicked him, I actually saw tears in his eyes.

I smiled with satisfaction, having taken perfect advantage of the situation.

We had a pact, and he hadn't patted his bottom. He looked at me knowing there was nothing he could do other than to say, "Son of a bitch—OW!"

Everyone laughed.

I returned to my desk, and Sunrise Huang stood up to let me back to my seat.

"Why," she asked, "would someone like you play that sort of prank on someone like him?"

I didn't respond.

"Well?" she insisted.

"What kind of person am *I*?" I shot back. "What kind of person is *he*?"

"His father works in the maintenance unit," she began to explain. "Their family has five children, and he's a rag picker who goes to the garbage dump every day, or scavenges lumps of coal from behind the boiler room."

I knew what she was getting at. Sunrise Huang was an only child, and so was I. In those days families with only one child were rare. Parents of such families were of either high status or the lowest. Students from households with many children could not hold their heads up high in school.

"Garbage Li never, ever bathes," she added.

"I don't go to the bathhouse every week, either," I said.

"How come?" she asked in amazement.

"Too much trouble."

"Every Sunday I'm there as soon as the bathhouse opens," she boasted. "I'm usually the second one in. I want to be first, but I'm always second."

I became curious. "Why?" I asked.

"Ahjitai is always first," she said.

My heart quivered. Ahjitai was a goddess.

"Garbage Li never bathes," she continued, "but he likes to loiter around the bathhouse, as if there's something mysterious going on there."

"He kicked me the other day," I blurted out. "When I was in the bathroom."

She stopped chatting with me. She opened her English textbook and began to concentrate on her work.

VI

A month later, or maybe two, we had learned the entire English alphabet and a few common phrases. I think we also had been taught the entire International Phonetic Alphabet, or maybe just some of it, I am not sure. All I can remember clearly is Sunrise Huang. She was the first to get the hang of those phonetic symbols.

I have to talk about her because she was an important figure in my life. Without her, the story of my English teacher and me would have been very different.

Sunrise Huang.

As the only child in her family, she was always well supplied with snacks. During class she would quietly pop things into her mouth from time to time.

Sitting next to her, it was really irritating to see her do that. I would gulp saliva, close my eyes, or simply avoid watching her. . . . I tried all sorts of methods to fend off my cravings for food.

Second Prize Wang also noticed this habit of hers, but he tolerated it. He favored petite, delicate-looking girls with fair skin, especially the smart ones—all male teachers do.

Sunrise Huang had obviously mastered all of the International Phonetic Alphabet since she could already pronounce words like *Father, motherland,* and *river.*

In the middle of his classes, Second Prize Wang would ask Sunrise Huang to go to his room and fetch the phonograph and records. She became our English class representative. One day, after she had put the phonograph at the front of the classroom and returned to her seat, I questioned her. "Did you go into Second Prize Wang's room?"

She nodded.

"I walked past his room the other day and could smell cold cream," I said.

She smiled. "His room doesn't look like a man's room. It looks nice."

"What else is in there?" I probed.

"What else?" She thought about it for a moment, then said, "There is also a large dictionary. An English dictionary. Mr. Wang said we don't need it yet."

After the lesson I finished cleaning the classroom. It was my turn that afternoon. Out of the blue, thoughts of Ahjitai came up. I had not seen her since she stopped teaching. For some reason, at that age, I felt an inexplicable sadness whenever I thought about a female teacher like Ahjitai. She didn't smell of cold cream, but her scent would make you feel sad. It brought on a sense of heaviness that is hard to describe.

I walked along the dark school corridor. The lights overhead were like the eyes of wild cats. I heard somebody laughing just as I was turning the corner. The laugh came from Second Prize Wang's room. It was Sunrise Huang's voice. Second Prize Wang was also laughing.

Then the phonograph started to play. It was a man reciting in English. I heard Sunrise Huang repeat each sentence after him.

I suddenly became angry with Second Prize Wang. All male teachers in the world are the same: They like to give one-on-one classes to girls.

I heard more laughter—Sunrise Huang had made a mistake reciting. I leaned against Second Prize Wang's door and tried as hard as I could to peek through the newspaper-covered window. I could not see a thing. All I could hear was that sound. It was the sound of English. I gave up. Feeling dejected, I left school for home, alone.

He smells so nice, I concluded, because he wants to attract girls like Sunrise Huang, girls who would never use Chinese characters as phonetic crutches. His scent must be irresistible to those girls, and just as little scraps of paper get caught up in the wind, they will end up in his room.

The sound of English again wafted from Second Prize Wang's room. The corridor was quiet. Strange English words followed me as I walked. They were traces of Sunrise Huang.

I don't know why, but I started to miss even more the days when Ahjitai taught us Uyghur.

VII

I forgot to tell you that Sunrise Huang's family lived in the same building as I did. Her father had renounced the KMT, the Nationalist Party that lost the civil war in 1949 to the Communist Party. He was a major general. I am not sure if "renounce" means the same thing to you as it means to me. In my city, "renounce" does not mean that someone from the KMT merely turned his back on the party. It means that he contributed to the other party's victory.

The building I lived in was filled with former KMT generals—Liu

Xing in Unit 1 was a major general. Ma Ping-lin in Unit 2 was also a general—a lieutenant general, I heard; he was a division commander. Huang Zhen, Sunrise Huang's father, lived in Unit 3 and was a brigade commander.

My family lived in Unit 3 on the fourth floor. Sunrise Huang's family lived on the ground floor because her father had injured his legs riding a horse during the war.

When we moved into the building two years earlier, my father often complained to Mother, "I, a chief engineer trained by the Communist Party, am forced to live on the fourth floor. He was injured fighting the Communist Party, and he gets to live on the ground floor."

"You can't really claim you were trained by the Communist Party," Mother would say. "Didn't you go to St. John's University? The fourth floor isn't so bad. It's quiet. We don't have to worry about noise from upstairs."

"Of course I was trained by the Communist Party," Father would counter. "I was a Tsinghua University graduate student after the liberation. Otherwise, why would they send me to the Soviet Union? I didn't go to the UK, the USA, France, or Japan. I went to the Soviet Union."

Ever since I was a child, I could tell Father had a sense of superiority, even haughtiness, when he talked about the Soviet Union. Thinking back, I can remember his face glowing, like a statue in a church bathed in heavenly light. I thought it was inappropriate for him to act like that—he was forgetting his origins. My grandfather—my father's father—was also an architect. The buildings he designed are still standing in Nanking and Shanghai. My father went to schools run by missionaries from the time he was a child. He then went to St. John's University. How could he claim to be trained by the Communist Party? If he had to link his education to a party, that party would have to be the KMT, not the Communist Party. But what about the Soviet Union? He did go there to study, he loved Russian architecture, and he edged his way into the Communist Party after much effort. But Sunrise Huang's father would never be able to join the Communist Party. He would forever be an outsider.

Let me tell you more about what I think of my father. As time went on, I realized he was very good at climbing the ladder of success. He loved me and loved my mother even more. But more important, he managed to become a "red engineer," somebody the party would favor the most; he was eager to show he was progressive; and to demonstrate his determination, he even shed tears in front of his superiors. I heard that when he was in the Soviet Union, he denounced his roommate during the Anti-rightist Campaign. That man was labeled a "rightist" and sent to dig coal in Dahong Gully. He later died in a coal gas explosion. It was horrible—his head was crushed by large slabs of coal. Over the years, Father never showed any remorse for what he had done. He simply told me, my mother, or himself, "That Wu Zhi-fang, he was just too careless when he talked."

It was as if the man's death had nothing to do with Father's denunciation, as if Wu had simply talked too much and died at the hands of bad people—people, in Father's eyes, like Director Fan, the man who had slapped him.

And just like that, Father was awarded the project of designing the Nationalities Theater. He became so full of himself that he would come up with lines like "I have built myself a monument."

However, Sunrise Huang's family got to live on the ground floor, and we had to live on the fourth floor. Father would sigh. "Sometimes it seems that joining the KMT carries more weight than being a member of the Communist Party."

I wanted to go out after dinner. Mother asked where I was going.

"Sunrise Huang's."

Mother appeared hesitant.

"What for?" Father asked.

"I want to learn the International Phonetic Alphabet from her."

Father's eyes lit up. "She has already learned the International Phonetic Alphabet?"

I nodded. "The English teacher gave her one-on-one lessons."

"Is the teacher a man?" Mother asked.

I nodded again.

My parents exchanged a glance.

Father then said, "Forget about it. Huang Zhen hasn't been in a good mood lately. You won't be welcome there. Also, what use is English?"

"I want to go," I insisted.

Father was about to lose his temper.

"Let him go," Mother interceded. "Maybe one day English will be useful and the Russian you worked so hard to learn will be useless."

"No matter how much the Soviet Union fights with us," Father argued, "it still deserves our respect because it's a socialist country, even though it happened to stray down the path of revisionism. But English . . ." Father stopped. He sighed and sat down, closing his eyes. I saw an opportunity and quickly slipped out.

I knocked on Sunrise Huang's door. She was happy to see me. "Come in," she said. "Be quiet. My father has been in a very bad mood lately."

We went to her room. I said, "I want you to teach me the International Phonetic Alphabet."

"How did you know I learned it all?"

"Didn't Second Prize Wang give you extra lessons?"

"You saw me go into his room?"

"Are you afraid of being spotted?" I asked back.

"Mr. Wang is worried about being spotted."

"Why? Does he worry that the boys in our class will be angry with him?"

Sunrise Huang smiled. "Are you angry with him?"

"A little."

"He is not afraid of the boys," Sunrise Huang explained. "We are just kids, what's there to be afraid of? He's afraid of the adults. The math teacher said Second Prize Wang is morally suspect. He told me to stay away from him and warned me against going to his room alone."

"So what do you think?" I asked her.

She thought about it for a moment, then said, "I think he is a good person. I have been to his place a few times, and all he talked about was English. He is interested only in English, nothing else."

"Will you go back to his place?"

"Of course. But now he doesn't close his door when I am there. He keeps it wide open."

I grinned. "He must have something sinister in mind."

"Why do you say that?"

"If I were him, I would have something sinister in mind if I were alone with a girl."

"So what about you and me?"

"We are different. We live in the same building. And we're just kids."

All of a sudden we heard Sunrise Huang's parents arguing in the other room.

"You're talking nonsense," her father said. "I have confessed everything to the party. What else is there for you to say? You think they will let you join the party if you hang around with them all day every day and hand in an application once a week? You don't know me at all! You don't know how much pressure I am under!"

Her mother did not back down. They attacked each other, back and forth. Sunrise Huang covered her ears and closed her eyes.

"Let's go to my place," I suggested.

She nodded.

When we got there, my mother asked her politely, "How is your father?"

Sunrise did not respond. Her eyes clouded. Once again, Father and Mother exchanged a glance.

That was early June in Ürümchi. Summer had not yet arrived, and spring had not yet departed. A kind of flower grew on elm trees at this time of year. People called them "elm coins." In those days families routinely ran out of food. They had too many mouths to feed. They picked elm coins from the trees and mixed them with maize flour. The mixture gave off a sweet scent when steamed.

Sunrise Huang started to teach me the phonetic alphabet under the suspicious eyes of my parents. As she taught me, that sweet scent wafted in from the window, and my heart filled with joy. Maybe the joy was brought to me by the spring, or maybe it was because of Sunrise Huang. If you think hard, you will remember that young girls have a pleasantly cool scent—it comes from their hair, or their clothes. It would be a pity if you could not remember that.

My heart indeed swelled with joy. At that moment I forgot about Ahjitai. Perhaps it was English that brought me joy.

VIII

Sunrise Huang sounded snobbish when she spoke English. Other students were embarrassed to pronounce English the way she did. But not Sunrise Huang—she was unabashed. She imitated the timbre of Second Prize Wang's voice, mimicking his every intonation. I was already annoyed that she carried snacks in her pockets, and now I also found her pronunciation irritating. I fantasized about speaking English like her, but I never dared to. Any boy who spoke English like that would be mocked.

Life is full of "ifs." If it had not been for that incident in the Huang household, Sunrise would have remained class representative, my relationship with Second Prize Wang would not have changed, and none of what happened between me and my English teacher ever would have taken place.

Second Prize Wang announced that the next lesson would be about "family." The word carries a sense of warmth: home; hometown; family portrait.

"The best way to learn the new vocabulary," he said, "is to bring your own family portraits. Bring a full family portrait." No one knew what he meant. "A full family portrait," he explained, "is a photograph of every single member of your family."

Only one person in the class brought a full family portrait: Sunrise Huang. She rose from her seat and walked to the front of the classroom. As she approached the English teacher, a smile lit up her face like the dawn's glow. She then presented to Second Prize Wang a rather bourgeois-looking picture frame.

Second Prize Wang examined it for a moment. "This is the best full family portrait I've ever seen."

Sunrise Huang's face reddened with excitement. She could not hide her joy as she turned to look at us. Then she lowered her head.

I studied the photograph. Each member of her family was looking in a different direction. Her father was looking to the left and her mother to the right. Only Sunrise Huang was looking straight ahead. This photo gave me the impression that her family was not at all united. And *this* was the best full family portrait Second Prize Wang had ever seen? After I grew up and came into contact with foreigners, who out of politeness will say This is the best or That is the best, I realized it's just a figure of speech. Now, whenever I encounter that, I recall Second Prize Wang's comment.

Sunrise Huang was being a total show-off that day. As a smiling Second Prize Wang watched her, she held the portrait reverently. She pointed to the man and said, "Father." Pointing to the woman, she said, "Mother." Finally she said, "I love my family." As the class representative, Sunrise Huang led us in our raucous chants of "Father, father. Mother, mother. Home, home." I envied her because I wanted to be the English class representative. But I was not as adept at English as she was. She could stand up in front of the whole class and loudly say "father" in English.

It was raining that day. On our way home from school, Sunrise Huang walked in front of me. She had a willowy gait. Her hair swayed. Rays of sunlight streaked out from behind the clouds and then quickly disappeared. Silky strands of rain drifted down from the sky, glittering with colors. I was walking faster than Sunrise Huang, and as I was about to overtake her she said, out of the blue, "I saw your father being beaten that day."

I looked away from her. I was upset because I did not want other people to bring that up.

"All your father did wrong was leave off an ear."

I didn't respond and walked quickly past her. I wanted to be rid of her.

"Even if he painted it wrong," she said, "they shouldn't be beating people."

"In the end, my father added another ear and it turned out even worse."

She looked at me. "Do your parents fight?"

"No."

"What a wonderful family you have," she said. "Your mother is so nice to people. When I grow up I want to be just like her, a well-educated person who is warm and polite."

"Why are you telling me this?" I asked.

"My mother is awful. She fights with my father every day. My father says he's old and can't take much more."

I did not wish to continue in this vein, so I quickened my pace.

She continued talking from behind, but I did not hear what she said. We reached our apartment building. I sensed something was wrong the moment I entered the building. Someone was crying—it was Sunrise Huang's mother. But she was not merely crying, she was wailing.

Instead of going up to the second floor, I instinctively turned left and went toward Sunrise Huang's apartment. A large crowd had gathered at the doorway. They all peered inside the apartment, but no one entered.

I thought her parents were fighting again and rushed over to watch the fireworks. Everyone seemed overly quiet. Only her mother's breathing was audible. I squeezed in between some adults, or rather under them, and saw her father hanging from the ceiling. His tongue was poking out. It was enormous.

To this day, I still remember vividly the expression on Sunrise Huang's face when she saw her father hanging from the ceiling. First her eyes opened wide, as if she'd been spooked by a ghost, and finally she fell, like a high jumper performing a backward jump, only she landed on her back.

Someone yelled out, "Get him down!" At that moment the image of the full family portrait Sunrise Huang had just shown in class flashed through my mind.

I was frightened but at the same time excited. We didn't have much theater during my childhood; all we could watch were beatings and suicides, and to tell the truth, being surrounded by horror can sometimes be thrilling. It's like watching a play in a small theater and being in the midst of all the dramatic elements: the backdrop, the silence, the characters' movements, the sound, the lights, the actors' expressions, and most important of all—the script. The fear factor is always exciting, and nothing is more exhilarating than hearing that someone you know well is dead—it makes an otherwise dreary life more interesting.

Just as I was enjoying the horror, someone grabbed me from behind. I turned and saw it was my father. I didn't want to go with him, but he was determined to pull me away. He even grabbed my ear, in the same way that Commander Shen had grabbed his ear. In the end I was dragged away—away from the dead man, away from Sunrise Huang, who was on the ground in a swoon, away from her mother's operatic wailing.

Father dragged me home and commanded, "Don't go near anything like that ever again."

"Why do people poke their tongues out after they hang themselves?" I asked.

Father thought for a moment. "Maybe they couldn't finish what they wanted to say when they were alive."

"People's tongues are longer than pigs' tongues. I've seen pigs' tongues at the slaughterhouse. They're only this big," I said, indicating the size with my hands.

Father grinned. "You've seen pigs being slaughtered?"

I nodded. "After school, whenever they kill a pig, I go to watch."

Father smiled. "Huang Zhen should have died long ago." He seemed to be gloating.

I was shocked, wondering whether I'd misheard what he'd said.

Father paused for a moment. "Don't go to the slaughterhouse anymore. It's filthy there."

Mother came home with a delighted expression on her face. "Is Huang Zhen dead?" she asked.

Father nodded.

"The canteen slaughtered a pig today," she said to Father. "Quick now. Go and buy some polished white rice."

As Father retrieved an enamel pot he said, "I heard a gun was found at the bottom of one of his storage chests."

"Really?" I exclaimed.

"Don't go blabbing that when you go out," Mother ordered.

My parents' attitude astounded me. Why did a death in someone else's family put them in a good mood? Sunrise Huang had just said that when she grew up she wanted to be like my mother. She said Mother had a graceful and polite manner.

The canteen was packed with people. My parents and I lined up separately. Father stood in the line for stewed pork. Mother was in the line for polished white rice. We called white rice *polished,* but people don't call it that anymore.

I stood in line for the free rice gruel. Someone behind me tugged at my shirt. It was Garbage Li. He was carrying a serving of stewed pork and said jovially, "Today I'm going for broke. Gonna eat some stewed pork." His father was just a laborer. His family was poor, so for them eating stewed pork was a big deal.

Garbage Li saw that I was not responding and joked: "The three of you are lining up just for polished white rice? What's the big deal?"

I glanced over at my parents in the crush. Their greedy expressions embarrassed me. Garbage Li asked if he could get in line in front of me. I let him cut the line.

"I bet I could finish all of the rice in that bucket," said Garbage Li. "What do you think?"

"That's impossible," I retorted. "No one has a stomach that big."

"I'd stick my head in that," he replied, gesturing at the bucket, "and poke my ass out over the latrine. Eating and shitting at the same time, I could eat all the rice I wanted."

I laughed, then changed the subject. "Did you hear that Sunrise Huang's father died?"

Garbage Li looked stunned. Wrinkles like an old man's suddenly appeared on his gaunt face. "We just saw her full family portrait in class," he said. "How did he die?"

"He committed suicide," I said. Neither of us spoke. After receiving our rice we left the canteen in silence.

On the way home it was obvious our neighbors already knew of the death of Sunrise Huang's father. They greeted my parents and gossiped about what was going on: The Revolutionary Committee had sent someone; the nature of the issue had been decided. I didn't understand what all this meant, but I could tell that everyone was excited.

I entered the building and carried the rice to the door of Sunrise Huang's unit. The door was still open, and there was quite a crowd inside. Her father's corpse had already been removed. Sunrise Huang lay on her bed crying.

Garbage Li was standing at her side, holding a serving of rice topped with meat and vegetables. He was prodding her back with the bowl to encourage her to eat, and he didn't notice me watching him. I turned on my heels and left Sunrise Huang's unit. Garbage Li's act of kindness left me feeling guilty.

At home our family of three enjoyed a hearty meal. My parents chewed noisily, as though they had never before eaten stewed pork with polished white rice, as though they were laborers like Garbage Li's parents, not educated professionals. People are strange. Sometimes when you observe your family eating, and listen to the sounds they make, you want to whip them. You want to whip them as hard as you can until they can no longer eat.

I felt distracted, perhaps because of the death of Sunrise Huang's father. Suddenly I thought of something: "Tell me, is it true what people say, that Chairman Mao will live for two hundred years?"

My mother's expression immediately changed. She whacked me hard with her chopsticks. It happened so fast, I didn't have time to flinch. "How should we know?" she snapped.

Father looked at me. His face had turned ugly.

I was in pain. At that moment I thought I could hear the sound of a Hunanese folk song drift into our unit from afar. It lingered, and mingled with the wails of Sunrise Huang's mother and the terrified expression of my mother. I couldn't imagine how this kind of question could provoke such a strong response from my mother. She had hit me savagely, as if I were not her son, as if she had never felt so tenderly about me as to want to name me Love Liu. I covered my head with my hands, and squirmed and cried in pain, to show them just how much it hurt.

Father was finally taken in by my sulking. "You must never, under any circumstances, ask questions like that," he intoned seriously. "You hear me?"

I didn't respond.

"Do you hear me?" he said, raising his voice.

I looked at him. There was a ferocious glint in his eyes. "I hear you."

The room was hot. Mother opened a window. The sound of singing drifted in. It was the girls of the propaganda troupe:

We Communists are seeds
The people are our soil
Wherever we go
We must unite with the people

Their song was leisurely, like a folk ballad. Accompanied by the tremolo of a harmonica, their voices made me think of reeds rippling on the surface of a lake. I'd never heard such beautiful singing before. It was like a hymn emanating from heaven. Of course at the time I knew nothing of churches, only mosques, but their singing was angelic, full of faith and purity. I forgot the pain of the beating at my mother's hand. This was the first time I remember being so profoundly moved by music. Just hearing the girls' voices, I could imagine their bright eyes. It reminded me of an occasion when I was small, when I accidentally saw Sunrise Huang urinating. She was at home, squatting over a basin. She was naked—maybe her mother had just given her a bath—and her whole body appeared to glow in the bright light. . . .

I ate. I listened. I contemplated. Suddenly Father spoke.

"That Huang Zhen had his good points, too," Father began. "Last time when he was the first to be 'struggled,' they glued a humiliating high hat on his head, but when they ordered him to kneel down, he refused. He finally knelt down only after someone kicked his calf from behind."

Mother did not speak.

"I'm not that stupid," Father continued. "I'll kneel right away when told to."

"Don't talk about that," Mother pleaded. "Don't talk about that—it's frightening even to think about it. Huang Zhen just didn't have a good marriage. His wife must have been so hard to deal with. But remember the time she came upstairs to return the purse I'd dropped in the first-floor hallway? And then another time, when Love Liu ran away from kindergarten, both of them helped us look for him until midnight. . . ."

"As I've said before," Father lectured, "any man who kills himself is actually killed by his wife. Just like in a Stanislavsky method drama, a man who kills himself does so just for others to see, and his wife is the most important audience. Huang Zhen, in his desperation, wanted to use his death to call out to his wife, so that she would treat him better. Before he committed suicide he had already visualized the grief his wife and child would experience."

Mother suddenly became extremely upset. Tears welled up in her eyes. "Don't worry," Father said, holding her hand. "I won't die like that. I want to live until the day things return to normal. No one can imprison springtime and sunlight forever." As he spoke the words *springtime* and *sunlight,* his eyes filled with anger as if he wanted to kill someone. Gradually, his eyes turned soft and sad. "I . . . Xuan-qi, listen to me. I may not have done anything significant in my life, not the Nationalities Theater, not the school building. They are not my achievements. A monument—well, only Pushkin is entitled to a monument. . . . My greatest achievement in this life was finding you, finding a woman as loving as you. If it weren't for you, I would not have been able to hold on when things began to go bad."

Mother was now sobbing audibly. It hurt to witness that. I had already forgotten she had hit me. I did not want to see my mother cry.

THREE

I

I recited an English text that I knew by heart. I tried to imitate Sunrise Huang's and Second Prize Wang's voices. I had stopped using Chinese characters as phonetic crutches.

Sunrise Huang helped me a lot with my pronunciation. To this day, I still believe that girls are geniuses at learning languages. Their mouths are created for talking, regardless of the language they speak. And boys' mouths are created for eating, regardless of the food they eat. There is a local dialect in Ürümchi. It is a mixture of dialects from such provinces as Gansu, Shaanxi, and Ningxia. There are also elements in the dialect developed by Uyghurs in Xinjiang, inhabitants of Yangliuqing, a town close to the city of Tianjin, and Mongols who live in Xinjiang's Börtala region. The language is very different from Mandarin, or the Common Language, the language used in programs on the Central People's Radio Station in Peking. Moving a mountain is easy, people say, but learning Mandarin is hard.

I've always known boys and girls are two different species. Girls learn to speak Mandarin when they are young, but boys just don't care. Some even stick with the Ürümchi dialect throughout their lives, without ever realizing how much it makes them sound like country bumpkins.

It's the same with English. Nobody will mock a girl if she speaks English in accordance with the International Phonetic Alphabet.

And if the girl has fair skin and beautiful eyes, the audience will go silent the moment she begins to speak. This was the case when Sunrise Huang first recited English. But I was treated differently.

When I recited English the same way as Sunrise Huang, the boys in the class immediately started laughing, and the girls joined in, too. I don't know where I got the courage and the determination to recite that way. Even though I broke into a sweat, I persisted, as I knew I was speaking correctly. Before her father poked his tongue out, Sunrise Huang must have taught me the lines a hundred times. In my home, in her home, under the eyes of our parents—while those unscrupulous adults were exchanging ambiguous glances—I mimicked her intonation and did my best to speak English as a smart girl would.

The laughter in the classroom became louder and louder, like the infamous eerie winds of Urho in the Kalamay Desert—you may not notice it at first, but the whistling sound will gradually drive you mad. Eventually, a faint smile appeared even on Second Prize Wang's face.

I kept reciting until I finished the first paragraph, then waited for the laughter to die down so I could continue. The laughter faded, but the boisterous mood lingered. Standing at my desk, I raised my eyes from the book and scanned the classroom.

"You motherfuckers! What's so funny!"

The laughter erupted again. They acted as if my vulgar outburst was not about their mothers but just another English sentence.

II

Second Prize Wang came over to my desk. The seat next to mine was empty because Sunrise Huang had been absent from school ever since her father died. I thought Second Prize Wang was going to scold me for cursing. I waited. I did not know what he was going to say, but I knew what I had to say. It was something I had wanted to say to him for a long time: You are laughing at me, too. You are not a teacher. You're just another Garbage Li.

I waited patiently for him to speak. Instead, he took my book and examined the pronunciation notes I had written in using the International Phonetic Alphabet. The smile on his face became more noticeable.

I lowered my head.

"Please continue," he prompted.

I took back the book and started reciting again. He stood beside me, nodding from time to time in encouragement.

I suddenly realized I was surrounded by silence, just like Sunrise Huang was when she recited English. There was no sound other than that of my classmates' breathing. I spoke confidently amid the silence. Streams of words came out as smooth as silk, and my voice became loud and clear, just like that of the great Italian opera tenor Beniamino Gigli reciting a poem in praise of heroes.

I imagined myself standing center stage under a spotlight, or being the brightest light in the midst of darkness. I was excited by the sound of my voice. The lingering shadows disappeared. All eyes seemed to be looking in my direction. In fact, all eyes were fixed on me. No one was laughing.

I finished reciting.

Second Prize Wang had stood beside me the whole time. He stopped smiling and looked at me for a moment, then scanned the classroom. He returned to the front and wrote a sentence in English on the blackboard.

"Do you know what this sentence means?" he asked the class.

Nobody said a word. I stared at the sentence, my heart pounding, not sure if I understood its meaning correctly.

"Learn from your classmate Love Liu," said Second Prize Wang, telling us the meaning loudly in Chinese.

The class started to bubble with excitement. Everyone was talking at once.

Second Prize Wang approached me. He was about to speak, but then something outside the window caught his eye.

Ahjitai was walking out of the school gate with a bag in her hand. Apparently she had packed her things and was finally leaving our school. She was wearing a Uyghur skirt that appeared to have been altered to the Russian style. She walked away, calm and proud, but something in her manner gave off a trace of sadness.

Second Prize Wang stared out the window, forgetting about me and the rest of the class. Once Ahjitai had faded into the distance, he turned his head back, lost in thought. Then the bell rang, and everybody jumped up.

Second Prize Wang did not talk to any of us. He collected his things, left the classroom, and stepped into the dark corridor, alone.

III

The door opened. Sunlight flooded out of the room, making me dizzy. I was a bit out of breath because of the excitement. For the first time I was walking into the room that only girls like Sunrise Huang had been in. It was Second Prize Wang's dormitory.

This was the luckiest day of my life.

Second Prize Wang was before me, facing the other way. He unhooked a striped towel from the back of the door and wiped his face. He did it in such a refined manner. Then he glanced at himself in the mirror. His face was clean shaven, otherwise he surely would have had a bushy beard. Ever since I was a child I've never liked men with full beards. I thought they look messy. As an adult I've had many friends with beards. Once I even tried to grow one. It was a fad. At that time, if you wore your hair long like I did, it made you feel the promise of a new beginning. We believed new ideas could change the world and that life would be free of hardship because young men like us dared to let their hair and beards grow.

Second Prize Wang never let his beard grow. His refined style was like a piece of Baroque music, balanced and modest.

Standing behind Second Prize Wang in his room for the first time, I could smell cold cream, and even a trace of cologne. The scent of mint also pervaded the room. The combination was overpowering. It made me feel ashamed of myself for being so filthy. I stank. I had not changed socks or taken a bath for at least a week. Even though Mother constantly nagged me about it, I just did not want to bathe. But at that moment I felt regret and started to blame myself. Later in life I tried many different brands of cologne, but none made me smell like Second Prize Wang.

"The phonograph is over there. Be careful when you carry it—the pickup is a little unreliable."

My eyes were busy scanning the room. I saw a brightly colored tin printed with the design of a couple, a foreign man and woman. I had seen similar objects at home when I was small. My parents had gotten rid of them a long time ago.

I also saw Second Prize Wang's clothes hanging on a line over his bed. There were quite a few well-tailored suits, some appearing to be made of wool. In those days, when we wanted to say someone was well dressed, we would say he was dressed in a trim outfit. That phrase seems to be less common now.

And I saw his shoes on the floor at the end of his bed. I think there were two pairs, both leather. They were highly polished.

"What are you looking at?" he asked with a smile.

My eyes were glued to a small bookshelf against the north wall of his room. There were some English textbooks, but what caught my eye was a thick book with a navy blue cover. I wanted to see it better, so I stepped closer.

He guessed what I was drawn to. "Do you know that word? *Dictionary?*"

"English dictionary?" I asked.

He nodded.

"Is it a comprehensive dictionary?" I asked.

"When you know all the words in that dictionary, you will be able to live like a real English gentleman. You can even have a better life than ordinary folks in England because you will be well educated."

"What does a gentleman look like?" I asked.

He thought for a moment and then said, "Like your father."

His answer disappointed me. Like my *father*? What kind of man is my father? I thought of the glasses he wore and the frightened expression that was always on his face. Still, I had to ask, "Do you know my father?"

"I've looked closely at the buildings he's designed. When I went past the Nationalities Theater the other day, I had a good look at it. It's tasteful. I chatted with your father when we were in line at the canteen. He was very polite and did not push and squeeze like the others."

I lost interest in Second Prize Wang's description of my father. And for a long time after that, I did not have positive associations with the word *gentleman.* If my father could be considered a gentleman, what was the point of being one?

Second Prize Wang appeared to have something else to say. I stroked the spine of the book nervously and was afraid I might be upsetting him, since what I was doing would upset my father. He would not allow me to touch the illustrated materials he brought back from the Soviet Union.

Second Prize Wang looked at his watch. "We still have two minutes. You can take a look if you'd like."

I took the dictionary off the shelf. It was heavy. Inside, there was text in both English and Chinese.

"This is an English-Chinese dictionary," he explained.

All I could do was stare at the book. And then the bell rang. I reshelved the dictionary and picked up the phonograph. Second Prize Wang followed behind me, holding two records. We left his room, leaving behind the scent of cologne.

IV

All eyes were on me when I stepped into the classroom. My classmates could tell I was being treated like the English class representative, even though it was not an official appointment. Sunrise Huang was the real class representative. I was not even the designated acting representative. However, I was already accorded the privilege of carrying the phonograph. This was not such a big deal to the boys, but it bothered the girls. For a while the girls in my class were jealous of Sunrise Huang, but her father's death freed her from their jealousy. Now I was their target. The moment I put the phonograph down at the front of the classroom, nearly all of the girls stared at me.

"Look! Look! His face is red," Garbage Li blurted out.

At that moment Second Prize Wang walked in, and everybody stood up. Second Prize Wang first played a record. The speaker's accent was different from what we were used to hearing.

"What you heard earlier was Chinese people speaking English. What you are hearing today is standard Linguaphone English," he explained. Second Prize Wang looked excited and sounded foreign when he said the word *Linguaphone,* as if it were the name of a religion.

We listened in silence. Standard English was like sunlight: It brightened his eyes, which shone with dedication, faith, and a determination to propagate authentic English pronunciation.

I noticed that Second Prize Wang's accent was slightly different from that of the man on the recording. Now, years later, I know there is a peculiar flavor to the English that Chinese people speak. The accents of people from different countries all have their own quality. Chinese accents give you a taste of Chinese herbal medicine. As for the accents of Japanese and Koreans—when they speak English, their heavy accents always give me the creeps.

When class was over, almost every boy could copy Second Prize Wang's accent and yell out: "Linguaphone."

Lin-guo-feng-wong.

Yes, that's right. This time they did very well using Chinese words as phonetic crutches. The sound of the word echoed around me for a long time. Like a pair of Sennheiser headphones, it will stay with me forever, accompanying me till the end of my life.

V

"Why are you called Love Liu?"

"'Cause my mother wished I was a girl."

"But it's not necessarily a girl's name."

"Yes, it is."

"Do you know what 'love' means?"

"It means when boys and girls . . . No, I don't know."

"No, not any of that. It means compassion."

"What is 'compassion'?"

"It's . . . it's . . . how should I put it . . . ? It means you can feel pain when you see others suffer."

"That's impossible."

Guess whom this conversation was with? Well, you are slow! It was with Second Prize Wang, of course! He started it one day when I helped him carry the phonograph back to his room.

He smiled. "Why do you think it's impossible?"

"Why would I feel pain when others have bad luck? I would feel happy."

He seemed shocked and disappointed. "Why would you think like that?" he said, shaking his head.

"My parents are like that," I answered matter-of-factly.

He looked at me in dismay. "Will you please go with me after school to visit Sunrise Huang?" he asked. "She hasn't come to class in over three weeks."

VI

It was dusk when we arrived at Sunrise Huang's. Yamalike Hill was blanketed with red clouds, and faint rays of sunlight shone on the family's small Red Flag brand radio and on Sunrise Huang's pale face.

"You should come to class," said Second Prize Wang. No response. "For the time being, Love Liu is doing the class representative work on your behalf," he continued.

Sunrise Huang raised her head, looked at me, and then looked back down. Second Prize Wang glanced at the photo of her father on the desk.

"Where is your mother?" I asked.

She shook her head. "At work."

"You can see the Tianshan Mountains from your window," said Second Prize Wang.

I followed his finger and looked out the window. The magnificent Bogada Peak was in the distance, glowing like gold in the sunlight. Second Prize Wang started to say something but was interrupted by Sunrise Huang.

"Have you started with Linguaphone English?"

"Yes. Today we listened to the record. I have been imitating the pronunciation all day," I said. Sunrise Huang lowered her head. She'd started to cry.

Second Prize Wang's face was clouded. He attempted to say something but was at a loss for words.

"When're you coming back to school?" I asked. She did not look up.

Second Prize Wang gripped her shoulder. "I will help you to catch up later."

"When're you coming back to school?" I repeated.

"I don't know," she finally said. "My mother says I have anemia and can't go to school."

While we were talking, her mother came home. She looked younger since the death of her husband. Unlike Sunrise Huang, she did not have a trace of sorrow on her face. She looked energetic. Yes, that's right: She was a widow in high spirits. She scrutinized me and Second Prize Wang.

"I am Sunrise Huang's English teacher." Second Prize Wang introduced himself. Her hint of a smile disappeared instantly. She just nodded.

"Sunrise Huang is anemic and can't go to school for the time being. Thank you for your concern," she said icily. Then she started to sweep the floor, as if she wanted to sweep Second Prize Wang out the door. He sensed her hostility, said good-bye, and left the unit. I followed him. Sunrise Huang's mother slammed the door behind us and immediately began to scold her daughter.

"Everyone says that man is indecent. I've told you this many times. Stay away from him or you'll be sorry."

Sunrise Huang wept. "But I want to learn English."

Thwack!—that must have been a slap on Sunrise Huang's face. Second Prize Wang turned around. He was about to knock on the door, but then he held back. For a long time he just stood at the door. I pretended I hadn't heard anything.

With eyes darkened like a snowcapped mountain cast in shadow at dusk, Second Prize Wang stood as still as a sculpture. Then he turned around and walked away without saying a word. His steps were somber, as if the whole building resounded with funeral music because another big shot in the central government had just died.

VII

At the dinner table that night, I asked Mother a question.

"What does indecent mean?"

Mother was shocked. "What are you asking that for?"

"I just want to know. What does it mean?"

Mother became agitated. "I don't know!"

Father glared at me. "Eat!" he ordered.

I kept my mouth shut for some time, then asked, "What is love?"

My parents were momentarily speechless. "Love?" they repeated, exchanging a glance, but they couldn't give me an answer.

"Does it mean 'compassion'?" I asked.

Father looked at me for a long time. Then he grinned. "*Compassion?* Where did you get that word from?"

I did not respond.

Mother looked at me with worried eyes. "This child. What should we do with him?"

Father sighed. "Compassion, love . . . We can't explain these to you. You are too young to understand. Who taught you these words?"

I looked down and remained silent. Father seemed overcome with sadness.

I could not sleep that night. Sunrise Huang's anemic face kept flashing inside my head. Suddenly, I heard Father tell Mother that he wanted to listen to music. To my surprise, this time Mother said, "Me, too."

The music played for a while at a low volume. I heard Mother say, "I washed his sheets last Sunday. They were stained. Isn't it too early for him? He's still young."

"Children these days mature early," said Father.

The sound of the music eventually dragged me into my dreams. A word echoed in my head throughout the night. *Compassion. Compassion . . .*

FOUR

I

Beyond the north gate of Ürümchi lies the Hunan Cemetery. We lived right next to it. It's an important part of my childhood memories.

The Hunanese who entered Xinjiang in 1877 with General Zuo Zong-tang were buried there after they died. The place was full of elm trees and weeds. There were wild rabbits, wild cats, wild birds, and weasels. I often heard their nocturnal calls. They had Hunan accents, just like the man Father painted many times. Really, I'm not making this up: The little animals all chattered with Hunan accents.

The Hunan Cemetery was gigantic. Apparently quite a lot of Hunanese died in Ürümchi—before *and* after General Zuo Zong-tang came along. I heard that General Tao Zhi-yue was also Hunanese and that many who came with him were from Hunan, especially his high command—people like Sunrise Huang's father, Huang Zhen.

Huang Zhen was buried in the Hunan Cemetery, his name inscribed on his tombstone. He committed suicide to escape punishment for secretly possessing a gun. Yet after his death he was still admitted to the Hunan Cemetery. Does such an honor prove that heaven is merciful?

"My father wanted to be returned to his hometown in Hunan," Sunrise Huang told me. "He said he didn't want to be a ghost in Ürümchi. But Mother doesn't have the money for that."

Whenever I was closest to the Hunan Cemetery, I was farthest from Second Prize Wang. It was the best place for me to go when classes were suspended, and in those days I played in the Hunan Cemetery every day because classes had ceased again. Many said that classes had been suspended this time because the "overall situation" had changed, and that classes in Peking had been the first to be suspended. But others said that schools in Peking were holding classes as usual, and that the overall situation had not changed. It was only our school—the People's Liberation Army Memorial Day Middle School—that had ceased classes, and the reason was clear: Counterslogans had been discovered on the school grounds.

What is a counterslogan, you ask? A counterrevolutionary slogan. What is a counterrevolutionary slogan? It's when you spot something written on a wall like "Down with Chairman Mao."

Even now, writing those words makes me quake in fear of being executed by a firing squad.

II

The morning that classes resumed, Garbage Li suddenly emerged from a hiding place to kick me in the backside. I was inside the school not far from Second Prize Wang's dormitory and had let down my bottom-patting guard. Garbage Li laughed raucously and ran off. It hurt so much. Sometimes you don't want to cry but tears come out anyway. I was not angry with Garbage Li, because we had a pact—don't pat your bum and a kick will come. Instead, I blamed my father: What a bastard he was for designing such a dismal building, I thought to myself. The corridors were as dark as a tomb, and all manner of evil could occur . . . and it was at that moment, as I was rubbing my sore bottom, that I saw the counterrevolutionary slogan.

My heart raced furiously as I read the words. I went looking for

Second Prize Wang so I could report it to him since he was a teacher. I knocked on his door for a long time, but he was not in.

I went back and stood in front of the slogan. I was going to rub it out, but instead I stupidly picked up the piece of chalk discarded on the ground and drew an *X* through each word. That was not satisfying enough, so I wrote in large characters "Down with Garbage Li" next to the slogan. After writing those words the pain in my backside seemed to disappear, which is how I came to a lifelong understanding that pent-up feelings must be released.

Another morning that summer I sensed something was amiss the instant I stepped into the classroom. First of all, I saw that Sunrise Huang had returned. She sat by the window in the seat next to mine, looking outside at the snowcapped mountains. Her face was pale, and her eyes were still filled with sorrow. She was obviously thinking about her father. When you were young, you probably hated your father like I did, and his very existence held you down. He would come into your room at night while you were masturbating and interrupt your climax; he would touch your face and kiss your forehead while you pretended to be asleep. He would look at you lovingly, just as you looked at your little penis, hoping he would just go away. The next night you would just want to go to sleep, preferring not to know whether he entered your room. You were exhausted from his affection because it was repeated every day, and we all know that repeated affection is a torment.

And then all of a sudden, on a sunny day, you'll lose him forever, and he will no longer enter your room at night like he used to. How would you feel then? Sure, you can now masturbate freely at night, but what about your days? I am sure you would stare dumbly at the Tianshan Mountains just like Sunrise Huang.

I walked over to Sunrise Huang to cheer her up, but she ignored me. Now that she had returned, I felt the end had come for me because my career as the acting English class representative was over.

For a moment it made me miss the days when her family's luck was at its worst: her father dead, Sunrise Huang suffering from anemia, her mother forbidding her to attend classes—it all gave me an opportunity I wouldn't have had.

"People say you wrote the counterrevolutionary slogan on the wall. Did you?" Sunrise Huang suddenly asked me.

"No. They're bullshitting."

"Well, why did you write 'Down with Garbage Li' next to it?"

"I was playing in the school when Garbage Li kicked me in the butt. It really hurt. After he ran off, I came across the slogan on the wall. It said 'Down with Chairman Mao.' There was a piece of chalk on the ground. I was really scared. I used it to cross out the slogan. Only after that did I write 'Down with Garbage Li.' "

"They're both written in the same style."

The bell rang. Second Prize Wang rushed in. He was carrying the phonograph himself. That was strange; he usually asked me to fetch it. He trusted me and would give me the key and let me go to his room to get it.

I looked at the phonograph on the table, then at Second Prize Wang's serious expression. I knew something was wrong. Second Prize Wang walked toward me. When he saw Sunrise Huang, his eyes lit up. Seeing his eyes light up like that, I knew there was no conspiracy between them. He was genuinely surprised to see her, proving they had not been in contact.

Sunrise Huang averted her eyes from Second Prize Wang, as if she were apologizing to him for her father's death. Second Prize Wang came up to me. He looked like he had a lot to say. I looked at him as if awaiting his verdict. Perhaps he was going to say: "I've given it a lot of thought. Although Sunrise Huang has come back, her mind is deranged. She just stares out the window and can't concentrate. The foreign language team has thoroughly considered the matter and has decided to make you the English class representative."

I really did imagine he would say that because I loved studying English. I was one of the few boys—no, I was actually the only boy—who was aware that the Ürümchi dialect was extremely unsophisticated.

I could see that Second Prize Wang had not slept a wink the previous night. His eyes were bloodshot, as though he'd been sleepwalking and had flown to the Hunan Cemetery to eat the dead.

He looked at Sunrise Huang and then at me. "Go to the principal's office," he said softly to me. "The principal wants to see you."

Now I was nervous. The principal wanted to see *me*? What could that be about? I was just an acting class representative. He wouldn't need to see me even if I were the class monitor.

I jumped up, intending to depart immediately. Sunrise Huang was in the way and seemed oblivious of the need to let me out. Second Prize Wang had returned to the podium at the front of the classroom and was writing something on the blackboard. I nudged Sunrise Huang, but she didn't seem to notice.

"Get up, the principal wants to see me."

She stared at me blankly as if she didn't understand what I'd said. Although I desperately wanted to know why the principal had summoned me, I was secretly thrilled by Sunrise Huang's weird behavior. She's gone crazy, I thought. They'll never let a nutcase be the English class representative.

In my excitement I leaped up onto the desk like a high jumper and hopped down in front of her. The entire class watched me; no one laughed. They looked at me as if I were going to the North Pole or the Party Headquarters in Zhong Nan Hai in Peking, not the principal's office.

There was a hugely popular song at the time that went:

They illuminate the world, the Zhong Nan Hai lights
Under them our beloved Chairman Mao all night writes

As I walked along the corridor, many possibilities flashed through my head. I did not know whether something good or bad was about to happen.

The principal did not look at me when I walked into his office. His head was lowered, and he seemed deep in thought, as if he were planning something big. Our class supervisor, Guo Pei-qing, was also in the principal's office. He told me to stand next to the principal.

I walked over and stood next to the principal, who reeked of sweat and tobacco. He ignored me, but then suddenly he stood up, flared out his chest, and glared down at me from on high like a mountain towering over me. I was frightened and could barely control my nerves. He spoke to me in a soft voice.

"Did you write the counterslogan?"

I was shocked. I knew that the job of English class representative did not require the principal's approval, yet somehow I'd imagined I was being called down to the principal's office to be designated English class representative. "Counter—counterslogan? What counterslogan?"

"Counter. Revolutionary. Slogan," he said, clearly articulating each word.

"What counterrevolutionary slogan?"

"The one written on the wall near the English teacher's dormitory," said the class supervisor. It all became clear to me. The principal had worked so hard to scare me so that when he brought up the slogan I'd be intimidated into confessing. I relaxed and began to play dumb.

"What was written on the wall?" I asked.

"'Down with Chairman Mao.'" The class supervisor said it for me. The instant the words left his mouth he became terrified. Guo Pei-qing was a timid man from a "bad" political background in Shanghai. His face changed color. "Mr. Principal, I—I—I intended nothing more than to remind him," he wailed.

The principal was furious. He glared at Guo Pei-qing and said, "I hereby proclaim that you are now an active counterrevolutionary!"

Guo Pei-qing was stupefied. "Mr. Principal," he blathered, tears spilling from his eyes, "I made a mistake. It was not intentional. My family are ordinary people from Shanghai, and we, too, were bullied by the capitalists. My mother was sold as a child into a brothel, where she was beaten, reviled, and never properly paid. She belonged to the laboring classes. We lived in the squatters' slum and then moved to the stinking swamps of Pudong. . . ."

"Shut up!" barked the principal.

But Guo Pei-qing kept going. "Pudong is infested with mosquitoes and flies. Once a fly got into my ear while I was sleeping and I couldn't get it out. The doctor said I needed an operation, but we didn't have enough money. . . ."

"Stop it!"

But the supervisor did not stop. The principal walked over to Guo Pei-qing and grabbed his ear, twisting it just as Director Fan had my father's. He opened the door and shoved Guo Pei-qing out. "You can leave now," he said. The principal then closed the door. Guo Pei-qing pawed on the door from the outside. Annoyed, the principal locked the door. But Guo Pei-qing could still be heard pleading.

"Mr. Principal, it was just a slip of the tongue."

The principal came back to me. His attitude to me was now lenient. Guo Pei-qing's voice became weaker. "Mr. Principal. I know I'm a pig. I'm dumber than a pig."

The principal snickered. He looked at me.

I looked at the principal and said, "But I did write 'Down with Garbage Li' next to it."

"I'm dumber than a pig," said Guo Pei-qing again through the door.

"My father says pigs aren't dumb. They're very clever animals," I said.

When the principal heard me say the words "my father says," his eyes lit up. "Your father said pigs aren't dumb?" he asked. "What else did he say?"

Suddenly aware of what was going on, I replied, "My father also said . . . also said, 'study hard and make progress daily,' " mouthing the adage by Chairman Mao that is emblazoned on the wall above the blackboard in every classroom in China. The principal appeared disappointed. He stared at me in thought. I was pleased with myself for seeing through the plot the principal was hatching against my father, and I quickly added, "My father never said anything else to me."

"The reason I wanted to see you is that someone accused you of writing the counterslogan."

"I wrote 'Down with Garbage Li,' and I drew the *X*-marks through the words."

The principal grinned. "Someone saw you write it."

"Make him come forward."

The principal was at a loss. He produced a sheet of paper and told me to write "Down with" on one side and "Chairman Mao" on the other. I was reluctant, wondering if this was another plot of his.

"Write it," he said. "Then you can return to the classroom." I didn't move. "If you don't write it, you can't go home." I stood firm, convinced it was a trap. The principal lost his patience. "They wanted me to lock you up," he said. "I've been protecting you. Do you understand?" Dumbfounded, I looked at the principal in disbelief, certain I had misheard. Such a powerful person saying he was protecting *me*? "Go home and tell your mother to come see me. Tell her I want to talk to her." I did not respond. The principal waited awhile and then left, telling me I should think about it carefully. He locked the door from the outside.

Noon came and went while I was locked in the principal's office, and I became hungry. After the hunger passed I fell asleep. When I awoke, it was already early evening. I was exhausted, but as I was about to fall asleep again the door opened and Mother walked in. She rushed over to me and hugged me tightly. My tears flowed.

"I didn't write it," I bleated.

Mother did not look at me as she spoke politely to the principal. "You should have told me earlier. You shouldn't have locked him up. He's just a child. This is a school. You shouldn't treat me like this, also . . . the child." Mother spoke in a very cultured manner, and the principal was obviously a little embarrassed. But I detected something strange in her tone.

"The child is a bit confused. He needs more attention," said the principal.

Mother led me out of the principal's office. In the corridor she said to me, "Son, why are you such a troublemaker?" Her voice was soft, which made me feel even worse. Her words reverberate in my memory, ringing like a church bell or buzzing in and out of hearing like swarms of insects over a puddle.

"Son, why are you such a troublemaker?"

III

At the time I had no idea this incident almost caused my father to commit suicide.

Others related the following events to me many years later.

After he left his office, the principal went to my father's place of work. As he entered the east gate, he collided full on with someone he recognized as the famous architect Liu Cheng-zong, who of course was my father. My father recognized the principal and immediately forced a smile.

The principal did not smile. "Were you born with eyes up your crack?"

Father had lived in Xinjiang long enough to know what this

meant, but he could not fathom why an educated person like the principal would utter those words.

The principal glared at Father as if he were a punching bag. Father did not respond. Even though those were difficult times, he still could not understand why a usually courteous person would say something like that.

My father's clothes were splattered with paint. He wanted it that way because the paint was his talisman. He would never let Mother wash his jacket because the paint showed he was a busy man. Busy doing what? Painting portraits of the great man. In Ürümchi he not only designed landmark buildings, he also painted huge portraits. Every dynasty needs a Liu Cheng-zong; the people, the times, society, they all need him.

With hatred burning in his eyes, the principal barked at my father, "Did you instigate your son to write it?"

Father had no idea what he was talking about. "Who? Son? Whose son?"

"Stop pretending!"

"What was written?" said Father as if he actually understood now.

"A counterslogan."

"Where?"

"Where? Where? Where do you think? At the school!"

Father was horrified. "What did it say?"

" 'Down with Chairman Mao!' "

Father gasped in disbelief upon hearing these words from the principal, who, realizing what he'd just said, blinked pleadingly.

Thinking only of protecting himself, Father didn't take this up with the principal. "What's that got to do with my son?"

Relieved, the principal said, "He's been accused, and our investigations have concluded that Love Liu wrote it."

Father's legs gave way and he collapsed to the ground. The principal left Father there and entered a large bright room.

Director Fan, the man who had once slapped my father, said that Liu Cheng-zong had painted many portraits recently, and that while he didn't deserve a word of praise, he should be given credit for working hard. But the principal saw it differently. He said Father was "using the red flag to oppose the red flag."

Director Fan ordered a bystander to go out and summon Liu Cheng-zong.

IV

I will never forget the pathetic expression on my father's face and the fear in his eyes. He obviously wished he'd never had a son like me.

The evening meal was on the table, already cold. Mother sat next to me. She was afraid Father would do something drastic at any moment. Father's wretchedness transformed into ferocity. He was glowering at me.

Mother stood up in a flash, positioning herself between Father and me. Father's fists were clenched, but Mother looked determined when she said, "We didn't write it, so we can't admit to writing it, no matter what."

I often wonder why women can withstand torment, whereas men are weak and destined to become traitors.

"Do you really think denying it is possible?" said Father. "He's targeting *me* this time, he's targeting *me*."

"In that case," said Mother, "I'll go to him."

When Father heard Mother say she would go to the principal, it was like being pierced with a needle, and his whole body became tense. I didn't know what to do. I felt terrible for writing "Down with Garbage Li" next to the counterslogan. Suddenly Father rushed at me, his fist raised. I ducked, and he fell to the ground like a toppled wine bottle. Mother stood in front of me, glaring down at Father as if she were facing the enemy. I also looked at him.

Father lay on the floor and began to cry pathetically. He hit his own face, bemoaning that in a past life he had not . . . but now he had a son like me. "I confessed," he then announced. "I had to. I know Love Liu didn't write it, but I had to confess. I'm done for, I won't live long now. I wish I could die here and now."

He kept on slapping himself in the face, behaving like a spoiled child in the hope that Mother would stop him. But Mother did not budge. Her fear transformed into hatred of Father.

Receiving no sympathy made Father want to hurt himself even more. He began to strike himself harder. Each time his hand found its mark, the sound was like the crack of a Kazakh horseman's whip on a horse's rump. He continued to slap himself while at the same time expecting Mother would stay his hand. He hoped to tease some tenderness out of Mother.

But Mother did not budge. That day she hated Father. His behavior upset her. For the first time she said to him, "I'm disappointed in you."

V

Mother's disappointment in Father utterly shamed him. He hated himself, and he hated Mother, too, because he couldn't bear to look her in the eye.

"I didn't confess," I said to Father, "because I didn't write it. And you certainly didn't incite me to write it, so why did you confess?"

Father did not speak.

Late that night, as I pretended to be asleep, expecting to hear my mother's moans as she embraced Father, I heard instead the sound of slippers as Father approached my bed. I knew he was looking at me, but I kept my eyes closed, feigning deep sleep. He stood there, his body brushing up against my arm, and started to stroke my face and my hair. Then he kissed my forehead and my face fervently.

Tears streamed down my face, and I opened my eyes.

"You're not asleep?" my father softly asked, surprised. I shook my head.

I looked at Father and spoke. "Why did you confess? The truth is I didn't write it, and you never told me to."

Father thought for a moment, then said: "Your father confessed so it would be only your father's problem and would have nothing to do with you anymore. You're still young. They can only come after me. You just need to study hard."

"But I didn't write it, so why did you confess?"

Father forced a wan smile. "After I'm dead, when you are old, you will understand."

"Where's Mother?"

"She went out."

"To do what?"

"Don't know. Anyway, she's gone out."

Father then hugged me tightly. "Give me a big hug," he said.

I extended my arms and hugged Father tightly. He smelled of sweat, and of paint. I felt I had never before hugged my father so tightly.

VI

The next day I went to school as usual. The principal was already in our classroom when I arrived. His attitude toward me had clearly changed. He examined me closely as he spoke.

"You don't look like your father. You're more like your mother."

I thought this was strange. Why would the principal say something like that? What did it matter to him if I looked like my mother and not my father?

The supervising teacher stood on the podium and made an announcement: "Today every class in the school is going to take a little test. Each student will receive a sheet of paper, and he'll write 'Down with' on one side and 'Chairman Mao' on the other. Pay attention now: Write 'Down with' on the front and 'Chairman Mao' on the back. You must not write all the words on the same side of the paper. Anyone who does is a counterrevolutionary."

Just then I saw Sunrise Huang drag herself into the classroom. She moved slowly toward me and sat in her seat. She appeared despondent.

Guo Pei-qing looked at Sunrise Huang and spoke again: "You missed what I just said, so I'll repeat it. We'll give you a sheet of paper and you'll write 'Down with' on the front and 'Chairman Mao' on the back. Do not write it all on the same side."

Sunrise Huang lowered her head and did not look at anyone. She just looked at her feet.

"Distribute the paper," said Guo Pei-qing.

Paper was issued to the front row of desks and passed backward. When the paper reached where I was sitting, I noticed that Sunrise Huang did not seem to see the pile of papers on her desk.

"Hurry up," the student behind her called out. Sunrise Huang heard him and instinctively rolled her eyes.

"Pass the rest back," I said to her.

She rolled her eyes again in response. I couldn't help chuckling. She actually laughed with me.

I took my sheet of paper. I was excited because I thought it made sense, since people's handwriting did not change. It was a smart test. I stared at the sheet of paper and was about to write, but I hesitated. Should I use my normal handwriting? I wondered. I could change it a little. But then I felt that would be too clever by half and might backfire on me. Many students had already completed the task, so I could delay no more. I wrote the required words on each side of the paper.

The teacher began to collect the sheets of paper in the order they had been distributed. Sunrise Huang appeared absentminded. She was leaning forward, daydreaming, the sheet of paper obscured by her body.

"Have you finished?" asked Guo Pei-qing when he got to her.

Sunrise Huang nodded.

"Then give it to me."

Sunrise Huang shook her head as she looked up at the teacher. Everyone laughed. We all thought she had been behaving strangely ever since her father committed suicide.

"Stop laughing," bellowed the teacher. Guo Pei-qing extended his hand like a beggar. "Give it to me," he said.

Sunrise Huang slowly sat up and passed the sheet of paper to Guo Pei-qing. He took the paper, glanced at it, then suddenly shrieked.

I looked at his ashen face. He completely lost control: His eyes went blank and the sheet of paper quivered in his hand. All eyes were riveted on the paper that had flabbergasted the teacher. On the front were the words *Down with Chairman Mao.*

After an eternity the teacher recovered and shouted, "Arrest the active counterrevolutionary!"

The whole class heard the order and rushed at Sunrise Huang. She began to cry. I felt the heat of everyone's bodies and got goose bumps.

The second lesson of the day was the English class. When Second Prize Wang entered, there was no call to rise. Sunrise Huang had already been dragged off to the principal's office. Everyone was chattering excitedly, as if they didn't see him. He stood at the front looking at us, unsure of what to do. He waited a long time, but it was clear the class would not settle down. He came over to me and asked, "Where's Sunrise Huang?"

"She's a counterrevolutionary," I answered. "She's been taken to the principal's office."

He immediately rushed out of the classroom.

VII

Half a year passed in a flash.

Ever since that day, we stopped learning English yet again. Not only did we stop learning English, we even stopped going to school.

The school gate was locked, and the light yellow building was full of dust and sunbathing spiders. It was deathly quiet inside, like a haunted house.

The days without school were great. I would get up in the morning and look out the window, completely relaxed, without the pressures of competition, without the burden of pride, without the ugly urge to show off to classmates. There was nothing, nothing at all.

And so I forgot about Ahjitai and even Second Prize Wang. Occasionally I saw Second Prize Wang coming out of the school building. He carried himself proudly and still dressed fastidiously. He'd disappear into the distance. I wondered what he was doing. Children always wonder what adults are doing, going back and forth like that every day.

VIII

The Hunan Cemetery became our playground. We played war games there every day. The games we played seem boring now. We divided ourselves into two groups, hid behind walls, and attacked the other side by throwing rocks. I imagined I would play at throwing rocks back and forth until the day I grew up, and then I would begin to walk back and forth like an adult.

Garbage Li was quick-witted. He was the only one of us who dared to peek over the parapets to observe the other side. Whenever the opposition threw a rock, he would see it coming and duck. No one else could do that, so Garbage Li became a hero. But heroes don't always see everything.

One day Garbage Li peered over the wall, but before he could observe anything, a rock struck his left eye. I heard a loud squeal, and Garbage Li began to bawl. I watched in astonishment as Garbage Li screamed beside me and rubbed his eye with his hands. Blood oozed out from between his fingers. Both sides held their fire as we all encircled Garbage Li. His face was contorted in pain.

"Quick," I ordered. "Take him to the clinic."

I was surprised to see Sunrise Huang again at the clinic. She was getting an injection, and her eyes lit up when she saw me. I had not seen her in our building for days. She became mentally deranged after being labeled an active counterrevolutionary. The hospital diagnosis was a nervous breakdown. Rumors were flying. Some people said she had been sent to the Dahong Gully coal mine. Some said she had been sent to a labor reform camp at Maralbishi County in southern Xinjiang. Others said she was just a child, and that even murder is not against the law for someone under fifteen.

"It's been a long time," I said to her. "Where have you been?"

"I just returned from my ancestral home in Hunan province. What happened?" she asked.

"Garbage Li injured his eye," I answered.

"You still play those games?" she said scornfully.

"What else is there to do?"

"I study the English textbook every day."

"I've lost mine."

"Your father didn't beat you?"

"Only your father beat you."

She stopped talking to me. I knew it was wrong to say that. Actually, I didn't mean to mention her dead father. I really wanted to say to her that with school closed, what was the point of studying English?

I thought for a moment. "I just saw your father's grave when we were at the Hunan Cemetery." Instantly her eyes filled with sadness. She didn't speak.

I went to see Garbage Li. His left eye was covered with a gauze bandage. He seemed back to his usual self.

"What're you gawking at?" he said.

I smirked. "Just wanted to check if you were blind."

"I saw Ahjitai the other day," he said out of the blue.

My heart fluttered. "Ahjitai?"

"Her butt is bigger than before," he said, "and she seems taller, too."

"Where did you see her? What's she doing now?"

"Not telling you. You might get all flirty."

I didn't respond.

Thinking back now, that was a very important day, because that was when she reappeared, the Ahjitai I had nearly forgotten about.

We left the clinic. Under Sunrise Huang's aggrieved stare I walked proudly, just like Second Prize Wang.

Garbage Li and I returned to the Hunan Cemetery. We scampered up a gnarled old elm tree and looked out at the snowy peaks in the distance.

"Didn't Ahjitai go off to southern Xinjiang? I heard she left for Kashgar, where her mother lives."

"Do you have a boner?" asked Garbage Li.

"You do!" I retorted.

"My dick gets stiff," he said unabashedly. "I wake up every morning before seven, and whenever I think of Ahjitai I get a boner."

Garbage Li articulated exactly what I felt. Every morning at seven, or just after six, or even while still asleep, I would experience what he was talking about. Ürümchi time is two hours behind the rest of China. When I say seven it's actually five. And six is four. At such an early hour a child can have erotic dreams just like an adult. Scary, isn't it?

IX

I couldn't sleep that night. Ahjitai kept appearing before my eyes—her breasts, her waist, her skin. As I thought about her, I couldn't help caressing my genitals.

The next morning at six I awoke from a dream. Garbage Li was right: We were just a bunch of boys with hard-ons.

After breakfast, my parents left the house. I immediately raced off to the store. I could see from a distance that there was a crowd of boys hanging around, talking and laughing while waiting for the store to open. As I rushed over, Garbage Li saw me first.

"What are you doing here?" he asked.

"I'm here . . . to buy some sunflower seeds."

"To buy fucking sunflower seeds? You're here to gawk at Ahjitai."

"No, you are!" I countered. The other children laughed.

The store opened, and we all charged in. But Ahjitai had not yet arrived. We wandered around the store, bored.

Garbage Li picked up a glass item. "What's this?"

"It's a breast pump," I replied.

"What's a breast pump for?"

"When your mother had your sister," I explained, "she produced too much milk, just like a cow. So she had to use one of these pumps to get the milk out. Otherwise her breasts would have swelled up and hurt."

"Kids nowadays," guffawed a saleswoman, "you know about everything."

"Oh yeah," Garbage Li said to me, "well, your mother's breasts are swelled up, too!"

Just at that moment Ahjitai entered through a door from behind the counter. She lit up the shop like the sun.

Ahjitai came over, apparently recognizing me. "Are you here to buy something?" she asked.

I didn't know what to say. I opened my mouth but just stammered unintelligibly.

Ahjitai grinned. "How is your English coming along?"

"I learned all of the International Phonetic Alphabet," I replied. "And now I've forgotten it all."

"I've heard classes will soon resume. You can study English again."

I wasn't interested in hearing her talk about school. I just stared at her face. I don't know where I got the courage to look at her like that.

Ahjitai became aware of my staring, and her face reddened. She reiterated: "Did you hear me? Classes will soon resume."

I could see only Ahjitai. Garbage Li and the other children momentarily disappeared, and I saw only Ahjitai.

FIVE

I

Autumn arrived, and our school's main gate finally reopened. I sensed something unusual when I entered. I walked into the foyer, up a few steps, and into the terrazzo corridor. The floor glittered, and walking on its colorful geometric designs made me feel as if I had just entered a palace. I thought of my father and had renewed respect for him.

No one's eyes could adjust to the sudden change if they ran from Hunan Cemetery, illuminated by bright sunlight, into our school's dark and narrow corridor. My vision would become blurry whenever I did that. A riot of colors would sway like crops in the wind. They would come and go, making me feel like a blind person who was scared of bumping into something. I thought again of my father, only this time I lost respect for him.

Summer not only tanned my skin, it also erased from my memory most of the English words and all of the International Phonetic Alphabet I had learned in the spring.

The moment I recognized Second Prize Wang's face was when a sliver of sunlight shot through the crack of the partly opened bathroom door and lit up the school's dark corridor. The melody of "The East Is Red," a song that was the de facto anthem back then, came to my mind that day:

Second Prize Wang is like the sun,
Wherever he shines, there is light.

Wherever Second Prize Wang is,
Hurrah, hurrah. . . .

Second Prize Wang walked toward me at a brisk pace, as if he was late for a celebration, and before I knew it I was in front of him. I wanted to slip away, as I thought he would not recognize me. But Second Prize Wang did notice me, and he slowed down.

I remember the way his hair bounced the moment he stopped. He could have chosen to ignore me, as if we had never met, as if his scent had never affected me, as a way to shame me for being so filthy in his presence.

He looked at me, but I was too nervous and shy to greet him. We just stood there. After a long moment he said, "Classes have resumed. Are you happy?"

"Are we still going to have English class?"

"I'll still be your English teacher," he answered.

There was the same scent of cologne on him. He set his eyes on me the way he usually did, as if he had just met an interesting person. He appeared to be in high spirits. His eyes were bright, like stars in a clear sky, like the glinting rocks on the Tianshan Mountains.

It is hard for me to imagine even today how an adult could be so upstanding in the company of a child. Didn't he feel tired at some point? Where did he get his high spirits? He always smiled and dressed neatly. His trouser creases were always well pressed, and the hint of a white shirt was often visible above the collar of his jacket. Why did he do that? Was it because of love?

The world of teachers is a mystery to students. What adults do every day is beyond a boy's imagination. Maybe everything Second Prize Wang did was for love. Perhaps there was a woman in his life, and he kept himself clean and fresh because he loved her. Or maybe there was no particular reason—keeping himself clean was just his way.

"I've forgotten all of the International Phonetic Alphabet," I confessed.

"All of it?"

I nodded.

"You don't remember a single one?"

I hesitated for a moment, then nodded again.

"Don't worry. We'll start all over," he said encouragingly.

II

The classroom was again filled with cheering and laughter. Everyone looked excited, like they had just come back from a great vacation.

We quickly picked up those lost English words and the International Phonetic Alphabet. Once again I could recite English texts, mimicking the voice on the record. Second Prize Wang was as happy as a farmer at harvesttime. He praised me when I finished reciting.

"Love Liu has the manner of a gentleman. The boys in the class should learn from him."

The class was quiet. Everyone turned to look at me. The word *gentleman* sounded foreign. You have to understand that we were in Ürümchi.

Second Prize Wang wrote the word *gentleman* on the blackboard. He asked us to repeat it after him a few times, then explained, "A gentleman is a man who has a dignified manner."

Ever since that day, my classmates stopped laughing at me when I spoke English with the same accent as the voice on the record. Sunrise Huang showed me more respect. Garbage Li was the only one who still laughed at me. "What an asshole," he'd say. Once he even made a comment like that in front of the class. I stopped reciting and glared at him, then continued.

Garbage Li stood in the corridor after class and gossiped about Ahjitai. His face was beaming with pride.

"I waited at the door because I knew what time Ahjitai finished work. I waited for a long time that day, but she didn't come out. So I went in. She was in the courtyard behind the store, changing her clothes. She didn't ask me to get out when she saw me. She wasn't wearing much, only a singlet. I walked in just at the moment when she raised her arm to put on her shirt. I saw her here—"

Pointing at his armpit, Garbage Li announced: "Right here. I discovered that her hair there is really long. Much longer than my older sister's and my mom's."

Boys surrounded him in the corridor, roaring with laughter.

Garbage Li was annoyed. "What are you assholes laughing at? You don't believe me?"

"Who? Who doesn't believe him?" someone chipped in.

Garbage Li continued. "When Ahjitai saw me, she asked, 'How's your English class going?' I said, 'Nah! English is fucking boring. It's worse than Uyghur.' She grinned, then said, 'English—' "

Wu Guang interrupted him at this point. "Stop talking about damn English. Let's get back to Ahjitai. She didn't ask you to leave with her?"

"Of course she did. Guess what she said?"

We waited for the answer. Garbage Li looked around and lowered his voice. "She said, 'Come to my place tonight. I live alone.' "

The boys burst out laughing and said he was making it up.

Garbage Li's face turned red. "Don't believe me. It's up to you."

I walked up to him at that point. He stared at me.

"Who's an asshole?" I demanded.

"You are!"

The boys standing there could tell I was provoked by Garbage Li's remark. The air became tense. They stepped back and encircled me and Garbage Li.

Garbage Li sneered. "Take a look at yourself when you recite English. What boy looks like that?"

I felt I was cornered. And his attitude made me even angrier.

Garbage Li started to mimic me and did it perfectly. He even had the text memorized. He was such a genius. I still believe that if he had worked hard, he would have been the best presenter on a foreign language program. His pronunciation was perfect when he said "There is a radio on the desk." His articulation and intonation were exactly like mine. He even reproduced my nervous breathing. Though he exaggerated a bit, everyone could tell that it was me.

Garbage Li then mimicked the way I blinked my eyes. The onlookers roared with laughter each time he blinked. Even the girls skipping rope nearby joined in.

I watched his performance, then suddenly threw a punch at his face.

At first Garbage Li was stunned. When he realized what had happened, he touched his face and then jumped on me with unstoppable force. We tussled with each other and fell to the ground. By the time Guo Pei-qing managed to separate us, there was blood on both of our faces.

Guo Pei-qing ordered us to go to the bathroom and clean ourselves. We went together but did not say a word. The fight showed that neither Garbage Li nor I could gain the upper hand over the other.

We were summoned to the principal's office after we came out of the bathroom. This time the principal was sitting there, smoking a cigarette while reading the *People's Daily*. The editorial caught his attention. He commented to a teacher sitting next to him: "This is exactly right. When you think about it, many people still embrace bourgeois rights—I myself am no exception. What it says about 'total dictatorship' also makes a lot of sense."

"What you said is exactly right, Mr. Principal," Guo Pei-qing chimed in.

"What's right?" the principal asked.

"Bourgeois rights and total dictatorship," Guo Pei-qing offered. The principal smiled.

Garbage Li and I stood in front of him for a long time before he finally got around to glancing our way. When he recognized me, a strange expression came over his face. He said to Mr. Guo, who was sitting next to him: "You can leave now. Let me have a few words with them."

Garbage Li fixed his eyes on the ground. I was looking up at the ceiling. I heard the principal say, "It's you. Were you two fighting?"

"Mr. Principal, he hit me first," Garbage Li declared.

"Shut up! I am not asking you!" the principal barked. Garbage Li lowered his head. The principal then turned to me. "What did he say to you?"

"He said, 'You're an asshole.' "

The principal was infuriated, as if he were the object of the remark. "Li Jian-ming, did you say that?"

"Mr. Principal, I didn't say *you're* an asshole. I said *he's* an asshole."

The principal pounded on the desk and boomed, "You are not allowed to say that to anyone, period!"

Garbage Li and I were silent. The principal paused for a moment. "You! Go back to your classroom now and write a self-criticism statement. It has to be thorough and soul-searching!"

Garbage Li walked to the door. He then stopped and turned around. "Mr. Principal, what is a soul?" he asked.

The principal was about to say something. "Soul . . . ," he began, then changed his tack. "Don't worry about what it is, just go and write your self-criticism."

Garbage Li finally left, feeling wronged.

What is a soul? What is soul-searching? I wondered, too.

The principal's attitude to me was much more lenient. "Take a seat, Love Liu," he said. "You are called Love Liu?"

I nodded.

He lit a cigarette, then asked, "How is your mother?"

I was puzzled—why was he asking about my mother? He looked at me, expecting an answer. Thoughts were spinning in my head: He asked only about my mother. Why didn't he ask about my father?

He drew hard on the cigarette. "How's your father?" he asked.

"I don't know."

He paused for a while. "What has your mother been designing lately?"

I remembered the drawings my mother was working on every day. "Air-raid shelters."

"Air-raid shelters must be well built, and they will be, with your mother's design. But it's just a bit of a waste, considering her talent. By the way, I heard you tend to show off in class. Is this true?"

I did not say anything.

"Humility helps one to go forward, whereas pride makes one lag behind," he lectured, quoting Chairman Mao. "You must be friendly with your classmates and must not be arrogant. In particular, you must not show off. People say your father likes to show off. Look what he ended up with! The title of Reactionary Technical Authority!"

I remained silent.

"I am doing my best to help you by telling you all of this. Did you hear what I said?"

I still did not say a word.

He took two long drags from his cigarette, then said, "You may go now. Give my regards to your mother."

Garbage Li was still outside of the principal's office when I came out. He smiled at me. He clearly was not someone who bore a grudge. I smiled, too.

"What did the principal say to you?" he asked.

"Nothing."

"Nothing? I heard it all. He sent his regards to your mother. Why only to your mother but not to your father?"

"I don't know."

"Did he ask you to write a self-criticism statement?"

"No."

"Then why did he ask me to write one, and want it to be *soul-searching*?"

We made our way down the long, dark corridor back to the classroom.

III

Sunrise Huang still sat next to me. She seemed to have returned to normal and to be as smart and happy as before. People had forgotten about her father, and if you mentioned her father, she would no longer cry.

But for me, Sunrise Huang returning to normal meant she was once again my strongest competitor, and she would be likely to regain the post of English class representative.

Second Prize Wang did not appoint the English class representative right away. He seemed reluctant to make a decision, and this gave me hope that the opportunity would come to me this time. Even Second Prize Wang's occasional looks in my direction, when he led us in recitations, would stoke my hopes.

It's weird when I think back: Why did I want to learn English when so few of my classmates had an interest in it? Was it because I was born with a love for the language? What kind of power did English possess to captivate a kid at that age, when everything was so confusing? I had been hungry for power ever since I was a child. If I were not appointed a class monitor, class representative would do, especially English class representative. Why was I so eager?

In those days, Second Prize Wang would go to his room and carry the phonograph to the classroom by himself. He asked neither Sunrise Huang nor me to help. I observed Sunrise Huang closely and saw that she apparently was not bothered by not being asked to help. But I was upset: I wanted to help Second Prize Wang carry the phonograph. Why was that? Was it because I wanted to learn English so badly? Or was it just because I wanted to wander around in Second Prize Wang's dormitory?

Sometimes I would loiter near Second Prize Wang's room, hoping to bump into him, so I could say to him, "Let me be the class representative!"

IV

As I was walking home from school with Sunrise Huang one day, she asked me out of the blue, "Do you want to be the English class representative?"

I nodded.

"None of the other boys in the class are like you," she sneered.

I was surprised because I did not expect Sunrise Huang to express her resentment this way.

"Think about it," she went on. "Is there anyone else like you among the boys? You are different from the others."

"But why do I have to be like them?" I countered.

She looked at me, then abruptly changed the subject. "What do you want to do when you grow up?"

"Revolutionary work," I replied.

She grinned. "That's not what I'm asking. What do you really want to do?"

"Galili who lives upstairs said working as a lathe operator is not bad. You work for eight hours at night, and then you can do whatever you want."

"Then learning English would be useless," she pointed out.

I paused. "So what do you want to do?" I asked.

"I want to be an architect just like your mother. I really admire her. She's much more elegant than my mother. She always smiles and speaks softly to people. She's very patient. Also, she dresses differently. I heard your mother was the belle of her university, and your father met her when he lectured there. They then started a teacher-student romance. Is that true?"

I was shocked. "I don't know. Who told you this?"

"My mother. I think she's jealous of your mother."

"My mother's different when she's at home. She loses her temper all the time. Don't be like my mother when you grow up," I warned her.

She was puzzled. "Then whom should I want to be like?"

"Ahjitai. She's beautiful and nice," I proposed.

"Ahjitai is nice only to the boys, unlike Second Prize Wang, who treats everyone the same."

"He treats girls better. He gave you one-on-one lessons. But we boys didn't get any lessons like that," I objected.

Sunrise Huang lost interest in the topic. She suddenly thought of something and said, "The night before I went to Hunan, I saw your mother in the principal's office. That night, my mother took me to see the principal to get approval for my absence from school. We knocked on the door a long time before your mother came out. She had probably been crying because her face was flushed. She normally has fair skin."

What Sunrise Huang said made me feel uncomfortable. I was only twelve years old then, but I had a funny feeling that something was going on between my mother and the principal. What could it be? I did not want to think about it anymore, even though I already knew what could happen when a man and a woman are together in private.

"Are you upset? It's true. I'm not making it up. I wanted to tell you the next day. But I went to the hospital that day and straight back to Hunan after that. Then I forgot about it," she explained.

"Do you want to be the English class representative?" I asked.

"I do. Mr. Wang also wants me to. But my mother won't allow it. She says that Mr. Wang is an indecent man and that most people who come from large cities are morally suspect."

That made me feel even worse. I did not want to talk anymore.

Sunrise Huang looked at me and said, "Let me talk to Mr. Wang and recommend you for class representative."

My eyes lit up. I raised my head and looked at her. "Really?"

She nodded.

V

Father turned on the radio, but he irritably turned it off once he heard a woman singing Peking Opera.

"Just tune it to another station and listen to the news," said Mother.

"What news! It's just the same old stuff!"

"Don't talk like that in front of Love Liu in case he blabs when he's out." Father did not utter another word. He took out the drawing he did years ago when designing the Nationalities Theater, lit a cigarette, and started to admire his work.

Mother cast him a contemptuous look. In the past Mother would often join him in admiring what they considered a masterpiece. Back then, as an architecture student over ten years his junior, Mother had worshipped him. This man, despite lacking a noble background, was charming: He understood music, architecture (of course), and women. He could spend long hours talking about Pushkin to women like my mother, and let's not forget that Liu Cheng-zong could recite poetry. Mother became excited by the musical rhyme of his words and fell in love with him.

But in this moment the eyes Mother set on him were filled with resentment and contempt. Father was sensitive. He could easily sense the lethal sharpness of her look but pretended not to see it. Mother made an exaggerated cough when Father exhaled smoke from his cigarette. Father raised his head, glanced at her, then went back to his drawing. "How could I be so brilliant? How? All of this now seems just incredible to me," he said.

Nobody was interested. He was just talking to himself.

"I really hope I can be given another opportunity to work. I am not asking for anything else, just let me work," he continued.

As a matter of fact he had been working every day—he painted portraits. It was a sacred task. What he just said was clearly reactionary.

He did not want to stop, however. "I may be working, but I am not really working. I have been painting imbecilic stuff every day. It's torture," he griped.

Mother had an expression of despair on her face. She looked at me, then stood up and looked out the window. When she opened it, noise from outside flooded the room. It was the sound of a broadcast over loudspeakers. The words were distorted by the distance but were sufficient to muffle Father's mutterings.

Father was probably annoyed by the noise. He looked out the window, then glanced sharply at Mother and turned back to his drawing. But Mother did not close the window. She waited for Father to say something.

But Father did not say anything.

Mother looked a bit lost. She took out the architectural drawing of the air-raid shelters she was working on and started to examine it. "The area where the Hunan Cemetery is located has always been a wetland. Waterproofing is crucial given the underground water problem," she said.

Father ignored her.

"With this type of soil texture, what's the most cost-effective approach to building the shelter's structure?" she continued.

Father disdained talking about the air-raid shelters. "Please! Don't torture me with air-raid shelters!" he implored.

"What do you mean by 'torture'?" she countered. "Air-raid shelters are meant to protect people in wartime."

Father laughed sarcastically. He sounded like a magpie. "War? They talk about war every day. War with whom? With the Soviet Union? What's the point of building air-raid shelters? What a waste! What's the point of being cost effective? We're being wasteful every day. It's criminal. And we dare talk about being cost effective?"

Mother ignored him. She put down the drawing and turned on the radio. She started to sing along with the revolutionary Peking Opera. She had a great sense of musical rhythm and sang very well. *"I am seventeen, old enough to help Daddy, why not, you see, thousands of pounds are on his shoulder. . . ."*

Father burst out laughing. "You are seventeen? Then I am eighteen. . . ." He rushed over and turned off the radio. I thought Mother would turn it on again, but she did not. Then there was silence. No one said a word for a long time.

I started to practice spelling. When I came to the word *mother,* I read it aloud. Then I thought of something and said to Mother, "Mom, the principal asked me to give you his regards."

Mother immediately seemed uncomfortable. She looked at me and said, "Hmm, all right, keep practicing."

Father stood up. He glared at me and held his stare for a long time. Finally, he came over to me and asked, "Where did you see the principal?"

"In his office."

"What were you doing in his office?"

I suddenly tensed up. I hesitated and did not want to tell the truth. Father stepped closer. Mother also came closer. She looked nervous.

Father asked again, "What were you doing in the principal's office?"

"I had a fight. I was reciting Engli—"

Father's hand, heavy with hatred, came down before I could finish speaking the word *English.* He hit me once, then twice more.

I did not flinch. I glared at Father. He had hit me hard, and it hurt, but I would not take my eyes off of him. I thought of the faces of revolutionary martyrs when they were confronting the enemy. My heart was filled with the same heroic determination to resist.

Father was clearly provoked. He jumped up and started to look all over the place for something he could hit me with. He was not very good at hitting people. He had never hit me before. He was an educated person who had a gentle and scholarly manner. But at that moment, Father looked like he was about to kill me.

He jumped around the house as if he were dancing. Blue veins stood out on his neck, and he jittered like a fighting cock. Finally he found a feather duster under the bed. The beautiful bronze red feathers were fluttering like the wings of a dragonfly. Father clenched the duster like a weapon, then lunged at me.

I charged at him, grabbed the feather duster from his hand, and yelled, "If you dare hit me one more time, I will report you, say you—"

Father was dumbfounded. He glared at me and hissed, "Say it! What will you say about me? Say it! Report what?"

"I'll say you said you've been painting imbecilic stuff every day. That it's torture."

Suddenly Mother leaped toward me and slapped me in the face. The slap was ruthless—*smack.* The sound echoed around the room.

Father's eyes were glued on me. He looked at me as if he had never met me before.

Mother wedged herself between Father and me and pleaded. "Hit me if you want to hit somebody. Don't hit him anymore."

Father raised his hand high. His eyes were on Mother, but his lips were trembling. Tears welled up in his eyes, but he held them back.

I rubbed my neck. It really hurt. I did not look at Father again.

VI

Right at that moment someone knocked on the door. I heard Sunrise Huang cheerfully calling my name. I did not move.

She called my name again and yelled, "Open the door, hurry up! I have something to tell you."

Although I was scared of Father barking again, I opened the door and stepped outside.

Sunrise Huang came up to me in the corridor. "What happened to your neck?"

I didn't answer.

She then announced, "Mr. Wang wants you to be the one to go to his room and fetch the phonograph. He has agreed to appoint you the English class representative."

I looked at Sunrise Huang but somehow couldn't manage to feel happy. Father's paranoid face and Mother's guilty look kept hovering in front of my eyes.

All of a sudden Father came out and tried to drag me back into the room. I resisted. He became terribly frustrated.

He yelled at Sunrise Huang: "Don't ever come to my house again!"

Mother rushed out and scolded Father: "How can you talk to someone else's child like that!" She looked tenderly at Sunrise Huang and stroked her hair. Then she turned around and said to me, "Love Liu, go back inside."

Sunrise Huang stared at Father's burning eyes and seemed not to know what to do. She was stunned. Her mouth was ajar, as if the man standing in front of her were an owl and not my father.

At this point Mother pulled Father back into the room. Feeling embarrassed, I glanced at Sunrise Huang and said, "You should go home."

Sunrise Huang looked back at me and asked, "What happened?"

I did not answer. I went back inside our apartment and closed the door.

The silence was unbearable. And then there was another knock on the door. Father and Mother looked apprehensively at each other.

I really hoped someone would just walk in at that moment. The person was still knocking, but harder now.

Father opened his mouth. "If it's Sunrise Huang's mother, I will apologize to her."

But we heard a man call out: "Liu Cheng-zong? Chief Liu?"

Father was surprised: In those days he would be grateful if someone called him Liu Cheng-zong. Chief Liu was how he was addressed back when he was a chief engineer. The man at the door was either out of his mind or from another planet.

Mother also seemed puzzled. She looked at Father and me, then opened the door.

VII

The visitors were Director Fan and a People's Liberation Army officer, whom Director Fan introduced as a senior officer from the Malan base. They sat down.

Director Fan first spotted the feather duster on the floor. He then noticed the tearstains on Mother's face and the expression on mine. "Did you two have a fight and hit the child? See! They say we educated men and women are different, that we're civilized and don't argue like the workers and peasants. Some difference! We eat the same grains and wear the same cotton clothes. I often jokingly declare that I am one with the masses of workers and peasants." He laughed aloud.

The army officer laughed along with Director Fan. "But you intellectuals don't quarrel the same way as us soldiers. Mr. Fan, you're a Peking University grad, right?"

"No—this is embarrassing: It was Tsinghua University. Those American bastards set up the school. It really is embarrassing for me. Back then I was eager to get high marks, and I did end up with high marks. I was so cocky. Thinking back, I was really naive. We must thoroughly reform our thoughts," said Director Fan.

"We are all here to serve the people. Director Fan, you don't have to be hard on yourself all the time. All right, why don't you brief Chief Liu," the officer said.

Director Fan put on a serious face. His expression reminded me of how he looked the day he slapped Father. He started to talk. "The party has made a decision. I wanted to tell you yesterday but didn't have time. In short, we are going to build a nuclear weapons research complex on the base, and we need a chief engineer. Liu Cheng-zong, as an architect who's overseen new construction, you've been chosen. You have the experience and are also a technical . . . I can't use the term *technical authority* anymore. . . ."

"But we also need technical knowledge," the army officer added soberly.

I was listening in on the conversation, and from that moment on I had a great impression of the People's Liberation Army. They were set up not to fight wars but to do good deeds. The soldiers would fight floods today and provide relief to earthquake victims tomorrow. And on that day, they walked into our home and liberated my entire family.

Father seemed unsure of what to do. First he rubbed his hands, and then he sprang up and started to pace around the room. He wanted to serve the visitors some tea, but we had run out of tea. He looked anxious.

Director Fan grinned and explained: "Liu Cheng-zong's a bookworm. That's the way he is."

The army officer also grinned, saying, "That is exactly the type we need."

Mother had only some boiled water to offer our guests.

Director Fan went on. "When you arrive at the base, you'll have the same benefits as an army officer, including salary, uniform, an extra issue of sugar, and a pound of cooking oil."

Father's eyes brimmed with hope. "I'll be in charge of construction and the structural design of the complex?"

The army officer and Director Fan both nodded.

"I wish to thank the party for trusting me," said Father, his face glowing with gratitude, "but I have one request."

"What's your request? Just let us know if your family has problems, and the army will do its best to solve them for you," the officer offered.

A smile appeared on Father's face, the kind of smile our revolutionary martyrs had before they died. "I want to ask the party to rescind all the extra benefits. Just let me work."

Many years have passed, but Father's words still hit me like the north wind, swirling above my desk, ruffling my pen and paper.

I can still hear Father's trembling voice: Let me be responsible for the whole project. The whole project. The whole project. . . .

VIII

I was awakened that night by a sound, a creaking noise coming from my parents' bed. I heard Mother's cry first, then Father's.

After that I heard Father say to Mother: "I am not asking for anything else. All I want is to be able to work until I die. Even if I die of exhaustion, I want to die at my desk."

Mother laughed in a way that sounded licentious to me. "Then I promise to buy you a new desk," she said.

Father started to cough. It was a cough of joy.

SIX

I

One day after I'd taken the phonograph back to Second Prize Wang's dormitory and was about to leave, he asked me to stay a moment. I didn't want to be rude to him, but I was a little tired that day and kept yawning.

"You don't seem very alert today. You must have gone to bed late last night. What were you doing?"

Second Prize Wang was just making conversation, but I didn't know how to respond.

What *was* I doing the previous night? It's actually embarrassing to talk about: I was following my mother. My suspicions had been growing daily, especially since Father left home three months earlier to work on the base. Mother seemed to be behaving strangely. That night she even put on a pair of high heels that had been stored in a trunk for years. Father was away, so whom was she wearing high heels for?

Before Mother went out she told me to go to bed early. She was pleasant to me. She had just combed her hair, and it was still wet. I thought I smelled perfume.

"Where are you going?" I asked.

"I have to attend to something."

I pretended not to notice she was wearing high heels, but they glimmered like the moon.

"I'll be back soon."

I nodded.

As soon as she left, I hid at the window to watch her walk out of the building and toward the school. I went down the stairs and followed from a distance.

When she entered the school gate, I hesitated. Was it right for me to be doing this? But then I heard the sound of her high-heeled shoes; she had already gone up the stairs and was headed somewhere on the second floor.

Following her in the dimly lit corridor, I saw her slender silhouette swaying. Mother was tall, and the high heels made her look even taller. She had to be up to something, wearing high heels at night.

Her pace quickened. To my surprise, she stopped when she reached the principal's office. The door opened before she knocked. "Now you come!" I heard the principal say. "I waited downstairs for ages."

The door closed. I gingerly went up to it and listened intently.

"Do you like these shoes?" Mother asked.

The principal did not respond.

"Why are you being so impatient? It took me a while to find these shoes."

Then no one said anything. The floorboards creaked, and soon I heard Mother moan. It was a soft sound, but I heard it clearly. I could definitely visualize what was going on inside. I should have called out, but I stood frozen.

Many years later, when Mother repented to Father, she explained she had to do what she did to protect us. In those days anyone who put up counterslogans would be executed by firing squad. Although she was defiled, she said she was motivated by her love for us.

Father forgave her. Not only that, he treated her better than ever. In Father's mind, because she did what she did, her heart must have been bleeding. The suffering she experienced must have been worse than the pain of torture. When the revolutionary heroine Jiang Jie was tortured in prison, the needles pushed under her fingernails caused only physical pain, but Mother suffered psychologically. What Mother suffered was the pain of our people.

Father was an idiot. He had been cheated and cuckolded for a long time, yet he worried about the whole country's pain? Don't you think he was being an idiot?

To avoid upsetting Father, and because I pitied him for the increasing number of wrinkles on his face, I never told him that Mother had worn high heels that night, that she had not been forced to be there but had actually enjoyed herself.

That autumn, Mother had relived her spring. She was thirty-something but had experienced the passion of a woman in her twenties. This is the deepest, darkest secret of my life.

II

It's not nice to gossip about one's mother. Really, it's terrible.

During those three months that Father had been away, he wrote to Mother a lot, and she also wrote to him. Later I read all the letters. They gushed with affection, and it was not completely false. But let me ask you: If your mother did the same thing as my mother, would you speak out? Mother's twisted behavior reflects the abnormality of the era. But if I did not attribute her behavior to the tragedy of our nation, would you criticize me? What should I do? Would it be better not to say anything and let the secrets stay buried in graves, like the ghosts of the wronged in the Hunan Cemetery whose stories were not told in their time, and were only partly recorded in a few of scholar Ji Xiao-lan's anecdotes two hundred years ago?

Was that the happiest time in Mother's life?

I must not jump to conclusions. Though Mother was also an architect, she was not as well known as Father. She did not get to go to the Soviet Union to study after graduation. She was too young, and when Father bragged about his experiences, he took up her entire field of vision. Her eyes were filled with affection, curiosity, and admiration. She knew her heart was conquered instantly, that she had fallen in love with this passionate old man, although he was only slightly over thirty years old.

At that time, Mother was vying against another girl for the title of campus belle. Mother was good at reciting poems onstage. The other girl, whom Mother had photos of, was good at basketball. The term *campus belle* was no longer in use when I was young, but Mother often used it nostalgically from time to time, as if people still cared about her grace and beauty. To be honest, she could not compare with Ahjitai—but that's just my opinion.

Anyway, that was the background of my parents' relationship. Father paraded around the campus of his alma mater, Tsinghua University, like a hero. Mother had only a short time to study him from behind. Then a fair wind blew, they greeted each other, and before she knew it she was in the palm of his hand. She was not madly in love; she simply thought the man who had just come back from Xinjiang had an air of greatness about him. She was drawn not only to his fame but also to his virtue. When he talked to Mother about humanity in architecture, he also talked about music, literature, and even philosophy. He dropped a lot of names, names women like Mother had never heard before. They were all foreign names.

I learned all of this from Mother's diary.

One night Father claimed the fruit of victory. He took Mother to the ruins of the old Summer Palace, burned down by foreign troops over a hundred years earlier. On the rubble that represents the humiliation of our entire nation, Father launched a fierce attack on Mother. He not only kissed her lips but also nearly tore her pants off.

Beneath the fluttering flags of victory were the tears of my mother, then just a college student.

After that, they kissed for a long time.

In his diary, Father recounts the same night at the ruins of the Summer Palace.

As the party who launched the attack, Father did not waste much space in his diary describing the scenery at the old Summer Palace. He just emphasized how discontented he felt after he kissed Mother for the first time. He wrote: "I did not think kissing her would be so disappointing." He didn't expect her mouth to be so wet. Then, when he tried to touch her private parts, she struggled. He said he immediately wanted to wash his hand.

The two of them, a sensitive man and a sensitive woman, were not mindful of each other's feelings. All they thought about was themselves. This was probably the reason they were later deemed to be in need of thought reform.

Before long it was dark in the garden park. The visitors had gone; only the couple remained, standing there as if frozen. They felt a little chilly and avoided each other's eyes for a long time, as if they'd be blinded if their eyes met.

At the end of the night, Father walked Mother to the entrance of the university. He offered to walk her to the gate of her dormitory, but she rebuffed him. She was confused and needed time to think; she wanted to be alone for a while. Father went back to where he was staying.

Both of them mentioned in their diaries that for dinner that night they'd had stir-fried Peking-style pasta that was drizzled with a layer of rancid oil. Father had diarrhea and wrote about having to go to the bathroom three times in the middle of the night. Mother made no mention of anything like this in her diary.

For years Father and Mother had a house rule: Each had their individual space, including drawers of their own that they rarely opened, and they never read each other's diaries. But then they had me, the fruit of their love. I inherited a slim body and fair skin from my mother, and a complicated mind from my father, and I never cared about my parents' privacy. At a very young age I opened those drawers and read my parents' secrets inside out. I never felt ashamed of what I did. Was being shameless a sign I was regressing?

Why did my mother do what she did? Even if she was initially coerced into that affair—she had to protect me and my father because the counterslogan incident was destroying our family—why did she go back to the principal's office again and again? Maybe the principal was not as self-centered as Father. Maybe he was more refined, and that's why even in difficult times like that, Mother put on high heels. Nobody wore shoes like that in those days. People either wore rubber shoes or canvas shoes. I can't think of anyone else who wore leather shoes—except, of course, Second Prize Wang and Ahjitai.

That night I pretended to be asleep when Mother got home. She quietly came up to my bed and stood there for a while. She gave off a strong fragrance that I'd never before noticed her wearing. Beneath that aroma, though, I could smell her skin, a scent that was familiar to me from when I was a young child. An overwhelming sadness came over me. Fearing I would not be able to hold back my tears, I acted as if I was disturbed by the light and rolled over. Mother switched off the light and went to her room. I wiped away the tears that were streaming down my face. My cheeks were soaked with the resentment and confusion I felt toward the woman I called Mother.

III

Father was back.

He was walking along the avenue of our compound, the Hunan Cemetery Residential Compound. He wore a full People's Liberation Army uniform with collar flashes and a red star insignia on his cap. Although the uniform was authentic, his bearing, unfortunately, did not match the uniform at all. He was short, he wore glasses, his neck looked elongated, and his back was slightly hunched. Some people would look majestic in a uniform like that, but Father was the opposite—the uniform looked so heavy on him, as if it were weighing him down and pressing him into the ground.

But Father was beaming with pride, like an unscrupulous person who has just come to power. He walked at a brisk pace, bouncing along with a spring in his step. Even though he did not have a hint of an erect carriage about him, he was "full of vigor and vitality," in Chairman Mao's words, "like the sun at eight or nine in the morning," with all hope being placed on him. I later realized that people must not be given too much power, nor blessed with too much luck, because once they get them, they will definitely change.

A perfect example of this was my father, who now wore a military uniform and was designing a building at the Malan base. I feared I would be the next to change. I was his son: How could I turn out any better?

The way Father walked should have invited the derision of other grown-ups, but no one laughed at him. Many even resumed addressing him by his old title of chief engineer.

One day in class, Sunrise Huang suddenly said to me, "Look! Your father!"

I looked out the window and peered at a black dot enlarging as it approached. It did not look like my father at all. "That's just a soldier." I chuckled.

"You can't recognize your own father?" Sunrise Huang retorted in disbelief.

I looked again at the black dot and still did not recognize him. Then the bell rang. It was class break.

"Look, look!" Sunrise Huang announced to the class. "That's Love Liu's father. He's a PLA officer now." Everyone crowded in front of the windows to gawk at the impressive officer.

I finally recognized Father because of the reflection of his glasses. As he approached, his skin looked darker, but his eyes were aglow.

"Love Liu, your father is a genuine army officer now," my classmates marveled.

All except Garbage Li: "His uniform looks like it's stolen." He snickered as he watched the way Father walked. His comment elicited some laughter.

As I watched Father coming closer, I could actually feel an adrenaline rush. I wanted to call out to him, but I could not open my mouth, and my throat seemed to be blocked. Father was no longer someone who painted portraits every day. He used to hunch his shoulders, but now he looked as proud as a peacock. He used to be the one who'd be slapped, but now he could probably hit others.

Sunrise Huang asked me, "Why don't you call him over?" I ignored her. "If I were you, I'd call him," she said. Then her eyes reddened. I knew she was thinking about her dead father.

My classmates seemed to be curious about the man in the PLA uniform. They surrounded me as if I were some sort of celebrity, but the stage was outside, and there was only one actor. The old elm we usually never gave a thought to, the spiky *Alhagi sparsifolia* bush in front of the building, the sunlight, and my father's shadow on the ground all composed the stage. Everything seemed so surreal.

Father walked toward us along the road outside the school. Once, for a brief moment, he glanced at the window where I stood. I thought he spotted me. I became slightly emotional because I had not seen him in over three months, but he had not seen me—his glance in my direction was an aimless one.

"Why don't you call to him?" Sunrise Huang urged again. "He's gonna walk away if you don't."

I remained silent. I was embarrassed even to think of calling out to Father. He walked through the school gate. I could imagine him walking along the school's corridor from the west to the east and exiting through the other gate. He designed the building, so he must be used to its darkness.

We began to drift away from the windows. I suddenly felt a bit tired from the excitement, as though I had just finished running in a school race. I sat down, staring aimlessly into the distance. "His uniform looks like it's stolen." Garbage Li's comment came to mind. My anger started to escalate. I glared at Garbage Li. I knew he had just been trying to be funny, but still I felt humiliated. Just as I was mulling over whether I should get even with him, Garbage Li came up to me.

"I didn't know that was your father," he said. "Don't be mad at me. I was just talking trash."

I didn't expect his apology, and I've never forgotten what he said.

"People look great in uniform," he continued. "Not many people in uniform come to our compound. I want to be a soldier when I grow up. I'll wear an army uniform, carry a gun, and go to Khorgos on the border with Kazakhstan."

Suddenly, a miracle happened. Father appeared in the doorway of our classroom. He scanned the room, looking for me.

Sunrise Huang quietly gave way to me. As I walked toward Father, my heart pounded so hard it almost jumped out of my chest. I felt like an actor onstage. I stood right in front of him, but he did not recognize me. Instead, he continued to scan the classroom. I could tell he recognized Sunrise Huang, so I nudged him. He looked down, dazed for a moment. Suddenly, a smile appeared on his face.

"You seem to have shrunk a bit."

I didn't know how to respond. Maybe he had grown taller.

"Give me the key for the house," he said. He grinned at me as I handed him the key. "You really did shrink," he reiterated.

IV

Father bumped into Second Prize Wang just as he turned around. Second Prize Wang nodded to him, and Father nodded back.

In the years since, Second Prize Wang told me more than once that this had been a greeting between two gentlemen.

Second Prize Wang initially was surprised to see Father in an army uniform, but he soon accepted the fact that Father now had a degree of authority. He gave Father a smile and extended his hand. Father hesitated at first, then smiled and extended his hand.

Ever since I was a child, it always bothered me to see grown-ups shake hands—what if they had just pooped? What if they had just wiped and smudged some poop on their hands? What if they had not washed their hands or not washed them thoroughly? These things could easily happen.

They gripped each other's hands for a long while. I thought they were trying to imitate Zhou En-lai, then the prime minister. Their eyes were piercingly sharp, their gestures authoritative, their chins lifted, and their chests puffed out. Their handshake was rhythmic, and it is burned in my memory. It was the first encounter between them I had witnessed, and it was like two rivers finally converging. Maybe they would go their own ways eventually, maybe they would both end up in the ocean. But in that long moment the sparkle of their smiles was like the foam of rushing whitewater misting in the sunlight. Finally, they let go of each other. Father turned and headed into the dark corridor he had designed.

The smile did not disappear from Second Prize Wang's face. "Can you go and get the phonograph?" he said to me. "We are going to learn something new today, and I need to play a record." He sounded more excited than usual. He handed me the key as he spoke.

I was thrilled when I saw the key. He even trusts me with his key, I thought. He doesn't worry about me stealing things from his room. He believes I'm an honest boy.

I dashed up to him, took the key, and ran along the dark corridor to his room. I came across Father again as I approached the principal's office. He saw me, and just as he was about to smile, the principal came out of his office. Sunlight was shining on the principal's face. He looked healthy and spirited, unlike Father, who had a sun-dried appearance.

Father turned to the principal. A chilling glint flashed in his eyes. Then he appeared calm again. The principal saw Father but did not recognize him. He must've thought Father was just a PLA officer. Nonetheless an army uniform represented authority, so the principal put on a polite smile anyway.

Father fixed his gaze on the principal and, to my surprise, offered his hand. The principal then seemed to recognize Father and instantly looked nervous. And then he also saw me.

The principal was eager to end the handshaking, but Father seemed not to have had enough. He gave a lethal smile and gripped the principal's hand. Father's eyes reddened. The men's hands seemed glued.

Then the principal made an offer to Father: "Would you like to come in?"

"All right."

Father pulled on the door that the principal was about to close and stepped into the room as though it were his home. The principal looked hesitant for a moment, then reluctantly followed Father into his own office.

The door was still open, so I peeked in. Father was looking around the room. His gaze stopped first at the curtain. Then he continued to scan the room. Maybe he was looking for a bed, I thought, but there was no bed in there. It wouldn't have occurred to him that the wooden floor he was standing on was where things had happened.

The floor was made of red pine hewn from the forest deep in the Tianshan Mountains. Planks of timber four inches wide and an inch thick were laid wall to wall. The floor smelled like the forest and gave the room a homey feel. Two middle-aged Tsinghua University graduates, a man and a woman, often cuddled together and rolled around on it. And now another Tsinghua graduate was standing on those same floorboards, but he didn't think to look down.

I stepped closer to the door and stared at Father. I was hoping he would glance at me so I could hint at some secrets with my eyes, but Father did not look at me. A smile was still on his face. He accepted a cigarette from the principal while declaring he did not smoke and let the principal light the cigarette for him, anyway.

I opened my mouth but did not know what to say. Then the door was shut firmly.

It will forever remain a mystery to me what Father said to the principal after he finished the cigarette. What could the two men possibly say to each other in there? What could Father possibly do to the principal?

Father would be no match for the principal if he wanted to hit him; even though the principal appeared to be gentler than Father, he was much taller. Although Father could go into a thundering rage from time to time, or even slap himself, that was just him being hysterical. The principal did not have to do any of that. He just calmly smiled and did everything he wanted, including sleeping with my father's wife.

V

I felt rebuffed and retreated to Second Prize Wang's room. The scent of cologne seeped out through the gap between the door and the floor. I opened the door, and again that thick dictionary was the first thing I saw. It was as if the book were glowing, or were playing a tune I had never heard before. How else to explain how it could always catch my attention and make me walk over to it?

But it just lay peacefully on the bookshelf. I gazed at it and felt I had some kind of connection to it. With that thought in my head, I started to wander around the room like I had nothing better to do than kill time, just like people nowadays stroll the streets window shopping. I became curious about many things in Second Prize Wang's room: a nail clipper, a red shirt, shoe polish, a towel, a blue toothbrush, a tube of toothpaste, and a brown leather suitcase under his bed. All of these things fascinated me.

Then I saw a jacket he often wore. The material was good, probably wool. It was charcoal gray and well tailored, and it looked like something Prime Minister Zhou En-lai would wear to impress foreign VIPs. I remembered seeing Second Prize Wang walk through our compound in that jacket. He attracted attention because of things like this.

I picked up the dictionary and started to flip through the pages. I lost track of time, and then Sunrise Huang suddenly pushed the door open and marched in.

"What's wrong with you?" she fumed. "Mr. Wang is expecting you. Everyone's waiting for the phonograph." I quickly put the dictionary back onto the bookshelf.

She stepped closer and looked at the dictionary. "Mr. Wang told me he might give me the dictionary one day if I work hard on my English," she said.

For some reason what she said made me angry, almost furious. He would actually give the book to her? Why? It was because she had ivory white skin, of course.

"Hurry up!" she urged. "Everyone's waiting for you."

We came out of Second Prize Wang's room. On our way to the classroom, we passed the principal's office. With the phonograph in my arms, I made an abrupt stop at the doorway, trying to peek in and listen to what was going on in there.

"Your father has already left. I saw him coming out of the room," said Sunrise Huang. We then continued to walk. After a few steps she added, "There seemed to be blood on your father's face. He wiped it with a handkerchief, but there was still some left."

I was shocked. "Are you sure?"

"The corners of his mouth were red. There was blood."

I passed the phonograph to Sunrise Huang, turned around, and strode toward the principal's office. Just as I got to his door, I thought of something. I dashed to the bathroom, where I remembered seeing a rusted steel pole. Somebody had left it there after replacing the water pipe. I picked it up from behind a wastepaper basket and ran back to the principal's office.

Sunrise Huang was still standing there. "What's wrong?" she asked when she saw me.

I rushed at the principal's door and kicked on it. The door opened, and the principal's head jutted out. I swung the pole and struck.

"Ouch!" I heard him cry out. I also heard the thud of the pole hitting something and saw some blood, which looked pretty in the sunlight streaming into the corridor.

Sunrise Huang started to scream. The principal covered his head with his hand and seemed to panic. He had no idea what had just happened. When I raised the pole again, he realized what was going on. He dodged, then grabbed the pole from my hands and used his other hand to grab me. He was strong. I knew I was no match for him, so I waited for him to take his revenge.

Blood streamed down his face, but he ignored it. Instead he stared at Sunrise Huang and boomed, "Don't you dare talk about this to anyone! If you do, I'll take disciplinary measures against you. Now go back to your classroom!"

At that moment there was no other sound in the corridor apart from reciting in the distance. Sunrise Huang was terrified. She hurried to the classroom with the phonograph in her arms. The principal then turned to me. I could see murderous rage in his eyes. I glared back. My heart swelled with hatred and fear.

"You can go home now," he said to me.

I was astonished. I thought I must have misheard him. I expected him to beat the shit out of me now that the steel pole was in his hands. He could hit me as hard as he liked. I was prepared for a thrashing.

"Quick now, go home," he repeated.

Certain I had not misheard him, I started to step back but continued to look at him, horrified. I was worried he might change his mind. My rage-inspired bravery had evaporated, and I saw my behavior as just the desperate act of a sick person. I was not a hero; I was my father's son. I obviously had inherited Father's weakness and impulsiveness. I was actually a coward. The fact that I was so engrossed with learning English and standard Mandarin showed that I was not a real man.

"Go. Don't go back to your classroom. Come back to school tomorrow," the principal commanded.

Like my father, the principal at this point took out a handkerchief and started to wipe the blood from his face. I continued to walk backward but kept my eyes on him so that if he changed his mind I could brace myself for a beating. Once I was over ten yards away from him, I turned around and ran.

In the dim light I could see my shadow on the wooden floor. I was running away from death, faster and faster. I felt the wind rushing by. I could hear Second Prize Wang leading my classmates in English. Mingled with their voices, a voice from the phonograph stood out.

It was the sound of genuine Linguaphone English.

VI

I went home. Father was sitting in a chair in his bedroom. I felt strong again when I saw him. I stepped closer to see if he had completely wiped the blood off his face. There was not the slightest trace of blood to be found. He just sat there staring blankly. He didn't wear the jacket of his uniform. His shirt collar was unbuttoned.

I stood next to him and did not say anything for a long time. I wanted to look at him but felt a bit embarrassed after a while.

"What's wrong?"

I was silent.

He studied me closely. "Why aren't you in class?"

"We don't have any more classes."

"Don't you have two English classes in a row?"

"Not anymore," I said.

He was angry. He could tell I was lying. "What actually happened? Why aren't you in class?"

"I—I . . ."

Father stood up and grabbed the collar of my shirt. "Tell me," he demanded. "Is the school giving you a hard time again?"

I shook my head.

Father's eyes turned brutal. He looked ready to hit me, but he pressed on with his questions. "What happened?"

"I used a steel pole to hit the principal in the head. There was blood."

Father was shocked. He opened his mouth and wanted to say something, but nothing came out.

"Sunrise Huang told me there was blood on your face. I knew it was because the principal hit you," I continued.

Father lowered his head. He sat down again and did not look at me. He just sat there. I stood next to him and did not know whether I should stay or leave.

Suddenly he raised his head and looked at me with teary eyes.

At this point I could hear the squeals of pigs wafting in from the canteen.

VII

That evening pork stew was sold in the canteen. Pig squeals always brought good luck, I thought.

When Mother came home, the three of us lined up in the canteen. The difference from last time was that Father was now dressed in an army uniform. He stood out in the crowd. People did not take their eyes off him, even when the well-dressed Second Prize Wang walked in. Mother stood in another line. I could see pride in her eyes as she looked at Father.

After dinner I waited for something to happen in our house. I thought Father would say something to Mother, or ask her something.

But Father did not say anything. He was in a good mood and talked about things at the nuclear base where he worked. Mother enjoyed listening.

It was a peaceful night. I went to bed early. However, I kept dreaming of blood—blood on the faces of Father and the principal.

SEVEN

I

On the day before he left, Father went to my classroom again to drop off our house key. This time he did not look as ridiculous wearing a military uniform as he did before. I could actually see sadness in his eyes. His neck was no longer extended forward like a skinny goose, and he walked slower. When he gave me the key in the classroom doorway, I could tell he had a lot to say, which made me nervous.

That morning I had just stolen a five-yuan note from his pocket. That was a huge sum in those days, equivalent to fifty thousand yuan today. Is taking money from your father theft?

When you hate someone, you steal his money.

When you love someone, you steal his money.

Mother and Father were my parents, and they should have let me spend some of their money. But that's not the way they saw it. They thought it was enough just to buy me some basic necessities. I disagreed. Money can be yours and bring you happiness only when you are the one who is spending it, and I knew this ever since I was a child.

I thought Father had discovered the theft and, seething at being cuckolded, was looking for an opportunity to vent his frustrations. Perhaps he had come to bash me or humiliate me in front of my classmates.

But he did not say anything. As he turned to leave, he just hastily said, "It's autumn: You should put on more clothes."

I read sadness in his eyes and nodded. After I bloodied the principal's face, I noticed that Father had suddenly become melancholy. He stopped talking to Mother about things like music or architecture. He never discussed with her those things that happen between men and women. He had been visiting us at home for at least a week, but I never once saw him lose his temper with her. He remained sad and calm while his heart bled.

The night before Father was to leave, I heard my parents making love. During his final groan my father said, "I really can't help it; I love you."

Mother said nothing.

Then I heard Father repeat what he had just said: "I really can't help it; I love you. Did you hear me?"

Mother did not respond. She wept instead. But she wept so quietly.

Father continually repeated that nonsense, but Mother remained silent.

II

When Father turned to leave, he still looked young from behind. He really was young—forty-something years old—but even though his life had been destroyed, from behind he still looked younger than a forty-year-old.

Father did not expect to bump into Second Prize Wang when he turned around. They were in each other's way. Father's acute sense of smell quickly picked up the scent of cologne on Second Prize Wang, and he knitted his eyebrows. Later Father said to me, "You see, wearing cologne in those days was just asking for trouble."

Second Prize Wang gave Father a friendly smile, but there was something inexplicable in his eyes, as if he knew something, or maybe he didn't know anything. But either way he respected my father.

Father was the first to extend his hand. Second Prize Wang hesitated, then shook his hand.

Father spoke first. "Love Liu says you are a good teacher. This is the right age to learn English. If they don't learn now, they'll miss out."

"He's now my English class representative. He's very diligent. He likes English."

"Be strict with him," said Father.

Second Prize Wang smiled. He smiled because he thought Father was being polite or just engaging in small talk. Father did not seem to know why Second Prize Wang would smile. He was confused but smiled anyway.

Second Prize Wang sighed. "The learning environment is terrible now. There aren't any teaching materials."

"I'll see if I can find something," said Father, "when I get a chance to visit my hometown in Nanking, or an old classmate at Tsinghua University."

"There's nothing available even in the large cities," said Second Prize Wang. "I've looked around in Shanghai. There's nothing, nothing at all."

Father instinctively became nervous when he heard Second Prize Wang talk like that. Although he was wearing the "green hat" of a cuckold, this green hat was part of the PLA uniform, which would ensure a glorious homecoming, and this good fortune had to be cherished above all. He looked around and said, "I have to go now, back to the base. You are welcome to visit us when I return next time."

Second Prize Wang nodded, they shook hands again, and each headed off in his respective direction. Later Second Prize Wang often criticized the habit of shaking hands for no good reason.

I walked back to the classroom with Second Prize Wang. "Should I get the phonograph?" I asked. His mind was occupied with something, and he did not hear me.

Sunrise Huang got up to let me back to my seat, but just as I sat down Father opened the door and beckoned me over to him. I looked at Second Prize Wang, who was already writing something on the blackboard. I could not ignore Father, so I nervously went back outside to see what he wanted.

He did not look at me as he rummaged in his pocket. He pulled out a ten-yuan note. "Take it. When you're hungry, buy something you like. You're too skinny."

I hesitated before taking the money. I was moved and did not know what it all meant.

"Your father kissed you last night. Did you notice?"

I shook my head. He turned to leave.

My emotions churned up like crashing waves. As I said before, five yuan in those days was equivalent to fifty thousand yuan now. Ten yuan was like having one hundred thousand yuan now. I was rich.

I pushed open the classroom door, but just as I was about to enter, Father called to me yet again, as if this time he would leave and never return, as if he couldn't bear to leave me and had to say a final farewell. I looked at him and waited for him to speak. From a distance of a few paces, his eyes glistened with the compassion Second Prize Wang had talked about.

"How much money do you have now?"

Stunned for a moment, I answered, "Ten yuan."

"I mean, in total."

I hesitated awhile and answered haltingly, "Just ten yuan."

Father's eyes lit up with his big smile. "It's fifteen yuan. I know."

III

Evening came. The wind began to blow.

I was still outside, running around anxiously in search of Sunrise

Huang. She had just run away from home. Her mother was crying plaintively in the corridor. She had obviously been out looking for her a long time, but grown-ups are clueless about kids' feelings and where kids will go when they feel like crying.

Sunrise Huang's mother had a peculiar way of crying. It looked like she was laughing. The more bitterly she wept, the more it looked like she was laughing hysterically. When she cried, she would first grimace, then squint. Then sound would come out of her mouth intermittently, making people think she had begun to laugh. Then she would laugh even more violently, and all the muscles of her face slithered toward joy, until her tears gushed out.

That's how Mrs. Huang almost made me laugh. The grown-ups who were trying to comfort her were also biting their lips to avoid laughing, because they, too, had noticed her unique facial expressions.

IV

I had to look for Sunrise Huang because I had caused her to run away.

V

Sunrise Huang's mother quickly found release from the pain of her husband's death and had been seeing someone. One day I had forgotten to take my English homework to class, and I returned home during the break time. Just as I entered the corridor, I saw Sunrise Huang's mother hastily leading a tall man into her unit. Being excited, the couple didn't notice me. I stealthily approached the door of Sunrise Huang's apartment so I could listen through the door to what was going on inside. Sure enough, I soon heard the sound of Mrs. Huang moaning, just like my mother moaned.

I can't explain the reason, but that was one of the most exciting events of my life. I couldn't control myself. As I stood outside the door listening, I wanted to fondle my thing. Sometimes I wonder why I am always thinking of older women, why I love them so, why in the dark of night I hanker for their scent, the fragrance that comes from the body of a mature woman, a combination of fresh leaves and stewed pork. I was never interested in innocent girls. Their bodies smell like dog's piss. Do you have a dog? Take a whiff after your dog takes a piss and you'll know what I'm talking about.

I stood there listening to Mrs. Huang's moans, not wanting to leave. The building was quiet—adults were at work, children at school—but Mrs. Huang and the tall man were enjoying each other's bodies.

When I got back to the classroom, Sunrise Huang was reciting from the English textbook. She told me Second Prize Wang said to her that memorizing vocabulary is not enough to learn English, and neither is memorizing grammar. You need to recite the texts. That will help you acquire a feeling for the language. And, more important, you need to get into the habit of thinking in English.

"He told only you, right?" I asked.

She nodded. I was immediately overwhelmed with jealousy and resented Second Prize Wang. He never told me anything like that, and I'm the English class representative! I saw this as an extra favor these damn male teachers gave to girls.

But Sunrise Huang did not bother to chat with me. She concentrated on studying and knew the text inside out.

I spoke to her softly: "Something's happened at your place."

Her eyes opened so wide that they appeared entirely white. She just stared at me like that. I thought I'd better stop. I tried to retract: "Nothing happened. I was just lying to you."

"No you weren't. Now you're lying to me," she retorted. "Tell me, what happened at my place?"

I did not answer.

"Was my mother beaten up?" she asked.

I said no.

"So what was it, then?"

"Go and look for yourself."

She put down her English book and ran home. Halfway through the next class she returned to the classroom, red faced.

She sat down in her seat and said to me angrily, "You liar, no one's at home." I did not know what to say to her. She kept on repeating, "Liar! Liar!"

Second Prize Wang was talking about the present perfect tense. "I have just . . ." Then he interrupted Sunrise Huang's angry grumbling: "Please summarize for the class what the present perfect tense is."

"It is for just completed actions," she responded.

I almost burst out laughing. Didn't the present perfect tense refer precisely to what her mother had just done? Second Prize Wang asked her to write an example on the blackboard. She got up and walked to the front.

After class she kept asking me why I was playing a prank on her.

"I'm not playing a prank on you."

"Well, what happened to my mother?"

"I saw your mother take a tall man into your home."

She was speechless for a while, then said, "So what?"

"Just that."

"So why did you say something happened at my place?"

"I . . ."

"What?" she demanded. "What?"

I didn't want to say. I didn't want to hurt her.

She looked at me and said, "Don't do that again."

"All right, I won't."

She paused for a moment, then said, "You don't look like you're lying. Tell me, what did my mother do with that man?"

"I don't know."

"I'm sure you do."

"After school. Tonight. I'll tell you," I conceded.

VI

"What did you see my mother doing with that man?"

Sunrise Huang asked me that on our way home from school. I'm not sure if I mentioned it earlier, but our school was only a few hundred yards from the new four-story building where we lived. It takes only a few minutes to get home, even walking slowly.

Sunrise Huang was on edge. She wanted to find out on the walk home, before the snowy peaks of the Tianshan Mountains disappeared in the dusk, what exactly it was that her mother and that man had been up to. I looked at her anxious eyes and began to laugh.

"What are you laughing at?"

"You tell me what I'm laughing at."

"Enough of that. Just tell me what they were doing."

"You tell me—what could they have been doing?"

Sunrise Huang suddenly saw the light. She was silent for a long time, then lost her temper.

She glared at me. "You have a dirty mind." And then she began to run like crazy. Did you ever have a female classmate like that? Smart, good at math, really thin, and able to run so fast that none of the boys could catch her. That's the way she ran that day, crying while running like the wind, with me trying my best to keep up with her.

We arrived at the corridor, one right before the other. Mrs. Huang was collecting the tomatoes she'd left out in the sun to dry for her daughter's dinner. I could see her afterglow as she stood there humming the melody of a Uyghur folk song. The lyrics went something like "Salaam to Chairman Mao." Sunrise Huang glared at her mother. Mrs. Huang stopped humming, a little surprised at her daughter's expression.

"Have you already forgotten Daddy?" Sunrise Huang shrieked.

Mrs. Huang stood there in a daze, momentarily unsure how to respond to her daughter's outburst. She lowered her head. Looking at Sunrise Huang standing before her, Mrs. Huang was unable to fathom why her daughter would ask a question like that. She opened her mouth. The tray in her hand tilted so that the sundried tomatoes were in danger of spilling out.

Sunrise Huang suddenly stepped toward her mother and shouted: "You slut!"

Mrs. Huang responded instantly with a slap to her daughter's face. It was a hard slap. Like a wildcat whose tail had been stepped on, Sunrise Huang ran away squealing, dropping her school bag in the corridor. Mrs. Huang chased her daughter, almost catching hold of her skirt, but Sunrise Huang nimbly evaded capture. Mrs. Huang fell to the ground and watched her daughter disappear.

I stood to one side, not sure what to do. I regretted revealing to Sunrise Huang what I'd seen. Dusk was falling, and my mind was a total blank. Suddenly Mrs. Huang grabbed me, scaring me witless, as if my brain had shriveled up and dropped to my throat. She huffed and puffed, unable to speak. Her face was as frightening as my father's when he was furious. I felt guilty. I thought Mrs. Huang knew I'd told Sunrise Huang about her secret affair. I was so scared that I wanted to tell her I'd been wrong and beg her forgiveness. Half expecting Mrs. Huang would beat me to death, I closed my eyes in a panic.

Life is full of surprises, so you'll be pleased to know Mrs. Huang did not beat me to death. She actually begged me to help her. At first I thought I'd heard wrong, but then I knew I'd heard her clearly.

"Love Liu, I'm begging you. Please help me find Sunrise Huang. Please."

I looked at her, feeling very relieved, and nodded in assent. Mrs. Huang then ran off, calling her daughter's name, and disappeared into the darkness.

VII

I was hungry by that time. I went home, but Mother was not there, of course, because she was still at work.

Nowadays I often miss those times after school when I was alone. Father was away and Mother came home late every night. Her designs had received approval from her superiors. Director Fan and his colleagues were most appreciative of Mother's work: An air-raid shelter should not be a defense against only ordinary bombs but also atomic bombs and hydrogen bombs. The shelter has to be built like a fortress that will seem advanced even after hundreds of years, just like the underground sewage system in Paris, and must not be like the roads in some cities—dig up a bit, then fill in a bit. At the time I really found Director Fan's words irritating, but now I can see how visionary Mother and the other intellectuals were, including Director Fan. I once went to Hebei Province to look at the underground tunnels. It was obvious they were just crap built by peasants fighting the Japanese, not structures designed to be around for hundreds of years.

Mother was different. She would look at every task assigned to her as the ultimate goal in her career as an architect. One day she would dream about designing a building more than ten stories high, and then the next day she would direct all her knowledge and imagination to building air-raid shelters.

She was now highly valued, and came home later and later each night. At first I thought she was secretly visiting the principal, but after following her a few nights, I realized I had misjudged her. She might have visited the principal occasionally, but now she was definitely devoting herself to her work.

They used explosives to excavate a huge opening in the Hunan Cemetery, almost fifty feet deep. Then they used steel-reinforced concrete to build a dome, like a European cathedral, and they put the earth back on the structure to make it look like a small hill. You can stand hundreds of feet underground and look at the grand hall, lit with brilliant lamps, and then go along tunnels to each battlefield until you reach your assigned position.

Even in those tumultuous times, Mother was able to find a position for herself through her own efforts. And because Mother was busy, I was free.

VIII

I found two maize cakes at home, smeared some soy sauce on top, and gulped them down. As I ate I thought of Sunrise Huang. I knew her mother would never find her. Just as I was about to leave, Mother came in.

"Where're you going?" she asked.

"Sunrise Huang ran away. Her mother asked me to help find her."

"No," said Mother. "You can't go."

"But I already promised."

"I said no! You can't go!"

I stood in the doorway, looking at my mother's stern face, uncertain if I should go or stay.

"It's dark. And it's chaotic outside these days. I've heard that wolves have come to Ürümchi from Fukang."

I knew I couldn't disobey her. I was not scared of wolves from Fukang, but I was scared of Mother, who loved me.

Resigned to staying, I sat down. Mother sat opposite me.

"Father gave me ten yuan today. I want to buy an English dictionary."

Mother was surprised. "He gave you money? Ten yuan?"

I nodded. Tears welled up in Mother's eyes.

"Your grandmother has been sick, and for the last several months we've been sending her all our money. Your father had only fifteen yuan. If he gave you ten, he's got only five left for himself."

It was heart wrenching to hear that. I felt terrible. I regretted stealing Father's money. He gave me all of his money. How would he manage?

"There's nowhere to find a dictionary now," said Mother. "Not even a Chinese dictionary, let alone an English one."

I didn't say anything. All I could think of was Father retracting his neck in that pose of lost self-esteem. The image of him in his baggy uniform kept flashing across my mind. His face was black and gaunt. It looked like the glasses he wore belonged to someone else. Mother quickly wiped her tears and buried her face in her architectural drawings.

"Can I write Father a letter?"

Mother paused. Turning to me, she asked, "You have something you want to say to him?"

I shook my head.

"It's a top-secret institution. Best not to write to him."

I kept thinking to myself: I stole five yuan from Father, and he gave me another ten yuan, so now he has no money at all.

IX

An hour later I heard more crying in the corridor. It was Mrs. Huang. Mrs. Huang was wailing so that everyone in the building could hear. Mother hid behind our door and listened in silence. Finally Mother opened the door and headed downstairs. I followed closely behind her. She turned around and looked at me but didn't say anything.

All the neighbors had surrounded the wretched Mrs. Huang, discussing where they should go to look for her daughter.

Mrs. Huang had been squatting, but now she raised her head and pleaded loudly: "We're all good neighbors. I'm begging you: Help me find my daughter." She then knelt on the ground.

Mother stepped forward to pull Mrs. Huang up. She helped wipe her tears and said to Mrs. Huang, "I'll help you." Turning to me, she said, "Go home." And then she walked off.

Many of the adults followed Mother's lead and also headed off into the darkness. I vacillated, finally deciding to look for Sunrise Huang, too.

I went to the Hunan Cemetery. Ghostly blue flames flickered. I thought I heard the sound of wolves breathing in the black of the night. Overcome with fear, I started running, and then I thought, If I'm this scared here, Sunrise Huang definitely would not have come here.

I searched for a while, then thought of a place behind the school where Sunrise Huang and I loved to play when we were younger.

The night air was filled with the sound of adults calling out for Sunrise Huang. It was like ghosts crying and wolves howling. From that distant time the sound has entered my study and is weaving its way around my bookshelves.

EIGHT

I

Many of Father's colleagues were jealous and said his design for our school building was influenced by Russian architecture. If you look down on it from the sky, it forms the Chinese word for mountain, 山. Father often proudly explained that the shape of the school building had nothing to do with Russian architecture; it was simply to protect the old trees.

In my childhood there were many ancient trees in Ürümchi. I was skinny in those days and loved to climb trees and idle away the day up there in the branches. Trees grew differently back then. The elm trees were never straight and upright. Their gnarled shapes looked sinister. Branches would grow out at a low place and streak up toward the sky like steps to the clouds. One trunk split off into three branches, and I would sit up there, feeling secure and comfortable. This was Sunrise Huang's and my favorite place.

My father selected the design for the school building from his many drawings and persuaded the leaders to allow the trees behind the school to be preserved. He often said, "They've been there for hundreds of years. Neither Han Chinese nor Uyghurs should disturb them because trees know our past, and they know our future."

Many trees were preserved because of Father. But he could never have imagined that those trees provided his son with many unforgettable experiences.

II

One particular tree came to my mind the night Sunrise Huang ran away. I don't know how, but as soon as I left the Hunan Cemetery I was certain I would find Sunrise Huang sitting in that tree.

The tree was between the first and second block of the school building. It was probably the oldest of all of them. It had been struck by lightning many times, yet it still had a will to live. Its thick trunk branched off as if it were three trees, and the large boughs reached out in all directions. One branch even reached up as high as a second-floor window.

I stood below the tree and looked up. No one was perched up there. I was disappointed. If Sunrise Huang had not come here, then where could she have gone? I climbed up the tree and sat on the highest branch.

Gazing at the moon, I thought back on when we were small and had just entered the first grade. Sunrise Huang was the one who put a red cravat on me the day I joined the Young Pioneers. We climbed this very tree that day. She sat on a high branch, and I sat on a low one. She told me she wanted to be a teacher when she grew up. When she asked what I wanted to be, I looked up and saw her white underpants beneath her skirt. It was the first time I'd seen a girl's underwear.

Suddenly Sunrise Huang showed up, as if she knew she'd just appeared in my memories. She stood under the tree, staring up in an exaggerated way, as if looking at the sun in the morning sky.

"How did you know I'd come here?" she asked.

"I just knew."

"I knew you'd know."

"Can you climb up?"

"I haven't eaten yet. Have you?"

I suddenly felt hungry. "Yes, but I'm still hungry."

"Did my mother cry after I left?"

"Yes. Now all the grown-ups in the building are looking for you."

She stood there under the tree and started to cry. I watched her cry from where I sat and waited until her sobs subsided before speaking again.

"Can't you get up here? Don't you know how to climb a tree anymore?"

She finally smiled. "Of course I can." She began to climb. I can still remember what Sunrise Huang looked like when she climbed. First she sprang up and took hold of a thick branch. Then she climbed up the branch I was on. She clambered toward me quickly, like a cat, just as nimble as she had been all those years ago. When we were much smaller, Sunrise Huang had never played with the other girls. She had always hung around with us boys.

We happily sat next to each other on the triple-trunked tree.

"Did you see everything?"

"I was wrong to make up stories. Your mother was not with a tall man. I was lying."

"I know you're lying now."

"Do you know what men and women do together?"

She did not answer.

"*I* know what they do!"

"I'm cold," she suddenly said. "Let's go home."

"You can wear my jacket."

When she put on my jacket she said, "Your clothes stink."

"Mother doesn't have time to wash my clothes because she's working on the air-raid shelters every day."

"I'm still cold," she said. "Hug me!"

My face started to burn. I embraced her tightly. She leaned on me. I could smell the minty fragrance of her body. Her breasts were soft, and there were two large protrusions. "Are all you girls like this?"

"Mine are bigger. I'm just skinny in other places."

I felt excited and broke into a sweat.

"You're sweating. You're really sweating. Why are you so hot?"

Just when I was at a loss for words, a light in a nearby window came on, illuminating our faces. Sunrise Huang and I blinked, but when our eyes adjusted we were shocked: Second Prize Wang and Ahjitai stood in the light, their faces beaming.

It had never occurred to me that this old tree grew right outside of Second Prize Wang's window.

III

Sunrise Huang's face turned white, even whiter than it had when I told her about her mother. She stared through the window motionless, as if the slightest movement would cause her to fall out of the tree.

I was actually a little disappointed because I did not see anything that lived up to my fantasies. Second Prize Wang smiled his usual smile. His eyes seemed especially bright, shooting rays of light out of the room, through the night sky, and into outer space. He gestured for Ahjitai to sit down. She smiled. Her smile was radiant, as if the moon had appeared that evening not in the sky but on her face.

Though I could not hear what he was saying, Second Prize Wang's movements looked a bit exaggerated when he invited Ahjitai to sit. He held out his hand with a flourish and, as he did so, bent slightly at the waist. His hair quivered exactly on cue. Perhaps that was a gentleman's gesture. I was so close to him that when his hair shifted from its normal position, more of his brow was exposed, and it looked like it could have been the brow of Lenin or Mao. He stood close to the light. That forehead of his looked like one of the majestic snowy mountain peaks reflecting the moonlight.

Ahjitai continued smiling. I had no idea what the smile of a woman like her could mean to a man. Their story had not yet unfolded, and there was not the slightest indication of what might happen next. Ahjitai watched Second Prize Wang prepare a brown beverage. She then began to explore Second Prize Wang's room. She wandered back and forth and then suddenly picked up the English dictionary.

I gasped. Could Ahjitai possibly read the dictionary? I knew it was the only comprehensive English dictionary in all of Ürümchi, and now it was in Ahjitai's hands. But she seemed to treat it as just another book, casually flipping through the pages. I watched her carefully. Something on one page seemed to capture her attention. Her beautiful eyebrows were knitted slightly. She read carefully and pondered, as if an English word or phrase had reminded her of something important. Finally she put the dictionary back and picked up another book.

My nervousness passed, and as Ahjitai looked at the other book I heaved a deep sigh of relief. My attention then turned to Second Prize Wang. He finished preparing the dark brown drink for her. An attractive tin box with a colorful logo was on the table. It looked exotic and refined, and it influenced my aesthetic sense for the rest of my life. There was also a ceramic jar that surely contained sugar cubes. In my childhood years, anyone with access to sugar cubes would have to be a member of the nobility—what else could they have been? He put the two ingredients together and poured boiling water from a thermos. The beverage steamed.

Second Prize Wang seemed to think of something. He walked over to the window and looked out. At that moment I felt our eyes meet, and we looked at each other for several seconds. I thought he wanted to say something to me. Although there was a pane of glass between us, I broke out in a cold sweat. But obviously he thought he was looking out into the black night. He never could have imagined I was in the tree with Sunrise Huang, watching him court a pretty woman. He then looked down and picked up a glass bottle filled with milk.

Second Prize Wang must have prepared in advance. Otherwise, how could he possibly have everything handy? He must have gone out in the morning to buy the milk and then boiled it to prevent it from going bad. We didn't have refrigerators in Ürümchi in those days. He poured some milk into the mug containing the brown beverage. His lips began to move. He must have said, "Try it." He then took the beverage over to Ahjitai.

Ahjitai took the beverage but did not drink it. She was being polite. Second Prize Wang said something. Ahjitai stirred her drink with a teaspoon and took a small sip. Second Prize Wang watched her expectantly. She looked happy, a shy smile appearing on her face.

Second Prize Wang took out a pretty box of candy. We used to have things like that at home, but they were taken away from us. Only people from Shanghai still had such things. He removed the lid, and rather than take some out for Ahjitai, he offered her the box. She shook her head.

Second Prize Wang carefully selected a candy but did not remove the wrapper. He passed it to Ahjitai for her to help herself.

Such attention to hygiene surprised me because Mother had quarreled with Father over this issue. But Father was unable to meet Mother's standards, and I was no better.

Ahjitai seemed hesitant. Second Prize Wang bowed again and made another elegant flourish with his hand. Ahjitai took the candy and put it in her mouth. Watching her eat it, Second Prize Wang looked pleased.

They had an animated conversation about something, perhaps a film they had just seen. What had they seen? Must have been *Lenin in October* or *Lenin in 1918* or perhaps a newsreel of Prince Sihanouk with Zhou En-lai at yet another banquet, or chatting with a jubilant Jiang Qing, the wife of Chairman Mao.

I noticed Second Prize Wang move closer to Ahjitai. When Ahjitai was sitting on the bed, Second Prize Wang stood in front of her. Now he also sat on the bed. As their conversation became more animated, he moved closer until he was almost up against her.

Each time Second Prize Wang moved closer, Ahjitai politely shifted away a little. She obviously did not want to sit that close to him. But Second Prize Wang kept moving closer.

Ahjitai's smile soon vanished. She stopped talking and glared at Second Prize Wang. Still sitting close to her, Second Prize Wang said something, apparently a joke because he was laughing. But Ahjitai did not laugh. Her expression was icy.

Finally, something happened. Something I wish I hadn't witnessed. Second Prize Wang held on to her shoulder and began to embrace her. Ahjitai struggled backward. Second Prize Wang pulled her back forcefully, bringing her body against his. They faced each other. He cradled her head in his hands and attempted to move his face closer to hers. At this point the last trace of a smile disappeared from her face. Her anger suddenly erupted, and she slapped Second Prize Wang in the face. The smack was so loud we heard it from up in the tree.

Second Prize Wang was stunned. He did not touch his face. His gentlemanly deportment now descended into a pitiful state. He just looked at Ahjitai. Ahjitai looked back at him. The two of them stared at each other for a long time without exchanging a word. Then Ahjitai abruptly walked toward the door. She opened it and, without turning back to look at Second Prize Wang, walked out, slamming the door behind her.

Second Prize Wang stood alone in the room. Steam rose up from the brown beverage, and the candy wrapper lay discarded on the table.

I heard a branch break just when the door slammed. Then I saw Sunrise Huang fall out of the tree. She nimbly grabbed a lower branch and swung past me like a monkey. She held on to the trunk and slowly slid down to the ground. I followed her. Before jumping down I cast a quick glance back inside. I saw a lonely Second Prize Wang.

He stood in the room, eyes filled with sadness. It was the same expression I had seen on my father's face. I didn't understand at the time why men always looked sad. Was it because there are women in this world?

I jumped down from the tree. Sunrise Huang was standing in the darkness, apparently waiting for me. I walked over to her. Under the moonlight I saw tears all over her face.

We just stood there like that. What we had just seen was still before our eyes. The moon was high in the sky, but why weren't there any clouds?

I smelled the scent of dog piss on Sunrise Huang. It smelled fresh. The freshness of a girl.

NINE

I

Garbage Li usually rushed out right after class, not to mention at the end of the day, but that day he stayed behind. He was leaning over his desk writing something, as if he had an important task to accomplish. Just as I went over to look, something happened.

There was no one else in the classroom except Sunrise Huang and me—we were on cleaning duty—and Garbage Li. Second Prize Wang approached a daydreaming Sunrise Huang.

"Why aren't you coming to the supplementary lessons?" he asked.

Sunrise Huang was silent at first, then exploded: "I don't want to. I just don't want to."

Second Prize Wang was taken aback. "You're upset with something I did?"

Sunrise Huang ignored him. She picked up her school bag, stood up, and stormed out. Second Prize Wang, Garbage Li, and I were left in the classroom, puzzled.

I looked at Second Prize Wang, expecting him to get mad, but he didn't. This made me wonder: When a female student loses her temper at a male teacher, does it mean he is guilty of doing something to her?

Second Prize Wang stood next to Sunrise Huang's seat. He turned to me and asked, "Did something happen again at Sunrise Huang's home?"

Garbage Li cast an irritated glance at Second Prize Wang. "Her father just died. Are you hoping her mother dies, too?"

Second Prize Wang was annoyed. "Don't joke about a death in someone's family. It's not kind."

Garbage Li was quiet for a while. " 'Kind'? What do you mean by that?"

I still wonder how Second Prize Wang dared to use words like *compassion* or *kind,* even in those difficult years. Was it because he was an English teacher?

Second Prize Wang was still looking at me, waiting for my answer. I put on a secretive expression, which, thinking about it today, was the kind of expression that makes me ashamed of myself. It was the expression of a degenerate person, or a sleazy eunuch in a period drama. It was the sort of expression that often appeared on my proud father's face, and sometimes on my mother's. I cleared my throat. Looking at Second Prize Wang, I was reluctant. Should I tell him that when everyone else was off at work, Mrs. Huang and the tall man were in Sunrise Huang's home, under the eyes of her late father's portrait, doing what grown-ups always do?

"Perhaps . . ." I stammered. "Perhaps something happened at her home. I'm not sure."

"She's been very emotional lately. You live in the same building and share a desk with her. Hasn't she told you anything?"

As though I understood, I replied firmly, "I don't know."

Second Prize Wang was either disappointed or did not know what to do. He looked out at the mountains for a long time and said nothing. By that time Garbage Li had left. Only Second Prize Wang and I remained in the classroom. I didn't feel like staying any longer, either, and was about to head to the door when he suddenly spoke to me.

"Let's go. Take me to her home again. I'll ask her mother."

Now I was really hesitant.

"Let's go," he ordered.

I just stood there.

"What's wrong?"

"Sunrise Huang's mother," I sputtered, "her mother . . . is not an easy person."

"I can't watch such a good student continue on like this. I must go," he said.

"Have you forgotten how she treated you the last time?"

When Second Prize Wang heard that, he too became hesitant.

II

Mother had not yet returned from work by the time I got home. I took some meal coupons and was on my way to the canteen. As I reached the ground floor, I heard Sunrise Huang's shrill crying and her mother's loud scolding coming from their unit. I went to their door to listen in when suddenly it opened. Mrs. Huang loomed in front of me.

"I was looking for you," she said. "Could you please go to the school for me and get your English teacher to come here?"

I didn't know what to do.

"You're the English class representative, right? Just go!" She turned around and produced a large white steamed bun. She pressed it into my hand and said, "Just say Sunrise Huang's mother wants to see him."

I bit into the bun. It was stuffed with meat. I felt blessed because we rarely had a chance to eat buns like that in those days. Sunrise Huang's family status sure had improved. They had meat-filled buns. I knew I had been bribed, but I still tried to wriggle out by saying, "My mother will be mad at me."

"No, she won't. I have a big bun for her, too."

I bounded off to school and found Second Prize Wang in the corridor on his way somewhere. "Sunrise Huang's mother wants you to go to her place. She has something to say to you."

Second Prize Wang was puzzled. "Then why didn't she come to me?"

"I don't know."

He thought about it and said, "Of course I can go to her."

III

This was a bit unusual. If a parent wanted to see a teacher, the parent would naturally go to the teacher. Mrs. Huang, however, summoned Second Prize Wang to her home, which suggested he had something to hide. Otherwise he should have been annoyed.

We walked down the corridor together. All the lights were on. Second Prize Wang did not speak at all. When we reached the main entrance, we saw Ahjitai coming toward us.

Second Prize Wang seemed nervous. He stood still, frozen in the doorway, and looked away from Ahjitai. He looked at me instead, as if he had just remembered something important.

Ahjitai did not look at him, either. She just smiled at me. She walked past us gracefully and left behind a trace of her womanly scent. It overpowered Second Prize Wang's cologne.

Watching Ahjitai, I felt an unprecedented surge of self-satisfaction—she had ignored Second Prize Wang and smiled at me. She had done well to slap him that night. In the lingo of the day, she had "beaten down" Second Prize Wang's "air of authority" and "boosted the prestige" of an unfortunate child like me.

Second Prize Wang did not look back at Ahjitai, though his shoulders tensed. My eyes were still following Ahjitai when Second Prize Wang said, "Let's go."

We arrived at our building and saw the sunlight fall on the old elms outside the gate. "It's going to rain tomorrow," he said, squinting up at the sky.

That was a surprise. I thought: He not only speaks English but also speaks the language of the heavens and can tell what the weather will be like. "Can you tell fortunes?" I asked.

"I have no interest in that sort of thing."

"Then how do you know it will rain?"

"I listened to the weather report on the radio."

I was thoroughly disappointed and burst out laughing.

He did not seem to understand. "What are you laughing at?" he asked.

"I know how to listen to the weather report on the radio, too."

He was even more confused. "I didn't say you didn't know how to listen to the weather report. Why are you laughing?" he asked like a simpleton.

"It's funny."

"I really can't see what's so funny," he said earnestly.

I said nothing.

"Come on. Tell me what you think is so funny."

"You said that tomorrow it will rain, and it made me think you were a fortune-teller who could read the *feng* and the *shui* like a real shaman. But you just heard the weather report on the radio. Isn't that funny?"

Second Prize Wang stopped and thought about it seriously. He suddenly began to laugh—a deep belly laugh. He was so slow on the uptake I couldn't believe it. I thought he would only chuckle and that would be the end of it, but he laughed with more and more exuberance, until he began to stagger about. He's a strange one, maybe a little abnormal upstairs, I said to myself.

"Hilarious, hilarious. Truly hilarious," he said, continuing to laugh.

I, on the other hand, became nervous. "Mr. Wang, listen. Sunrise Huang's mother is singing."

The sound of her singing came from the corridor:

Oh, my b'loved China
My heart has not changed
It forever cherishes your . . .

Mrs. Huang's singing was full of passion, just like the day when she had wailed.

Second Prize Wang listened attentively. "Prince Sihanouk wrote the lyrics with genuine feeling. That's why many people love to sing that song." Her singing kept coming at us, like a flowing river. We listened.

"Why is her mother so happy?" asked Second Prize Wang. "Well, we'd better let her enjoy herself and finish the song before we go in."

"I don't know why," I said. "Ever since Sunrise Huang's father died, her mother has been cheerful like this."

I didn't realize I had just said something profound. Second Prize Wang studied me closely. Mrs. Huang finished a verse and began to sing the melody in notation: "so—la so mi so la do—la so mi so si la—so mi la do la do mi—"

Second Prize Wang grinned. "She sings in tune, all right."

"You don't really have to go in," I said. "I can just say I didn't tell you."

"We shouldn't approach things that way," he responded. "The most important thing is to help Sunrise Huang. If Mrs. Huang hadn't summoned me, I would have come anyway."

We arrived at Sunrise Huang's apartment. The door was open. I was about to step inside, but Second Prize Wang held me back. Standing in front of the open door, he knocked.

Sunrise Huang came to the door. Her eyes lit up when she saw me. Then she saw Second Prize Wang. Sadness, resentment, and disappointment welled up in her eyes all at once. She tried to close the door. I tried as hard as I could to push it open, but she turned it into a pushing match. We pushed the door back and forth like that while Second Prize Wang just stood there. Obviously Sunrise Huang did not want to let Second Prize Wang in, but I had no idea she was actually trying to protect her English teacher.

The noise finally caught Mrs. Huang's attention. "Who's there?" she called out. As she spoke, Mrs. Huang walked to the door. "It's you," she sneered. "You really did come."

"May I talk to you inside?" Second Prize Wang proposed.

Mrs. Huang turned to her daughter. "Go to your room," she ordered. Then she said to Second Prize Wang, "Very well. Come in."

Sunrise Huang would not give up. She kept pushing on the door to force Second Prize Wang out.

Mrs. Huang did not expect her daughter to behave like that. "Let go of the doorknob," she said.

Sunrise Huang disobeyed and continued to hold on to the door.

"Let go," said Mrs. Huang. "Did you hear me?"

Sunrise Huang still pushed against the door. Mrs. Huang raised her hand to smack her daughter. The heavy smack left a red welt on Sunrise Huang's face.

Second Prize Wang was outraged. "Why did you hit her?" he demanded. "She did nothing wrong. You can't hit her like that."

"You've got to treat children the same as you treat political reactionaries," Mrs. Huang asserted, watching Sunrise Huang retreat to her room. "If you don't beat them, they won't capitulate. Dust doesn't sweep itself," she said, quoting Chairman Mao.

After we sat down, Second Prize Wang began to speak. "I came today because I want to find out why Sunrise Huang hasn't been able to concentrate on her studies. Hasn't she recovered from her illness? She hasn't looked right lately, and I felt I should talk to you."

Mrs. Huang glared at Second Prize Wang. "I actually wanted to ask you about that. You tell me why she is like this."

Second Prize Wang shrugged his shoulders like a wicked foreigner in the movies. I could tell that gesture provoked Mrs. Huang.

"That's why I came to discuss it with you," he responded.

Mrs. Huang lit a cigarette and deliberately blew smoke into Second Prize Wang's face. He began to cough. I thought all this was a bit ridiculous, but I did not want to leave. I wanted to see what would happen next.

After exhaling several puffs of smoke, Mrs. Huang abruptly asked, "Are you her supervising teacher?"

Second Prize Wang shook his head. "No. No I'm not. Guo Peiqing is the supervising teacher."

"I know you're not her supervising teacher. And since you're not the supervising teacher, why are you poking your nose into this?"

"I just think she's a good student, far more intelligent than average. If she studies hard, she'll have great potential when things return to normal. Also, she's learning English better than the others. Her pronunciation is accurate, and her ability to mimic is excellent. I am an experienced English teacher. I can tell."

"The problem," said Mrs. Huang, "is that you're not her class supervisor. You're just an English teacher. It's none of your business."

Second Prize Wang was astounded. "What do you mean by that? I like this student and am concerned that something's wrong."

The word *like* infuriated Mrs. Huang. She glared at Second Prize Wang and abandoned all restraint. "Don't act as if you don't know," she snapped. "If you hadn't come, I would have gone looking for you anyway. You're here, and that proves you've got something to hide. Everyone says your morals are suspect, so why pretend to be innocent?"

Second Prize Wang's face reddened. He was at a loss for words.

"From now on," she continued, "don't ever ask Sunrise Huang

into your dormitory again, and it would be a good idea if none of the other girls went there, either. Supplementary lessons, eh? I know what degenerates like you are up to."

"And what is that?" Second Prize Wang mumbled.

"Depravity." She snorted. "It doesn't matter if Sunrise Huang stops learning English. As long as she has no more contact with you, I'll be happy. Now get out! Don't wait until I throw you out. We can still 'serve the people' as Chairman Mao requires without learning English."

"It does not matter whether she learns English," Second Prize Wang responded. "And I don't have to give her supplementary lessons, either. You are also free to say I'm morally suspect, if you like. I came here today just to ask why Sunrise Huang has been emotional lately and whether you wish to take her to see a doctor. I know a doctor. He's an expert in psychology and psychiatry. He was also exiled from Shanghai. His name is Wu Cheng-en—"

"That's enough!" interrupted Mrs. Huang. "Stop talking about people from Shanghai. I've had enough of you Shanghai people."

Second Prize Wang was baffled by Mrs. Huang's rudeness. I was, too. Mrs. Huang was not usually like that.

"You can go now!" she ordered. "Love Liu can stay."

"May I speak with Sunrise Huang?" Second Prize Wang pleaded.

"If you don't stop harassing her, you'll be sorry. I'll report you."

"For what?"

"Stop pretending to be innocent. You know what you've done."

Second Prize Wang sighed. "I have nothing to hide," he said. "I did give your daughter supplementary lessons, but I didn't have any ulterior motive. If you speak to me like that, I can say only that you are rude."

Mrs. Huang began to sweep the floor, filling the room with a cloud of dust.

"You are rude," Second Prize Wang said loudly.

He was just about to leave when a man emerged from another room. The man was tall, a head taller than Second Prize Wang. He wore a khaki military uniform without an insignia of rank, but he appeared to be very important.

As soon as he saw the man, Second Prize Wang looked intimidated. "Commander Shen," he stammered, "I didn't know you were here."

The tall man swaggered over to Second Prize Wang. He then grabbed my English teacher by the shirt collar and said, "You think it is all right to take advantage of a widow and her child, do you?"

"It is nothing like that, Commander Shen," Second Prize Wang explained. "Mrs. Huang asked me to come over."

"No," said the man. "I was the one who wanted you to come. I asked her to send for you because it wouldn't be appropriate for me to be seen at the school. Now tell me, what were you planning to do to Sunrise Huang?"

Second Prize Wang looked frightened. "I—I noticed that Sunrise Huang has been upset lately, and I wanted to help her . . ."

The tall man suddenly roared, "You degenerate bastard! I don't want to be hearing about this again. Watch your back, you mongrel." As he spoke, he lifted Second Prize Wang almost off the ground, dragged him to the door, and hurled him out into the corridor.

Second Prize Wang fell to the ground like a rag doll. The door slammed shut, and I heard Sunrise Huang crying again. I thought they were tears of hatred then, but with the passage of time, I came to realize they were tears of love.

"Did we make a mistake by coming to see Sunrise Huang today?" Second Prize Wang asked me after I came out to him in the hallway.

"I don't know."

"And I still haven't found out why Sunrise Huang has become so moody."

Second Prize Wang was now covered with a layer of dust. I felt sorry for him. Then I thought of that night when Ahjitai slapped him and Sunrise Huang almost fell out of the tree. I thought I knew the answer to his question but did not want to tell him. What would he think of me if he knew I'd been spying on him from a tree? So I did not say anything, but I knew Sunrise Huang's mood change had something to do with her seeing Second Prize Wang and Ahjitai together.

I want to add a few words about Commander Shen. He was a well-known figure. He commanded Xinjiang's bloodiest armed factional fighting during the Cultural Revolution. That happened when I was a child. The tall man now was the deputy director of the Revolutionary Committee of Ürümchi. Despite my reluctance to employ an appellation like that in this story, there is no way to make things clear without it. Being a deputy director of the most important revolutionary organ at the time meant he had unlimited power. If Commander Shen had wanted to have Second Prize Wang killed, my English teacher would definitely not have lived to this day.

Later, when we could talk freely, I asked Second Prize Wang, "Were you really scared of Commander Shen?"

"Yes," he replied.

IV

Second Prize Wang continued to teach us English, but he looked a little different. He still smiled, but from time to time he looked out the window, staring into the distance, with sadness in his eyes. To be more precise, I should say that this change occurred after Ahjitai slapped him. Nonetheless, he continued to give supplementary lessons to some of the girls, but Sunrise Huang was no longer one of them.

Sunrise Huang changed, too. At first no one noticed, but after a few weeks her behavior caused speculation.

Gradually a mood of resentment took hold. It was, of course, directed not at Sunrise Huang but at Second Prize Wang.

Sometimes, out of the blue, Sunrise Huang would erupt in front of people: "Bastard! What a bastard!" This of course begged the question: Whom was she cursing? Her mother? Or someone else?

Garbage Li asked her with a smile, "Who are you talking about?"

I wondered about it, too. Was it her mother, because she had that tall man? Or was it Second Prize Wang, because he used to give her one-on-one supplementary lessons?

Garbage Li was smart. He linked the mystery to Second Prize Wang and his supplementary English lessons. But now Sunrise Huang had stopped going.

At this time it was difficult to look at her face because it was so deeply pained.

Second Prize Wang had a bad habit that made people hate him. Many male teachers enjoyed giving private lessons to female students, but in those tense times the male teachers were very restrained—except for Second Prize Wang, who acted as if he were from another world, as if people from Shanghai were different from other people. Was it because Shanghai had once belonged to the Americans, who encouraged the people of Shanghai to develop some distinctive habits?

Second Prize Wang never tried to explain himself to others. His smile never left his closely shaven face. But you could see sadness hidden deep in his eyes.

V

I could still hear girls' laughter coming from Second Prize Wang's room. Second Prize Wang laughed, too, although not loudly. I could picture the smile on his face. Sunrise Huang was not among the girls anymore, but Zhou Yan, Wang Hui, Gao Yuan, Bai Yang, and Liu Hai-ping were there.

Recalling the names of my female classmates makes me experience a mixture of happiness and sadness—the same sadness I saw deep within Second Prize Wang's eyes. When my father left us to go to the nuclear base, his eyes had that sadness, too. But no one else seemed to notice the sadness in Second Prize Wang's eyes, and everyone began to wonder whether Second Prize Wang had taken advantage of Sunrise Huang.

While many people became suspicious of this English teacher from Shanghai, giving rise to countless animated discussions, Second Prize Wang seemed entirely oblivious. One day after class I carried the phonograph and followed him back into his dormitory. As soon as I stepped into his room, I spotted the tin box containing the brown beverage, and the English dictionary.

As I was about to leave, Second Prize Wang unexpectedly asked me, "Why doesn't Sunrise Huang want to take supplementary lessons anymore?"

"I don't know. You should know."

He did not pursue the topic. As I had no excuse to stay any longer, I headed toward the door. But for some reason, just as I was about to close the door behind me, I pushed the door back open and walked back into his room. In a hushed voice I asked him, "Did you ever get fresh with Sunrise Huang?"

Second Prize Wang did not hear me clearly. "What did you just say?"

"Behind your back, everyone is saying that when you gave the one-on-one supplementary lessons, you took liberties with Sunrise Huang."

"Everyone?" he said, looking at me wide-eyed. "Who is everyone?"

"Classmates. And other teachers."

He stared at me with those wide eyes. "Your supervising teacher?"

I nodded. "I heard my mother say that even the principal said it. My mother asked me."

His eyes returned to normal. "Do you think I'm that sort of person?"

I just looked at him without saying a word. "I don't know," I finally answered.

Looking demoralized, he cast a glance at me, then walked over to the window. The old elm was right before his eyes, stretching out its branches as if waving at him. I'd said what I'd wanted to say, so I went to open the door. As I was about to leave, he said, "Thank you for telling me this."

Once I'd gotten outside of his room, I breathed a sigh of relief. I realized that for the first time in my life I had spread some gossip.

VI

I no longer could hear girls' laughter coming from Second Prize Wang's room. Bai Yang, Zhou Yan, and Gao Yuan had stopped going, and whenever Sunrise Huang saw Second Prize Wang, she took a detour to avoid him.

On the way home from school one day, I sensed Sunrise Huang had something to tell me. "What's up?" I asked.

"Garbage Li wrote me a note."

"What did it say?"

She did not reply.

"Did he write that he likes you?"

She shook her head. "He wrote in English. Just one word: *Love.*"

I was speechless for a moment. Garbage Li had never studied hard, yet he used an English word. "What do you think?" I asked.

"I feel disgusted whenever I see him, just like when I see a fly," she said.

I couldn't tell if what she said was true, but I could see that she looked pleased.

"What will you do?" I asked. "Are you going to write him a note back?"

"I've already written one." She stopped and retrieved a piece of paper from her schoolbag. It was all in English. It said something like: We are good children growing up under the red flag of communism and should not be thinking about that kind of thing at such a young age.

"Garbage Li won't be able to read this."

"That's what I thought," she said. She then tore up the letter. When we reached the entrance of the building, she suddenly stopped and said to me, "I want to use Garbage Li."

Staring at her innocent, pale face, I asked, "How do you want to 'use' him?"

"I want him to poison my mother and that man."

My scalp tightened. "Murder will get you executed by a firing squad," I said, staring at her with my mouth open.

"I know," she replied.

"Don't you hate Second Prize Wang more?"

She shook her head.

"Did he ever touch you?"

"Never!" she said in surprise.

"Well, that's what everyone says. Look at the way your mother treated him."

"Second Prize Wang is bad, but my mother is worse. I'll get my revenge on her one day."

"If Second Prize Wang never touched you, why don't you tell people?"

"There's nothing to say. He deserves it."

"Do you hate him because he likes Ahjitai?"

A few tears escaped from Sunrise Huang's eyes. She nodded.

VII

Being poor, Garbage Li often rummaged through the trash. In those days we said that kids from poor families matured quickly, and it really was true of Garbage Li. After school he would pick through the trash, then go behind the boiler room to collect unburned coal from the cinders. His face was often black, but I did not know at the time that love was buried deep in his heart.

I'm talking about him now because he did something that affected Second Prize Wang, and also me and Sunrise Huang. It happened late one night when my mother was still at work. I was bored, so I walked to the old tree behind the school. Suddenly I heard people talking. It was Sunrise Huang and Garbage Li.

"Did you find the rat poison?" Sunrise Huang asked.

"I got a bag of it from my father's storeroom."

"So when will you do it?"

"I know they always go to your place in the morning soon after we start class. Give me your key tomorrow morning."

"Just poison the man. Don't kill my mother. Let her live."

"I'll do anything for you," said Garbage Li. "To me, you are just like the moon in the night sky."

Sunrise Huang giggled. "Tell me," she said, "how do you say 'moon' in English?"

"Second Prize Wang hasn't taught us that yet."

"Of course he has. It's 'moon.'"

"Moo-nah," said Garbage Li, mimicking Sunrise Huang.

Sunrise Huang laughed again. "What do you want to be when you grow up?" she asked.

"A bandit. A guerrilla fighting the Japanese," he replied, listing his favorite characters from popular revolutionary movies we had all seen.

VIII

The first class the next morning was English.

While Second Prize Wang was writing the new vocabulary on the blackboard, Garbage Li slipped into the classroom without anyone noticing. Sunrise Huang tensed up. She looked over toward Garbage Li. My heart filled with horror.

I was still nervous after school. "You're not going home?" I asked Sunrise Huang, who was busily copying English vocabulary.

"You go ahead of me."

I could see that Garbage Li was not about to leave, and as I knew they had something to discuss, I left the classroom. When I reached the entrance to our building, I heard the resounding wails of Sunrise Huang's mother. I knew then that another person in our building had died.

A security officer was in the corridor taking photographs of the scene. But no amount of photographs would reveal who poisoned the tall man. The legendary Commander Shen was dead. He would no longer secretly come to sleep with Mrs. Huang. I heard that someone from the Ürümchi Public Security Bureau came because they were determined to solve the case—as I said before, that tall man was an important figure. They suspected Second Prize Wang, but he had been teaching at the time, so they lacked evidence. They also suspected Sunrise Huang. But no one ever suspected Garbage Li, much less that he would have done it out of love for Sunrise Huang.

It was a love between a young boy and girl. A typical case of puppy love.

IX

Sunrise Huang was questioned many times. All she ever said was, "I don't know."

After she grew up, Sunrise Huang once said to me, "I felt like I was in exactly the same situation as revolutionary heroines like Jiang Jie and Liu Hu-lan." But Sunrise Huang was nowhere near as brave as she later described. She cried.

When the adults interrogated her and didn't let her sleep, they asked her why she was so emotional. Second Prize Wang had asked the same thing, but for a different reason.

Sunrise Huang was so desperate to sleep that she said something against her will. The grown-ups asked her whether Second Prize Wang had touched her during their one-on-one supplementary lessons. That night, with their prompting, Sunrise Huang said: "He touched me."

X

It was the same night that Sunrise Huang's mother unexpectedly knocked on our door. With tears streaming down her face, she begged Mother to exchange units with her. She said she was a jinx to men, and that things would be all right if they switched units.

Mother was caught off guard.

Mrs. Huang's voice brimmed with regret. "Why is it that every man I'm with dies? No matter whether he's a Communist or a Nationalist."

Mother was shocked and said she'd never thought about it.

"Do you believe in spirits?" asked Mrs. Huang.

My mother, the Tsinghua University graduate, laughed. "I'm an atheist."

"Well, do you believe in ghosts?"

Mother laughed even harder. "If this is how you feel, all right then, let's swap units."

TEN

I

One morning I arrived at the classroom very early. After cleaning the blackboard, I stood in front of it, admiring the fruits of my labor. The first class was English, and Second Prize Wang was obsessive about clean blackboards. Alone in the classroom, I was bored. I picked up a piece of chalk and wrote "soul," "love," "house," and "change." I thought about what each word meant, then one by one erased them until just one word remained—*love.* I left it on the board. Then Garbage Li came in. His face suddenly flushed. "What do you mean by writing that?" he asked.

"What are you talking about?"

He grabbed the eraser and rubbed the word out. The word *soul* was still just barely legible. Garbage Li retraced the letters and made them clear again. "What does that word mean?" he asked.

"Soul," I responded in Chinese.

"Ever since I was small," he said, chuckling, "I've had to write countless self-criticisms that 'must touch the very soul,' but I still have no idea what 'soul' is. Do you?"

"I don't know, either. They say that after you die, you'll know what the soul is."

"You're the one who's gonna die." He snorted.

I laughed, too, as if the word *die* was funny.

"Let's go to the East Hill Graveyard to watch an execution sometime," he proposed. "Maybe we'll see some souls."

I ignored him and erased the word.

II

The bell had already rung, but Second Prize Wang did not appear for ages. We all thought it was strange. Usually Second Prize Wang was as punctual as a clock. Even on the few occasions when he was sick, he did not want to miss classes and would soldier on, speaking to us in his Linguaphone English accent.

"Why hasn't he come yet?" I said to Sunrise Huang.

She did not respond. She became annoyed with me when I kept repeating the question. "How the hell should I know?" she snarled. "I'm not his mistress, you know."

Her use of the word *mistress* startled me. In those days we read a children's story called "The Cock That Crowed at Midnight," about a mean landlord named Zhou Ba-pi and his nasty mistress. Yet for Sunrise Huang to use that word surprised me.

After a while the principal and Guo Pei-qing walked in. The principal had a long face.

"Starting today," he announced, "you will no longer learn English."

Everyone was stunned. Quite a few students cheered. "Great!" they cried out in delight. But I felt devastated.

"It is because," the principal explained, "Second Prize Wang has committed a serious mistake."

I don't know why, but I suddenly flared up with rage. "How about stopping Chinese classes, too?" I shouted.

The principal glanced my way, and our eyes locked. He was obviously being easy on me and quickly diverted his attention.

"You may read silently for the remainder of this class," he instructed. "For future classes, the school authorities will give further notice once a decision has been made."

III

After class I ran as fast as I could to Second Prize Wang's room. When I reached the door I tried to peek through the decorative glass panels, but it was dark inside, and I could not see a thing. Joyful laughter echoed through the corridor.

I stood in front of the door. "Mr. Wang!" I called out. Nothing. I called his name a few more times, but there was still no response. Feeling disappointed, I was about to leave when the door suddenly opened, and Second Prize Wang stood in front of me. We looked at each other for a long time. Then he opened the door a little more to let me in.

It was dark inside, just like a bad guy's room. For the first time I noticed the absence of any fragrance in his room. Second Prize Wang looked ashen. Although his face was clean-shaven as usual, it reminded me of cement.

I sat on a chair. He remained standing. I wanted to ask him something, but his gray face scared me. It was the first time Second Prize Wang, the only person who could speak English in my childhood, looked monstrous. I almost regretted going there.

He looked at me. "You won't be learning English anymore?"

I shook my head.

"Who announced it?"

"The principal."

"What was the reaction?"

I hesitated a moment. "Everyone was happy."

Second Prize Wang looked hurt. It was not what he had expected me to say. Tears formed and were about to spill out, but he held them back. At first I thought I was mistaken, but there definitely were tears.

His tears scared me even more—I really hoped he was not someone who would cry. Could he really cry? I did not want to see him cry. I wanted to leave that depressing room immediately but felt too guilty to do so. When someone cries in front of you, can you leave before they have wiped away their tears? I did not know what to do except stand there feeling awkward.

A few teardrops escaped as his eyes blinked, but they quickly dried. All was quiet for a while, and then he broke the silence, speaking loudly and startling me.

"Actually, I'm not sad," he declared.

I looked at him and stood up. "Then I'll be going," I said. "Phys. ed. class is about to begin."

"You don't really like phys. ed., do you?"

I shook my head. But I thought it was strange that he knew I did not like phys. ed.

He paused. "During phys. ed. classes, I notice you tend to stand around and never kick the ball. You always look like your mind is elsewhere."

"Mr. Wang," I said, "I'm going now."

He nodded. As I was about to go out the door he said, "Wait."

That made me jump. I was terrified he might really be a bad guy. He walked over, pulled me back into the room, and closed the door. I did not know what he intended to do. I looked up at him as if awaiting a verdict.

He seemed to hesitate, pondering something. Then, slowly and deliberately, he asked me, "Why does Sunrise Huang hate me?"

I did not respond.

"Why does she hate me?" he repeated.

"She didn't . . . tell me . . . ," I stammered, "that she hates you."

He studied my face until he was sure I had nothing more to say. "Go," he said, opening the door. "And don't come here again. It's not good for you."

I walked out the door and turned my head to look back at him. He said, "And don't come here again. It's not good for you."

Those words hurt. I was suddenly overcome with sadness. I felt like telling him, "Sunrise Huang hates you because you like Ahjitai." But I walked away in silence.

The corridor was dark, my mood was dismal, and I despised my father's gloomy architectural designs.

IV

Without English class, I was lost. It gave truth to a popular saying about studying Chairman Mao's works: "A day without study and problems appear; two days without study and you're going downhill; three days without study and you're done for." I was probably done for.

When I was in other classes, I often took out my flash cards to examine over and over again the English vocabulary and the illustrations I had drawn for each word. For the word *face,* I had drawn Garbage Li's face in an exaggerated way. For *fate,* I had used a lightning bolt to illustrate destiny. For *father,* I'd drawn Father's crooked eyes. Bittersweet feelings came over me whenever I flipped through those cards.

One day it was raining again, and the Tianshan Mountains disappeared in the mist. Sunrise Huang saw my flash cards and wanted to take a closer look, but I didn't let her. While Guo Pei-qing was speaking to the class, the two of us grappled under the desk for one of the cards. In the end, it was torn in half.

I was furious. I completely forgot I was in class and yelled at Sunrise Huang, "Fuck!" My classmates were stunned. In their eyes I was a polite boy, so why would I swear like that, especially in front of our supervising teacher?

Sunrise Huang began to cry. Guo Pei-qing ordered me to stand up.

"Why did you swear?"

"She tore my card."

Guo Pei-qing came over and snatched the card from me. "Bird? A flying bird. A bird in English. A foreigner's bird . . . Looks like you've been poisoned by this English business."

Without warning, Guo Pei-qing violently opened the window. Rain splattered in, and my face was instantly drenched. He hurled the card out the window. A card with the English word for bird was thrust up into the sky, soaring higher and higher. Guo Pei-qing slammed the window shut and dismissed the class. The bell in the corridor sounded. Guo Pei-qing walked out of the classroom and did not seek me out.

Just when I was able to calm down a bit, Garbage Li came up to me and demanded that we go outside and fight. He looked irate, so I stayed in my seat and tried to avoid looking at him.

"Are you a man?" he taunted.

I still said nothing. The standoff continued until Sunrise Huang intervened.

"Go back," she ordered Garbage Li. Garbage Li glared at me, then looked at Sunrise Huang and obediently returned to his seat.

I took out a new flash card and wrote the word *bird* in English. "Damn bird," I said. I drew a bird with outstretched wings, flying up in the clouds. Just then I caught another glimpse of the Tianshan Mountains. They seemed to shudder in the rain, as if they were overreacting to the moist air and perhaps had caught a cold.

V

Mother's design for the air-raid shelter began to be built. Digging was under way in the Hunan Cemetery.

People in those days were terribly smart. Even though we were poor, we were ingenious in defending against foreign invasion. Rocks were piled up to build a blockhouse. Then dirt was heaped up in a mound on which trees and grass were planted. On the western side of the mound, they dug an opening like a cave dwelling's entrance and from there excavated the entrance shaft. From a distance it looked like a hill, and from above like a tomb.

This was Mother's masterpiece. For the first time ever, without any help from Father, she was able to exhibit her talents and creativity. I heard that Mother cried when she first saw her design become reality.

I forgot to bring my key that day, so I went to the construction site to find Mother. She would not have had time for me even if she had noticed me. She was earnestly discussing something with Director Fan and looked a bit impatient. As she debated with him, her face was in bloom like the flowers on the prairie. In July, flowers bloom in the grasslands north of Ürümchi. The Muslim Hui people gather in the foothills of the Tianshan Mountains to sing in pageants called Hua-er. If you have ever heard a cheerful accordion solo, you will understand what I mean. Mother's smile in front of those men was like the melodiousness of the accordion, like the beauty of the flowers. Her smile also proved that people do not always hold grudges. Trees have growth rings to record what happens in their lives, but people are different. Work made Mother forget personal feuds; she appeared to have no memory of Director Fan slapping Father. There was no question: Work made Mother luminously beautiful.

I stood to one side, waiting for Mother to notice me so I would have a chance to explain that I did not have my key and that I was hungry. In those days, my hunger was as profound and infinite as the sky. Like clouds filling the sky, hunger would descend on me less than half an hour after eating.

I planned my strategy to interrupt Mother's discussion with the men. I knew I had to be succinct and to say it all in two sentences: "There are no more meal coupons at home"—that would be the first sentence. Then I would say, "I forgot my key; give me yours."

But Mother's enthusiasm for her work made me suspect that even if I did manage to get out those two sentences, I could not make her listen. She was so excited to see her design become a reality that nothing else mattered.

From a young age, I understood that work could make a talented woman temporarily forget about her offspring. I was like a bystander in that bustling place, more composed even than the adults around me. Once I realized that Mother was not going to turn her attention to me anytime soon, my hunger pangs subsided.

VI

I began to wander around the air-raid-shelter construction site, examining like an archaeologist the unearthed objects. I saw a large fossilized shell. Again I realized my parents were right about Xinjiang once being a sea. The sea was gone, and parts had become a desert.

Why did it have to become a desert? Being reminded that I had still not seen the ocean brought wave upon wave of melancholy crashing down on my heart. And then I saw Second Prize Wang emerge from the excavation pit. He looked a lot darker and thinner and was not as fastidiously groomed. Wearing a khaki military-style uniform and a pair of large rubber boots, he looked like a different person, like the little tramp in a Charlie Chaplin movie.

I rushed toward him excitedly, but he did not recognize me right away. "I'm Love Liu."

"You've grown taller," he said in disbelief, looking me up and down.

"My mother designed this air-raid shelter."

"I can see that it was done by a professional."

"Why are you wearing rain boots?"

"There's a lot of groundwater seeping in down there, and we have to stand in it as we dig."

"It must be tiring, right?"

"It is." He nodded. "Are you still studying English?"

"I've forgotten everything."

"How's Sunrise Huang?"

"She's fine. She joined the propaganda troupe and practices with them every day."

"Practices what?"

"The Grasslands and Peking Link Hearts."

"How can the grasslands link hearts with Peking?" He chortled.

"Will you come back to teach us English?"

His eyes became gloomy. "I probably can't," he replied. "Next month I might have to move out of the school. Actually, I really like that dormitory with the trees outside the window and the views of the Tianshan Mountains, and the constant sound of students' laughter in the corridors."

"I want you to come back."

He was clearly touched. Just then Mother came over and stood between us.

Mother nodded politely to Second Prize Wang and then said to me, "What are you doing here?"

I was about to answer when someone called out to Second Prize Wang. He turned around and left. I gazed at his departing figure for a moment. Suddenly I rushed to him and blocked his path. He regarded me warmly and patted my head.

"I am sad to see you dressed like this," I said.

He looked down at his clothes but did not say a word. Then he patted my head again, gently moved me out of his way, and headed back down to the excavation pit.

Mother pulled me aside. "Of all the teachers," she said, "why do you have to spend time with him?"

"He's the English teacher."

"But his morals are questionable."

"What does that mean? Whose morals are not questionable? Are your morals perfect?"

Mother raised her hand in fury and slapped me. Before her hand landed on me, though, she managed to regain control, and by the time she made contact with my neck, the force of her blow was greatly diminished.

I fled, forgetting to take the key and the meal coupons. Thinking about it later, I was sure I must have spoiled her day—at work she could forget about so many things, and then I came along to remind her of her failures in life. I ran fast and soon arrived back at school. As I walked along the corridor, I heard the sound of singing coming from the small meeting room.

Oh, my b'loved China
My heart has not changed
It forever cherishes your . . .

Peering through the door crack, I saw Sunrise Huang and several other girls dancing and singing. Their manner was graceful. I saw Sunrise Huang's skinny frame bobbing about in a roomy khaki tunic. And when she turned around I noticed that her breasts seemed to be larger than they appeared just a few days earlier. It reminded me of the time up in the tree when I accidentally brushed against her breasts, and I suddenly felt hot all over. But as I watched her singing and dancing, I also thought about Second Prize Wang. A wave of rage rose up in my heart.

I watched the rehearsal with mixed feelings until Sunrise Huang and the other girls came out of the room. I hid behind a concrete column and saw them slowly walk away. Sunrise Huang entered the girls' bathroom by herself. Her hair and face were still wet when she came out.

I walked toward her. She saw me but did not speak.

"Do you know where Second Prize Wang is?" I asked.

She said nothing.

"He's digging the air-raid shelter."

She still said nothing.

"It's all your fault. You'd better do something to get him out of there."

"I'm busy rehearsing."

"All you have to do is go to the principal and say he didn't touch you."

Her face reddened.

"It's horrible there."

I walked toward the construction site, Sunrise Huang following close behind me. I walked fast, and she almost had to run to keep up with me. I saw beads of sweat on her forehead. She hid with me behind a tree not far from the construction site. We did not have to wait long.

Second Prize Wang came out in his muddy clothes. He did not look in our direction. Like a wise old man he just looked at the sky, as if something up there had caught his attention.

Sunrise Huang's face immediately turned ashen. She ignored me and stared at her English teacher. "He's darker," she murmured like a concerned mother. "And he's slouching a little."

VII

We returned to the old tree that night to discuss what to do. You might say it was a conference, a conference that marked a turning point, just as the Zunyi Conference of 1935 was a turning point for the Chinese Communist Party.

It was cloudy that night, and I could see nothing in the sky. The Tianshan Mountains in the distance were also covered in clouds. I thought it might rain again.

"I'm cold," Sunrise Huang said.

I took off my jacket and gave it to her.

"That's gentlemanly, right?" she asked.

"Second Prize Wang said that's what a gentleman would do," I replied.

"Do you get angry when people call you 'the gentleman'?" This had become something of a nickname.

"It makes me happy."

A grin appeared on her face. But then she said, "I really regret hurting Mr. Wang."

A light came on. Through the window we saw a despondent Second Prize Wang walk into his dormitory. He stood in silence for a while and then began to pack his belongings.

"They want to kick him out," I whispered to Sunrise Huang. "He can't live here anymore." Tears soon began to stream down Sunrise Huang's face.

Second Prize Wang had an impressive suitcase. He started putting some small objects into it—his razor, towel, and toothbrush—and then finally he reached for the English dictionary. My heart raced; I really loved that dictionary. He flipped through it. Then, apparently coming across a word that caught his attention, he sat down. He concentrated hard, mouthing the word silently. Suddenly, he laughed.

He doubled up laughing as we watched him. I wondered what word could make him so happy that he would forget about his difficult situation.

He must have thought of something because he stood up, paced the floor, and then stopped and looked at himself in the mirror. He changed into his well-tailored jacket. Retrieving a bottle of cologne from his suitcase, he carefully splashed a little onto his hand and applied it to himself. He was in no hurry and did everything in a deliberate manner.

Sunrise Huang watched him adoringly. From that young age I knew what it would be like when a young girl fell in love with her English teacher—and what kind of expression she would have on her face.

Second Prize Wang examined himself in the mirror one last time, then opened the door and stepped out.

"I want to confess to him," Sunrise Huang blurted out.

"Don't tell him," I said. "Tell the principal."

"What if the principal does nothing?" she asked. "What then?"

I had not thought of that.

"I ought to tell everyone in the whole compound," she abruptly declared, "that he never once touched me."

"How will you do that?"

She thought about it, then answered in disappointment, "I don't know."

We became disheartened. But when I heard my mother calling for me, an idea came to mind. "I do," I said.

Sunrise Huang looked at me, full of hope.

"There is a solution—we'll do what Chairman Mao did," I proclaimed.

VIII

Sunrise Huang stuck a big character poster in front of the administration building. It was titled "My First Big Character Poster," exactly the same as Chairman Mao's poster that started the Cultural Revolution.

The content of the poster was straightforward: "Second Prize Wang never touched me. At the time I was mad and spoke complete nonsense. I have wronged Mr. Wang and apologize to him. I will never falsely accuse a good person again. Signed, Sunrise Huang."

The news was explosive, and everyone in our compound was shocked. It was a thunderbolt out of the blue in their dull lives. People flocked to read it. Second Prize Wang came by and read it word for word. Bystanders stared at him as if he were from outer space. Second Prize Wang's face had turned bright red by the time he finished reading the poster. He ripped it down and tore it to shreds.

"How dare you interfere with the 'four freedoms of the Red Guards'—the right to speak out freely, to air one's views fully, to write big-character posters, and to hold great debates?" someone demanded. Second Prize Wang ignored the question and walked off alone.

"It's him," someone else said, "it's Second Prize Wang!"

Second Prize Wang was still wearing his large rubber boots and plodded along with a limp. He managed to move quickly, and from behind he looked scrawny. He seemed not to hear the chattering of those around him, as though his ears were filled with music.

The principal sought out Sunrise Huang for a talk. The conversation between Sunrise Huang and the principal went like this:

"Mr. Principal, Mr. Wang never touched me. I was talking nonsense."

"Then why did you say it?"

"They questioned me for days and wouldn't let me go home. They wouldn't let me eat and wouldn't let me sleep. I was fed up and spoke nonsense."

"Did Second Prize Wang give you one-on-one supplementary lessons every day?"

She nodded her head. "Not every day. Just occasionally."

"Then why are you nodding your head?"

Sunrise Huang laughed.

"What did he say to you?"

"English. Nothing but English."

"We will never treat a bad person unjustly, and we will never let a good person off. So be honest."

"Mr. Principal, it's 'never treat a good person unjustly and never let a bad person off.' "

"That's what I said."

"No, you didn't. You said the opposite."

The principal studied Sunrise Huang and sighed. "Students nowadays, what's with them?"

Sunrise Huang looked out the window and did not speak for a long time. Suddenly, she raised the pitch of her voice a full octave and announced, "If I am lying, I'll die like both of my fathers!"

"Don't say things like that," he implored. "Youth is full of vigor, like the sun at eight or nine in the morning. All hope rests on you. The world ultimately belongs to you . . . ," he continued, quoting Chairman Mao.

Sunrise Huang interrupted the principal's emotional outpouring: "Mr. Principal, if you don't allow Mr. Wang to come back to school, I will say *you* touched me."

The principal was stunned. His mouth was agape and he was unable to speak. "You—you—you—" he sputtered.

"And I'm not just saying it," she continued.

"By the way," the principal said, after finally regaining his composure, "who told you to write the big character poster?"

Sunrise Huang thought about it for a moment before responding earnestly, "Chairman Mao."

IX

I learned about the connections between the principal and Director Fan only after I grew up. They both studied at Tsinghua University and had "rebelled" together at the start of the Cultural Revolution. The principal saved Director Fan's life during the bloodiest factional battle among rival Red Guard groups in Ürümchi, the battle Commander Shen led. If it hadn't been for the principal, Director Fan would have been "martyred" in the attack on the No. 1 Middle School. For this reason, the principal also was a somebody in our compound. I found the following record in the minutes of a meeting:

PRINCIPAL: "Director Fan, Second Prize Wang has not breached moral standards. The girl called Sunrise Huang is mentally ill—two family members recently died, one after another, and she's become troubled."

DIRECTOR FAN: "Who's Second Prize Wang?"

PRINCIPAL: "An English teacher from Shanghai."

DIRECTOR FAN: "You people can deal with trifles like this. Are there still any English classes?"

PRINCIPAL: "They've been suspended."

DIRECTOR FAN: "We should still teach English. All the primary and secondary schools in Peking are teaching English. Ürümchi may be a long way from Peking, but we still should teach English."

PRINCIPAL: "Then I'll get Second Prize Wang to come back."

Are these just a few ordinary lines in the minutes of a meeting? No. This conversation changed the fates of Second Prize Wang and me. It even changed the fate of the city of Ürümchi, capital of the Uyghur Autonomous Region of Xinjiang. Do heroes make history, or do slaves? You may answer that it is heroes, but I insist it is slaves—from Director Fan to the principal, and Second Prize Wang and me and Sunrise Huang and my parents . . . not a single one was a hero. We were all slaves.

X

Once again Second Prize Wang walked the school corridors. Once again he wore his sharp gray suit and gave off the scent of cologne.

The lights in the corridor were dim, but Second Prize Wang strode toward me as bright as the sun.

Second Prize Wang is like the sun,
Wherever he shines, there is light.
Wherever Second Prize Wang is,
Hurrah, hurrah, the people are liberated!

ELEVEN

I

I cannot remember how I got my nickname "the gentleman."

Everyone called me this. Back then someone was called "Lord of the West," after a butcher in the sixteenth-century novel *Water Margin*, and someone else was called "chopper." One girl was called "ferocious shrew," and I was called "the gentleman." I am not sure who gave me the name—maybe it was Garbage Li, or maybe not.

I had changed, I really had. Was it English that had changed me? Or was it Second Prize Wang? All I wanted was to be a gentleman. I wanted to "follow my own course, and let people talk," to use a maxim Karl Marx paraphrased from Dante.

I began to change the way I walked, imitating Second Prize Wang. I was born with perfect eyesight and did not need to wear glasses, but I went to the city's Big Cross district, to the Red Sun Spectacle Store, which used to be called the Prosperous & Profitable Spectacle Store, and asked for a pair of eyeglasses.

The old man in the store was surprised. "For whom?" he asked.

"For me."

He was horrified. I could tell from his bespectacled eyes. "There are no other kids like you in Ürümchi. There weren't any before, and there certainly aren't any now," he said.

I took out a ten-yuan note and said, "I want a pair of eyeglasses."

He shook his head and grinned. "This is bourgeois stuff, you understand? If somebody asks you, don't say you got them from Prosperous & Profitable—no, no, I mean from Red Sun," he warned.

"Where?"

"Red Sun," he repeated.

"And who sold them to me?" I pressed on.

He now realized he had said too much. "Kids nowadays. They can trick me into saying anything." He sighed.

That was how I got my glasses. Whenever I had them on and walked along the school corridor or passed through the playground, I could hear the word *gentleman* being whispered around me, like leaves rustling in the wind.

I could hear the whispering wherever I went. Those glasses and the way I walked became subjects of derision for everyone. Like Garbage Li's line "Qiu, Qiu, as in Bethune's balls," my glasses and the way I walked inspired endless laughter.

II

I carefully retrieved a bottle of perfume that Mother had hidden at the bottom of a trunk. I gently opened the cap, poured out a few drops, and patted some on my hair. Then the fragrance started to fill the air around me.

It was a unique scent, the same one I was familiar with as a baby in my mother's arms. Cocooned by the scent, I felt a little dizzy.

Autumn sunlight stretched out along the floor. I looked out the window and saw that the elm tree's leaves had turned yellow. The azure sky brought back memories of being a baby, and tides of sadness washed over me.

I became aware that a chapter of my life had come to an end, and that a new chapter was about to start. Knowing this made me excited and disconsolate at the same time.

I could vaguely remember my mother's body. I could see her white skin, and the dark tips of her breasts. They danced before my eyes like little insects in the sky.

The scent of the perfume carried me into irresistible solitude.

My eyes returned to that green bottle. I decanted a few more drops and applied them to my neck. Then I shook the bottle a few times and breathed in as deeply as I could.

That was my first secret experience with perfume.

After putting the bottle back in the trunk, I marched out of the building and paraded down the road. There were few paved roads in Ürümchi back then. Dirt was everywhere. An autumn rain the night before had turned the dirt into black mud. I strode over the spongy mud, feeling the entire world was suffused with that perfume's fragrance.

In the distance the snowcapped Tianshan Mountains glowed in the sunlight. Elated by the perfume, I greeted the mountains: "Hello, my friends."

That evening, Mother detected the perfume as soon as she walked into the room.

She was in a bad mood that day. Maybe her design of a new air-raid shelter had not been approved? Her face was the color of ash, making her look like a sooty statue.

She glared at me for at least twenty seconds. "Why did you rummage through the trunk?" she demanded.

"I—I didn't," I denied, lacking the nerve to face her.

She walked up to me and pulled my ear. "Why can't you stop lying? Lying is disgraceful! Understand?"

"I didn't lie."

Straightaway, she smacked me on the head. "I could smell the perfume as soon as I walked in the door. If you didn't go through the trunk, how could you possibly have gotten the perfume out?"

My face reddened.

"You misbehaved and then lied about it. Why?"

I did not respond.

Mother rushed to the basin and grabbed a bar of soap. "I'll wash your mouth out with this," she barked, trying to stuff the soap into my mouth.

I turned my head. "You tell lies, too! Can you say you have never lied?"

For a moment she was dumbfounded. "I've never lied," she said coldly. While saying that, she began pounding me with her fists.

To this day I can't explain why she was acting like a sandstorm. Was she under too much pressure at work? Was it because Father was away? Was she going through menopause? But Mother was just a little over thirty years old. If she was not at the age of menopause, why was she so scary?

Mother stepped closer. Already frightened, I backed away several paces. "You reek of perfume. How dare you say you didn't lie? And you don't think I should wash your mouth out with soap?" Then she noticed mud on my shoes. "You went outside? Do you have no shame?"

I resisted her with silence.

"How come you're so different from other kids? What goes on in your head every day?"

There was nothing I could say. How could I describe what went through my head every day?

Mother suddenly raised her voice. "Did you learn this from your English teacher? Doesn't he like to wear cologne?"

I could not deny it. It was true that Second Prize Wang always smelled like cologne. When he walked past me the first time, the fragrance had made me realize there was something beautiful in this world.

"You don't 'unite with your classmates and participate actively in school activities,'" Mother said, using the standard phrases from our school policy. "Instead, you hang out with that English teacher every day. What exactly do you want? I hear he's morally suspect. Don't you know? You've gone down the wrong path with him!"

What she said about Mr. Wang incensed me. "How would you know he's morally suspect?"

"I just know!"

"He's morally perfect," I countered.

"People have told me everything. This man has serious ideological problems."

"Who?" I bellowed. "Did our principal tell you that?"

Mother was shocked. She had not expected me to mention the principal. She was silent for a while, and her face turned red. "Why am I being damned like this?" She wept.

III

There was a hubbub at the school entrance as I arrived the next day. A large crowd of adults were gathered—all parents of students.

From the distance I saw the principal explaining something to the crowd. As I moved closer, I figured out that the parents were protesting the school's decision to let Second Prize Wang come back. I can still vividly remember what the principal said: "He is an excellent English teacher. Because of a series of tragedies in the family of that female student, she became mentally disturbed, but she told the truth when she returned to normal."

"I heard he gives one-on-one lessons to female students. Is that true?" a voice from the crowd asked.

"Not just female students. He tutors male students, too," the principal corrected. He then spotted me standing to one side. "Love Liu, weren't you there for the sessions? What do you have to say?"

My face flushed. I was silent for a while, not knowing what to say. Finally I said, "Sometimes I was there, sometimes I wasn't. Actually, I wasn't there most of the time." The crowd roared with laughter.

The principal's face turned red, too. After glaring at me for a second, the principal said to the crowd, "All right. I promise you that from now on I will not allow him to give private lessons to anyone."

The parents finally left. The principal blocked my way and locked me in his stare. "Is your brain made of wood?" he asked. At the time I didn't quite know what he meant. But one thing was confirmed a few years later—my brain *is* made of wood. I know this because my father, the principal's enemy, became enraged with me and asked me the very same question: "Is your brain made of wood?"

But we can talk about that later. Now let us go back to Second Prize Wang.

IV

I walked into Second Prize Wang's room. The brilliant sunlight made me dizzy.

Second Prize Wang was standing in front of the window, lost in thought. He saw me walk in but did not move. Obviously, he knew what had happened at the school gate.

"We've finished preparations. Apart from Garbage Li and a few others, almost everyone can sing 'The Internationale' in English," I reported. He did not seem to hear me and continued to stare out the window.

"It is a lot of fun to sing in English, only sometimes it can be difficult to get both the lyrics and the tune right. Sunrise Huang is the only one who can sing it well," I continued.

He did not respond. Then, out of the blue, he said, "Did you hear what the parents were saying this morning?"

I nodded.

"So what do you think of me?" he asked.

"I think there's nothing wrong with you morally. But . . ."

"But what?"

"I don't like you giving private lessons to girls."

Taken aback, he stared at me for a long time. Then he smiled. "You'll understand when you grow up. It's natural for male teachers to want to give supplementary lessons to female students. But everything has a limit, and I know what I am doing."

"But what they said was horrible."

He looked serious. "As long as they let me go back to school, let me continue to be a teacher, and let me teach English, I don't care."

"And you won't care if they humiliate you?"

He shook his head.

"What if they beat you?" I persisted.

"Let's not talk about this. See if you can sing 'The Internationale' in English for me."

My face turned red because I was at that age when my voice was beginning to change.

"Go ahead," he prompted.

"Let's ask Sunrise Huang to sing it. She sings well," I suggested.

He smiled. "The teaching manual requires the song to be sung in chorus. On second thought, I don't really want you and Sunrise Huang to sing that song."

"Why?"

"You've asked too many 'whys.' But I like that you are inquisitive," said Second Prize Wang.

I was still watching him, waiting for an answer.

"Both you and Sunrise Huang are good students. You love English and should be taught with beautiful English. But don't tell anyone what I just said to you, all right?"

I nodded.

He paused for a moment. "In a truly beautiful English song, every note is perfectly arranged. It may not be a song for the masses; rather, it is something for the noble few. Eventually you'll come to appreciate its elegance and refinement."

He sounded passionate about this.

"Is perfume something refined?" I asked.

"There are many kinds of perfume. You can't buy good perfume in China. There isn't any."

"I tried Mother's perfume without telling her. She beat me when she found out."

He smiled. "You are still too young to use cologne."

"Then who should be using cologne?"

"A gentleman."

"Are you a gentleman?"

To my surprise, his face flushed. He thought about it for a while and said, "Go back to your classroom now. I have some things to do. I'll answer your questions later. But you must not tell anyone what we just talked about. It's between you and me. It's our secret. Promise me."

I nodded. Just as I was about to step out, the question we'd skipped came back to me. The bell for the next class had just rung, but I closed the door anyway and turned to him.

He looked at me with surprise. "More questions? You'll be late for class."

"Just now you said that all male teachers like to give supplementary lessons to girls. Why?" I asked.

He smiled again. "Why? There're lots of reasons. Some are easy to explain, but others I can't explain."

"So is it true that female teachers like to give private lessons to boys?" I continued.

Second Prize Wang thought about it carefully. "No, probably not," he said with a grin.

"Why not?"

"I don't know how to explain. This is a question for Freud. I heard about Freud on an English radio program. Too bad none of his books can be found here in Ürümchi."

I watched him, expecting him to go on, but he changed the subject.

"Why are you asking *me* questions like these? Why don't you ask your mother or father?"

"My mother is strict. She would beat me."

He smiled and said, "Your mother is a typical educated person. How strict can she be?"

"She's very strict."

"Then what about your father?"

"My father has no time for me. He's always under a lot of pressure. There're some things I dare not ask him, and there're also things I'm ashamed to ask."

"Actually, they know all the answers to the questions you just asked me."

I was about to leave at this point when he asked, "Does your mother know you come here all the time?"

I paused, then told a lie. "No."

To my surprise, Second Prize Wang appeared to be a little disappointed.

Many years later, when I take my long walks and reflect, a worldly me can still recall the disappointment on his face. He genuinely hoped my mother knew I spent a lot of time with him and believed him to be a good influence on me. He thought because both of my parents were educated, their thinking would be aligned with his. The fact is, he was wrong. Mother never had a good impression of teachers like Second Prize Wang. All she worried about was whether people like him might pose a danger to me and the rest of her family.

V

There is a song in English that goes like this:

> *Why does the sun go on shining?*
> *Why does the sea rush to shore?*
> *Don't they know it's the end of the world*
> *'Cause you don't love me anymore. . . .*

Second Prize Wang did not teach me this song. I heard it at a party when I was an adult, and the girl singing it was from the foreign language department of the Ürümchi College of Education. She sang well. For someone who had been stuck in Ürümchi for a long time, hearing it was like heaven. Her voice was so pure that I could somehow see beauty in its air of despair. It brought to mind a song Second Prize Wang had taught me years earlier: "Moon River."

I went to his room late one afternoon. There was a trace of cologne in the air. He studied my face for a while, then asked, "Why did you help me?"

I was startled. The serious expression on his face scared me. I did not know what he meant.

"Sunrise Huang has told me everything."

"What did she say?"

"She said you persuaded her to admit to the principal that she had lied."

"I saw you covered in mud at the air-raid-shelter construction site. I wanted to learn English."

He looked grateful. "Let me teach you a song in English," he said to me.

That was the afternoon he taught me "Moon River." In the light of the late afternoon sun, he wrote down the lyrics for me from memory. Then he started to teach me, line by line. He had a soft voice, possibly too soft, but he sang perfectly on pitch. I tried to imitate him and was deeply touched by the beauty of the song. Forever in my memory, the sunlight of that afternoon remains bright, and the moon river of the song remains calm, just like the voice of Second Prize Wang.

VI

What marked the start of my friendship with Second Prize Wang? Was it "Moon River"? Was it an English class, or that plot Sunrise Huang and Garbage Li hatched? Or did it grow out of English words like *soul* and *huckleberry*?

I have no idea how I came to make this bold request: "Mr. Wang, may I borrow the dictionary for a couple of days?"

There were some words in the song that I did not understand, like *huckleberry* in "my huckleberry friend." So I looked up both *huckle* and *berry*. The dictionary was a gold mine. I could even find words in it that would make me blush.

VII

It was Sunday. Nobody went to school that day. Mother left home early—she was to receive an award for her air-raid-shelter design.

Before leaving, she put on a colorful top and got out two pairs of shoes she hadn't worn in years: high heels and flats. She also took out that bottle of perfume.

Mother seemed unsure of herself. As she stood there examining those items, I heard her sigh. She put everything back into the trunk, and when she turned around, I saw tears in her eyes.

I was surprised by her tears. I even felt they were laughable. I had no sympathy for her, and don't even now, because she was so harsh to me when I was young.

In the end, Mother went to receive the award in her usual gray blouse.

My classmates and I lined up and streamed into the East Wind Cinema. Important officials were up on the podium, and ordinary spectators and children sat below. It was a gathering to celebrate victory.

I almost stopped breathing when the emcee called Mother to the podium to receive her award. Mother was smiling and looked so fit and lithe. She was like an athlete—in front of more than a thousand spectators, she hopped up onto the podium, full of youthful energy. Everyone sitting on the podium looked at her as if she were from another world. Though she was dressed the same as any other woman, her bearing was entirely different.

I thought to myself: Why do I look like Father instead of Mother? Mother was good looking; Father was not. I definitely inherited my parents' least attractive features.

Sunrise Huang and a few of the other girls from my class looked at me admiringly. "Your mother is beautiful," Sunrise Huang whispered to me.

My face felt hot. I did not look at her.

"It'd be great if my mother was like yours," she continued.

At this point Director Fan asked Mother to say something. Holding her award certificate, Mother remained quiet for a long moment. Then she began to weep. "I am grateful to the leaders and the party . . . for giving me this opportunity. There are few such opportunities in life. I am glad that I grasped this one, completed the design of the air-raid shelter, and finished the task given to me by the party and the people," she blathered in broken phrases, mouthing the political clichés of the day. "I promise I will keep working hard . . . to reform my world outlook . . . in order to become at one with the workers, peasants, and soldiers."

Mother's sobbing embarrassed me so much that I hoped the

ground would open up and swallow me. Seeing her cry always scared me, even more so with over a thousand people watching.

At this point, borrowing from something Chairman Mao once said—All reactionaries are paper tigers—an official up on the podium proudly announced: "The air-raid shelter we built will protect us not only from missiles and atomic bombs but also from hydrogen bombs. So all paper tigers will quake in fear before us." Someone then led the audience in chanting the slogan "Prepare for war!"

I noticed that supervising teacher Guo Pei-qing was dozing off and thought it was a good time to go outside for a breath of fresh air, so I snuck out. Phew! What a relief to get out. I felt I had just escaped from a hot oven into someplace cool. After ducking back inside to take a pee, I fled the East Wind Cinema for good.

VIII

I arrived back at school in no time. Walking down the long corridor, I came to Second Prize Wang's door. I could hear him singing "Moon River." The door was not shut all the way, so I gently pushed it open and saw him sitting in a chair, flipping through the dictionary. I was hesitant but went in anyway. He was surprised to see me.

"Didn't you go to the victory celebration?" he asked.

"I've just come from there. My mother cried when she received her award, and I didn't want to watch her cry."

"Those were tears of joy, tears of happiness."

"Can the air-raid shelter protect us from hydrogen bombs for sure?" I asked. Second Prize Wang did not answer. "My father's designing a hydrogen bomb research complex in southern Xinjiang, and my mother designed an air-raid shelter in Ürümchi. Are we really going to war?"

He shook his head. "I don't know."

"Are you scared?"

He looked at me and after a long time finally said, "Yes."

"Why?"

"Because other countries are more powerful than we are."

"But my father said we're going to have our own hydrogen bombs. He told me this when he came back last time."

Second Prize Wang looked lost in thought. "Many people will die if there's a war. And people like us will be the first to die," he finally said. We were silent for a while. Then his singing penetrated the silence. It was "Moon River" again. I sang along with him, and the sound of English filled the room.

IX

"Could you please lend me the dictionary?"

"No."

"One day, just for one day."

"No, not even for one day. I have to use it every day to prepare for class. I have very few reference books, and I rely on the dictionary."

I cannot think of another book that was as irresistible to me as that dictionary. It brought me more knowledge, or I should say joy, than any other book. If I rearranged the words in the dictionary, the entire world would open up before me.

To this day I can still feel the sting of that rejection. Upon hearing Second Prize Wang tell me no, I felt my face turn red, like Mother's face, and wanted to leave. I got up slowly from the edge of the bed. My legs felt heavy. I must have looked like a sick old man. Second Prize Wang probably noticed my pain.

"You can come here often and check the dictionary."

"You mean every day?"

"If I am here."

I did not leave. Instead, I sat back down on the edge of his bed. There was no more reason for me to feel nervous when I walked into his room. We were linked by fate. Even though he was an adult and I was a kid, even though he refused to lend me the dictionary, he treated me as his equal when I was in his room. It was a friendship between generations. Yes, that's exactly what it was—a friendship between generations.

I carefully turned the pages of his dictionary. It was the greatest book in the world, full of heartwarming words like *love, home, sunshine.* Suddenly, a word caught my eye: *masturbate.*

"What's 'masturbate'?" I asked.

Second Prize Wang looked startled and a little embarrassed. There was a pause. "It's hard to explain," he finally said.

"What is it? Don't you know?"

He smiled. "It's something that I have to do all the time. But I'm afraid it's not yet appropriate to explain to you."

"Is it a swearword? A dirty word?"

"I can't really say."

"Then what does it mean?"

"I'll tell you someday."

My heart was swollen with disappointment when I left his room that day.

X

Every morning, before the sun came out from behind the Tianshan Mountains, I felt cold and longed for someone's touch, for a woman to stroke my hair, my face, my entire body. Those days were torture, yet full of pleasure, and the women in my mind became vivid and familiar.

Two women would always appear: Ahjitai and Sunrise Huang. I would stare at the window every morning, waiting for their arrival. Ahjitai was full-figured, beautiful, and had a halo of warm mist, while Sunrise Huang was delicate, sensitive, and had a trace of crisp coolness. They arrived together each time, then turned into one person and came to me.

I waited for them with my eyes open. I knew if I did that, they would come. If I accidentally closed my eyes, I could miss my chance and lose my greatest happiness.

I was plagued with longing every day, and the passion wore me out. Mother did not seem to notice. As I said, she was very busy. The air-raid shelter design was her most successful work, and she did not want to disappoint all the people who had honored her with a prize.

I constantly felt guilty in front of Mother. She was exhausted and stressed out, and I let myself wallow in longing every day and never offered to help her. Was this a sin? My guilt made me want to avoid her. Thankfully she was always busy, and thankfully she came home late every night.

Sunrise Huang did not notice the changes in me, either. She even tried to speak to me in English, but I didn't dare make eye contact with her, fearing she might find out about the desire I had every morning and be able to read my dirty mind. Sunrise Huang's innocence made me ashamed of my filthiness. I had spasms of pain in my chest. I was no different from an old man, with a heart filled with grief and alienation.

But one person did notice the changes in me.

XI

"You look pale. Are you sick?"

"I'm awake early every morning and can't stop staring out the window."

Second Prize Wang came up close to me and studied my face. An understanding smile slowly appeared. "You hope someone will float into your room from out there, right?"

My face reddened. Apparently he could read my mind.

"You'll be ruined if it goes on like this."

"What's wrong with me?"

He did not answer. My tears gushed out. Agony crumpled me, and there I stood, like a sack stuffed with lumps of coal.

There was a long silence before he asked, "How long has it been going on like this?"

"A few months."

"No wonder you've been staring outside during class."

"I can't help it." Admitting my secret to someone was excruciating. Like I said, I was convinced I was filthy.

Second Prize Wang held me firmly in his gaze as if he were about to make an important decision. I went silent and picked up the dictionary. The word *masturbate* caught my eye again as I flipped through it.

Second Prize Wang leaned over and saw the word. "I've also experienced what you're going through," he said.

I was thunderstruck. A refined person like him was actually telling me he'd also felt the way I was feeling. What he said was like the first ray of sunlight after a storm, warm and unexpected, and I had to close my eyes because the light was blinding. If you were overcome by euphoria because you knew you were rescued, you would feel giddy and exhausted. And if there was nothing for you to lean on, you would collapse. That was exactly what happened to me—I collapsed on the edge of Second Prize Wang's bed.

I gawked at him until my brain started to function again. I'd heard what he said: He said he'd experienced the same thing. That meant I was not alone. If a gentleman like Second Prize Wang had the same problem, then I must not be the only filthy person in the world. I was rescued—my idol was just like me.

"Are you feeling guilty?"

I nodded.

"Actually, there's no reason for you to be so upset. Everyone goes through something like this." He sighed. "Unfortunately, your father's not around. He should be the one to tell you this."

"My father wouldn't tell me. I rarely see him; he is very busy." I was struck by grief. Sadness welled up inside of me. I missed my father: Where was he? He must still be at the nuclear bomb base. What was he doing there? He was designing the hydrogen bomb research complex for manufacturing weapons. In other words, Father was guarding our country. But he'd forgotten about me—his own son.

Second Prize Wang appeared at a loss after hearing what I'd said about Father. He wanted to say something but decided not to.

I was still holding the dictionary. It was opened to the page with the word *masturbate.* I blankly stared at the word but did not know if it had anything to do with me.

"Do you really want to know what this word means?"

I raised my head.

From the little conference room outside the door, I heard a woman singing a song accompanied by an accordion.

Looking up, we see the Big Dipper.
In our hearts, there is only you, Mao Ze-dong, oh, Mao Ze-dong.
Thinking of you in dark nights, we know where we are,
Thinking of you when we are lost, we know where to go. . . .

"You must learn how to masturbate," said Second Prize Wang, seemingly oblivious to the singing. Thinking back, I wonder what made him say this. What he said was inappropriate for a teacher to say to a student. So where did his courage come from? Was he also looking for emotional relief?

"Did you hear me?" he said. "You must learn how to masturbate."

XII

There was actually nothing to learn. Any boy would naturally know how to do it. My English teacher not only taught me how to sing "Moon River" but also let me understand it's all right to think of women and feel burning hot all over my body early in the morning.

I was finally liberated. My guilt was gone. That autumn, walking on the waterlogged roads of Ürümchi, my steps were once again full of life. Happy times had returned. Basking in the sunlight, I looked off in the distance and greeted the snowy mountains: "Hello, Mr. Mountain. How are you today?"

For the first time I was able to get through the morning. I did not stare outside at dawn or feel the burning urge in my body for the next few days. I repeated the motion a second time, then a third time, until one morning Mother discovered what I was doing and pulled my hair.

XIII

I opened my eyes that morning and knew I needed to do it again. I did not realize I'd forgotten to shut the door after going for a pee in the middle of the night. Whom should I think of today, Ahjitai or Sunrise Huang? I tried to make up my mind. Slowly, the two melded into one. She was walking naked in a cloud of thick steam, her long hair cascading down her back. It looked like she was in a bathhouse. At first I saw just her back and did not know who it was until the moment she turned toward me: It was Ahjitai. She was smiling, and I could see drops of water on her pearly white skin. Then I saw her breasts—they were right in front of my eyes. I also saw her legs and belly—they were snowy white. More than any other woman I've seen since growing up, Ahjitai was immaculate. Back then I had no idea about female anatomy and where their hair grows, but seeing Ahjitai's smile and her smooth belly was enough for me to speed up my motion. Nothing else mattered.

Mother came into my room right at that moment, but I did not notice. I was too busy moving my hand like a maniac. Mother probably observed me for a while, trying to figure out what I was doing. Then, shocked and outraged by what she saw, she charged up to my bedside and tried to yank the quilt off me.

Jolted out of my sweet reverie, I opened my eyes and got the fright of my life. Mother was standing right in front of me. Her eyes locked on mine, she was tugging the quilt as hard as she could, like an untamed beast. I struggled to hold on to the quilt, and eventually she gave up, since I was stronger than Mother by then.

Mother's fury retreated with her strength, like an ebbing tide. Her hysteria was washed away in her tears. Mother had completely given up on me. She had no idea that while she was living her busy life, her son was sliding into a degenerate pit. Tears blurred her eyes. She let go of the quilt and plodded out of my room.

Mother went to her bedroom and started to wail, just as she did the day her father died. Her father was crippled, and he drowned in a pond in his hometown. He was an educated man and had raised her well, sending her to Tsinghua University. Mother should have understood that her son was only doing what a man is supposed to do, but she howled nonstop. Her howling forced me out of bed. Even though I had not finished what I'd been doing, I could no longer continue, so I put on my clothes and went to her room.

I wanted to say something to her but was too ashamed. I should've said, "Mother, I'm sorry," right? I'd said it when I was a little boy, when my parents scolded me for breaking a bottle. But what had been broken that day was not a bottle; it was the bond between mother and son, and the trust Mother had in me.

Her tears flowed like the Ürümchi River, and I could do nothing but stand there like an elm on the riverbank. Time moved at a snail's pace. I felt many centuries had passed. Mother suddenly turned around and wiped her tears away.

"Did he teach you that?" she demanded.

"Who?" I answered defensively.

"Your English teacher."

I became even more nervous. I faltered, but the answer was written on my face.

Mother washed her face, combed her hair, and rubbed a bit of cold cream on her face. She then hurried out of the house. I could hear rage in her steps.

XIV

"Did you teach him that?"

"Yes, I did." Second Prize Wang actually admitted it. He was so composed, much like Liu Hu-lan and Xu Yun-feng, the revolutionary martyrs.

Mother landed a vicious smack on his face. Second Prize Wang did not move, and his eyes did not reveal even a hint of surprise.

"How dare you corrupt a child like that! I'll report you!"

"Go ahead."

"You'll be sorry!"

"No, I won't. I'm just a little disappointed in you."

"I'll never let my son step in here again!"

"I agree. I won't let him in."

"You promise?"

"I promise."

This confrontation took place in Second Prize Wang's room. I was spying from a branch of the old elm outside of his window. I saw the whole thing, and I'll never forget what Second Prize Wang said at the end.

"No one should treat a child like that. He needs help and friends, not what you are doing now." What he said fell on deaf ears. Mother fled his room as if she were running away from a monster. The door slammed shut. Second Prize Wang examined his face in the mirror. It looked a little swollen. He examined the welt closely and caressed it. Then he shook his head and smiled.

Later, I asked him why he did not slap her back. The same kind of smile reappeared. "She's a woman, and I'm a gentleman. A gentleman shouldn't even think of striking a woman," he answered.

"Then what is he supposed to think?"

"He should ask himself whether he was wrong. If he was not wrong, then he should just smile to himself."

TWELVE

I

My relationship with Second Prize Wang grew awkward because of my mother's interference.

That was the darkest period in my life. Mother was the bane of my existence. Of course she did what she did for my sake. But the thing is: Love can kill. Everyone knows that.

Mother went to the principal and asked for my title of English class representative to be revoked. On the principal's orders, Sunrise Huang was reinstated to the position. It was no loss for Second Prize Wang, since he was still surrounded by girls, but it was a total loss for me. Growing up in a backwater like Ürümchi was bad enough, and now I was cut off from my only claim to sophistication.

II

I remember vividly that it was a Friday. Fridays did not mark the start of the weekend in those days. Sunrise Huang was sick, and her mother had asked me to take her doctor's certificate to school. I saw an opportunity. After handing the certificate to supervising teacher Guo Pei-qing, I dashed to Second Prize Wang's room. My heart was racing when I reached his door.

I was hesitant to knock and pulled my hand back twice because I was too nervous to follow through. I finally knocked when the first bell rang.

Suddenly, sunlight flooded onto my face—just as I described before.

Second Prize Wang stood at the door. He didn't seem surprised to see me. I was astonished by his reaction and stared at him in disbelief, as if I'd just seen Lin Biao, Chairman Mao's deputy. I could not think of what to say and had forgotten what I was there for.

He could no doubt see how nervous I was, but grown-ups are masters at feigning indifference. Since I had nothing to say, Second Prize Wang turned around and closed the door.

I was again enveloped in darkness. Then I remembered the purpose of my visit. Again I knocked on the door, and again he opened it. By now the bell for class had rung a second time. "Sunrise Huang is sick. I am here to help you carry the phonograph."

"We're not using it today."

It took me a moment to come up with a new line. "I am here to carry the homework."

"I can do that myself."

He then locked the door and walked toward the classroom without saying a word.

Rebuffed, I walked behind him down the corridor, feeling cold through and through.

Second Prize Wang stepped into the classroom ahead of me. On his way to the lectern, he asked class captain He Qiu-yuan to return the homework to everyone.

He Qiu-yuan divided the papers into eight stacks and asked the students at the front of each row to pass them back.

Meanwhile, Second Prize Wang was writing new vocabulary on the blackboard.

I turned my head to the window and stared at the mountains in the distance. The sunlight seemed to be taunting me.

III

"My mother said it was wrong for her to slap you. She regrets it."

"Your mother?" As I stood in his doorway, Second Prize Wang looked at me and shook his head.

"She regrets it. She asked me to come here and tell you."

"No, no way. Women like your mother never admit they've done something wrong."

"Then I was wrong. I'm sorry."

"No, you didn't do anything wrong. You were wronged."

"It's been hard for me every day. I want to go to your room."

"No, you can't. I promised your mother."

"I want to hear you speak English."

"You can come see me when you grow up if you still want to hear me speak English. Not now."

"When I grow up?" It sounded like an eternity to me, and I started to feel dizzy.

For a moment Second Prize Wang seemed to have second thoughts, but in the end he just shook his head.

"I want to read the dictionary."

"No, you can't. You can't come in."

Feeling rebuffed, I left. Without looking back, I could sense that Second Prize Wang remained at the door, following me with his eyes as I disappeared down the corridor.

I was devastated. I had a dream that night in which I saved Second Prize Wang's life—he was coughing up blood, and I carried him to the hospital. The doctor, class captain He Qiu-yuan's father, told me, "It's all because of you that he survived. We are deeply moved by what you've done." In the dream, Second Prize Wang gave me the dictionary as a thank-you gift.

It was still dark outside when I woke up the next morning. As usual I looked out the window, hoping someone would float into my room. But the subjects of my imagination were no longer women. Ahjitai and Sunrise Huang were on the second tier. I now saw Second Prize Wang. He no longer had a cold expression but was smiling and singing "Moon River." And he held the dictionary under his arm. He smelled of cologne and said, "I was cold to you earlier. Last night I couldn't sleep because of it. I regret what happened. That's why I came at this hour."

I accepted the dictionary and opened it. Again the word *masturbate* was there. I trembled, speechless, like a counterrevolutionary hearing the good news of his rehabilitation. But Second Prize Wang disappeared. He left through the door instead of the window. As he descended the stairs, I heard his shoes tapping on the steps.

After the sound faded into the distance, I discovered that the dictionary had disappeared from my hands.

IV

The son of two architects, I was born to know how to plan. I came up with a plan to steal the dictionary.

Second Prize Wang's door was not made entirely of wood. The top part consisted of framed glass panels. All I needed to do was break the glass panel closest to the lock, unlock the door from inside, go in, grab the dictionary from the bookshelf, and run.

There were two routes. If things went smoothly, I'd exit out the door. If someone happened to walk past, or if something else happened, I would open the window, jump over to the branch of the old elm, and escape from there.

V

It was a clear night. The moon and the stars were aglow.

Mother had not yet come home, so I could go to school and

check to see if Second Prize Wang was around. He was rarely in his room lately. I noticed his light was always off. Where was he? Was he really busy? Was he busy with his job like my mother was with hers? Or maybe he was busy being in love. Whom did he love? Ahjitai, of course.

On my way to school, I tried to identify the constellations: the Great Bear, Cassiopeia, the Big Dipper. Don't assume I learned about them in science class. No, we did not have science back then. Second Prize Wang taught me about them—in English.

As I reached the school I became more nervous. Standing beneath Second Prize Wang's window, I saw that his light was off. My heart was racing wildly. Now was the time to do it.

The thought of stealing made me need to pee. I hated myself for being such a sissy. I glanced up at the moon and felt like crying. I did not know why I felt like that. I was sad, hungry, and cold. I peed against the wall.

The main gate of the school was shut for the night, but I remembered that a bathroom window on the ground floor was broken, so I headed over there. I stood outside the bathroom window for a while, hesitating, and then I climbed through it.

VI

I moved along the corridor like a real burglar. There was only one lightbulb dangling in the corridor—a light as bleak as my mood. I had always thought this building—my father's masterpiece—was too small, and also too gloomy. But that day the walk seemed endless.

My footsteps were almost inaudible. I nearly lost my nerve when I saw Second Prize Wang's door and the glass panel I planned to break that night.

Father's face emerged from the darkness like the moon. I saw love in his eyes. He seemed to be telling me, "You'd better not steal."

"I have no choice. I need the dictionary."

"But you'll break the law if you steal."

"The guy who hit you also broke the law. People break the law every day. Why can't I break the law?" Father looked disappointed. His eyes filled with tears.

Suddenly I heard someone walking toward me from the direction of the principal's office. I slipped into the bathroom. The steps came closer. I hid in the last stall and peeked out through the gaps. Sure enough it was the principal. He probably had been drinking and looked sad. His legs were a little wobbly while he peed. He glanced over in my direction as though he had seen me. I was terrified.

After the principal left the bathroom, he went to Second Prize Wang's door and stopped. He knocked heavily on the door. I stood at the entrance to the bathroom and watched. Suddenly, the door opened. Second Prize Wang stepped out.

"Why did you switch off the light at this early hour?"

"I wasn't feeling well, so I went to bed early."

I was startled and almost let out a gasp. He was actually in his room. Good thing I didn't break the glass.

"Put some clothes on and come to my office. We have somewhere to go," the principal ordered.

"Anything wrong?"

"Of course there is. You've been harassing Ahjitai, and the leader of her work unit has complained to me. Tonight we are going to her superior's place. You have to apologize to him in person."

"I am single, and I like Ahjitai. She doesn't mind talking to me when I see her. I don't need to apologize." Second Prize Wang was getting worked up.

"Lower your voice. Let's go. If you don't apologize, you'll be back digging at the air-raid shelter tomorrow."

Second Prize Wang fell silent and returned to his room. He came back out a moment later, fully dressed.

"I know how you feel," the principal continued. "I know how painful it is to be tormented by love. But look at the times we're in. Are they the same as your university days in Shanghai? Are they the same as the years when your father referred to a missionary as his godfather? If I didn't keep you on by insisting on having English classes and praising your pronunciation as the best, you wouldn't last here for a single day."

Second Prize Wang did not respond.

"You like to teach English, right?"

"Yes," said Second Prize Wang, nodding.

"Then behave yourself. Stop harassing Ahjitai. We're going to her superior's office. Maybe she'll be there as well."

Second Prize Wang waited for the principal at his office. A moment later the principal came out more formally dressed. As they were walking, he patted Second Prize Wang's shoulder and said, "Stay away from pretty women. If you think she's pretty, others will think so, too. And things will happen if there are too many people fighting over her. You'd better just behave yourself."

"How come you're still single? Why don't you settle down with someone?" Second Prize Wang countered.

The principal sighed. "There's only one love in my life. Forget it, let's not talk about this."

For some reason this conversation made me think the principal might not be such a bad guy. Otherwise, why would he talk to Second Prize Wang as if they were friends? The principal seemed to be a different person from the one I thought I knew. He had two identities depending on whether it was day or night.

They walked past the bathroom and were on their way out of the school. The building fell into silence. My heart raced wildly again: It was time to act.

I picked up a brick I found in the bathroom. Thinking *Now is the perfect time, there's nothing that can stop me,* I lifted the brick and struck the glass. There was not a loud sound. The glass panel did not break but fell inward instead, meaning it was removable to begin with. This will be smooth sailing, I thought.

I paused and listened. There was still nothing but silence. I put my hand through the hole and unlocked the door from the inside. I then stepped into the room as if I were entering my own home.

VII

The room was completely dark, and I didn't dare turn on the light. The smell of the room made me nostalgic. I had not been able to go in there for quite a few months, but that day I went in as a burglar.

I knew the place well, so I went straight to the little bookshelf and reached for the dictionary. But the thick book I grabbed was not the dictionary—I could tell just by touching it—though it also had a hard cover. A wave of panic surged inside me. Where was it? I broke into a cold sweat.

My eyes soon became accustomed to the darkness. By the light of the moon, I carefully went through the books on the shelf again and again. Although there were only a few dozen books, I simply could not find the dictionary. I then started to search around the room like a maniac—on his desk, on his bed, under the pillow, on the windowsill, on the floor, and even under the bed. The dictionary was nowhere to be found.

The room was not hot at all, but I was drenched in sweat. Ever since that day, I could fully understand why rooms visited by burglars always look like a bomb has gone off inside.

In the end I went berserk and placed all my hope on the suitcase. I pulled it down from the top bunk and opened it. Inside, there was nothing but photos. I looked closely and discovered they were all photos of Ahjitai. It was unbelievable. Second Prize Wang was usually frugal. I often saw him in the canteen buying only vegetable dishes, even on big days when stewed pork was on the menu. It was hardly a time to go on a diet—people were starving in those days. But Second Prize Wang used all the money he had saved to take photos of Ahjitai. He was incredible.

I went through the photos one by one. Many were taken at Mirror Lake next to Yuewei Cottage in West Park, some were taken along the Ürümchi River, some at the Yan-er-wo scenic spot near Wulabo Gorge, and some in front of the tombstones of the revolutionary martyrs Chen Tan-qiu and Mao Ze-min, the younger brother of Chairman Mao. Some were even taken in the pine forest and on the alpine plains in the Tianshan Mountains. Second Prize Wang had not only taken Ahjitai to all the beautiful places in Ürümchi but even traveled with her to the Tianshan Mountains.

I felt a stabbing pain in my heart. There was no way we kids could compete with these grown-ups—they could date each other and go out together. Us? All we could do was stare from a distance, our mouths agape like idiots.

I almost forgot why I was in the room. I finally pulled my eyes away from the photos and looked up. There's no doubt about it, I thought, the dictionary is gone. I'd better go.

I gingerly opened the door but heard someone approaching from the stairs. I tensed up. I shut the door and quietly opened the window. I heard people talking down below. I instantly shrank back.

Beneath the window, Garbage Li was bragging to Sunrise Huang about how he'd followed Second Prize Wang and Ahjitai. From what he said, I gathered that Ahjitai had rejected Second Prize Wang yet again. No matter how hard he tried, he still could not win her over. Ahjitai coldly pushed him away when he attempted to hug her in the West Gate Park. "He looked so pathetic squatting on the ground and pulling his hair," Garbage Li reported.

I felt sad when I heard that. At a time when hundreds of thousands of educated Chinese gave their love to their country, Second Prize Wang was hopelessly in love with Ahjitai.

I was getting bored. It was not possible to leave through the door because there was someone in the building. And I could not leave from the window, either, because Sunrise Huang and Garbage Li were standing beneath it. I was stuck. What should I do?

I sprinkled some of Second Prize Wang's cologne on myself, put on his nice jacket and leather shoes, and quietly paced around the room. For the first time in my life I felt I was walking like a real gentleman. Eventually I stood in front of the mirror and changed back into my clothes.

Again I heard the sound of footsteps. I could tell they were Second Prize Wang's, even from where I was in the room. I was familiar with the sound of his walk and could tell he was wearing leather shoes. I was scared witless and broke out in a cold sweat again. I must run no matter what, I thought. I rushed to the window. Sunrise Huang and Garbage Li were about to leave.

"I have to go or my mother will worry about me," said Sunrise Huang.

"Don't rush. Can you stay a bit longer?" Garbage Li pleaded.

"Enough! I don't want to hear about Second Prize Wang anymore."

Garbage Li was puzzled. "But didn't you say if I told you things about him, you'd spend more time with me?" Sunrise Huang brushed away Garbage Li's hand and headed home. Garbage Li followed her.

Second Prize Wang was approaching, and it seemed he was not alone. The principal was probably still with him. If that's the case, I'm done for, I thought.

I was in a panic. I climbed onto the windowsill, terrified. I was only about three feet away from the branch of the old elm. The distance should have been nothing for me—I'd been climbing trees since I was very young—except that panic seemed to have bound my hands and feet. Instead of grabbing the thick branch after I jumped out, I clung onto a small twig. It broke instantly.

While I was in the air, I noticed there was a full moon. In that instant I remembered I did not feel the slightest guilt for being a burglar. All I could feel was heartache. Pain flooded my heart and gradually submerged me. I then dropped to the ground and lost consciousness. After a short while I woke up. I opened my eyes and saw Second Prize Wang looking at me from his window, aghast.

I instinctively wanted to get up and run, but I couldn't move. I saw Second Prize Wang climb onto the windowsill. After a moment's hesitation, he jumped from the second floor like a superman and landed next to me. I was embarrassed to look at him, and the pain forced me to close my eyes anyway.

I remember the way he carried me was exactly like what we saw in those revolutionary war movies—a soldier carrying his injured comrade-in-arms, trudging beside Weishan Lake, along railroad tracks, across sorghum fields, through snowfields, over the top of unnamed hills, on his way to the land of hope, not the land of despair. I opened my eyes slightly and saw that Second Prize Wang's face looked pale under the moonlight. He was just about to put me down on a giant tree stump when pain took away my consciousness again.

VIII

When I woke up I found my face soaked in the sweat of someone's neck. A man was carrying me. I forced open my eyes and discovered that this sweat-drenched person was Second Prize Wang.

The agony of shame and physical pain bewildered me. I struggled to free myself, but Second Prize Wang gripped me tighter. "Don't move! You're still bleeding."

It was dark. Second Prize Wang and I were the only ones around. It felt eerie. "Will I die if I bleed too much?"

He laughed. "No."

"What makes people die?"

"Not wanting to live."

We stopped talking and kept moving. Second Prize Wang took a shortcut through the cemetery. While he was trudging through the weeds in the old elm grove, I glimpsed a blue flame flickering nearby. Second Prize Wang's steps became hesitant.

"Mr. Wang, there's a ghost or something behind the blue flame. Did you see it? It's fanning the blue flame."

"Close your eyes," he ordered. But I bravely kept my eyes open. The flickering flame became brighter, so I clung even tighter to Second Prize Wang's back.

Second Prize Wang was almost running by now. I could tell he was scared because his hair was standing up. The night wind blew stronger around us, and I shivered from the autumn chill. Gradually we increased our distance from the blue flame. We did not talk again. At last we saw the dim light of the hospital twinkling ahead. Second Prize Wang let out a long sigh of relief.

"Does it still hurt?" he asked.

I shook my head.

"For someone so slight, you sure are brave," he praised.

We did not talk for a while. "Did you see someone fanning the flame?" I asked. "Was it a ghost?"

"I did see that. But I have no idea what it was."

"But you know everything, right? How come you don't know about the ghost?"

"There are many things I don't know about," he said.

"When Chairman Mao said 'fanning an evil wind and lighting a ghostly flame,' was he referring to someone like that?" I asked.

"He probably meant more than that."

"Are you an atheist?"

"No, I'm not an atheist."

"Then are you afraid of ghosts?"

"Yes, I am," he responded.

I became worried as we passed through the hospital gate. "Will others find out about what happened tonight?"

"Do you want people to find out?" he asked.

"No, Mr. Wang, no."

"Then, no, they won't."

He didn't sound serious, and that made me anxious. "I didn't take anything from your room," I burst out.

"I believe you," he said.

In the hospital's emergency room, the doctor gave me an injection to relieve the pain. That put me to sleep before Mother arrived. I dreamed that the news of me stealing things had spread around school and throughout our compound. I imagined everyone in Ürümchi knew about it. But when I woke up I realized that because of Second Prize Wang's discretion, the incident remained between him and me.

Everybody did know about me breaking my leg, though. They thought I'd been up in the tree memorizing English words, and because I was so engrossed in studying, I forgot where I was and fell from the tree like a giant apple.

THIRTEEN

I

"You are not a gentleman."

Second Prize Wang looked like a wise man deep in thought whenever he uttered words like *gentleman.* He would stand with his hands behind his back and proudly raise his head. It never seemed to occur to him that his manner and tone were a bit over the top. It was just how he talked, and it always fascinated me. He knew so much more than I did, and would actually speak to me as his equal. He was happy to talk to me about anything and everything, and, most important, he was happy to listen to me.

Suddenly I felt sad. Mother had ruined everything, and Second Prize Wang had helped. I shouted to him in my head: Why did you listen to her? Why did you take her side? She doesn't love me or care about me. Don't you know? She loves only herself and her air-raid shelters. And all she cares about are preparations for war. Don't you know?

My silence left Second Prize Wang at a loss. I could tell he wanted to know what I was thinking. He crossed his arms, making him look even more like a foreigner. Squinting at me, he said, "You once said to me you wanted to be a gentleman."

I remained silent, ashamed of myself.

"Didn't you say I was your best friend? That you could talk to me about things you couldn't talk to your parents about?"

"You stopped talking to me first."

"That was at your mother's request. She asked me not to talk to you, and I obliged."

"Why? I'm the one who wants to be your friend, not her."

"What is it you want? What do I have that could be worth you ending up like this?"

I went quiet again, hoping to muddle through and escape his grilling by keeping my mouth shut. Why couldn't I admit I wanted to steal the dictionary? Perhaps stealing a book is not the most shameful thing imaginable, but I was too ashamed to admit it, especially to my English teacher. I could not understand myself. Why couldn't I admit it? What made me want to keep it a secret? I couldn't breathe, and my face flushed. Second Prize Wang's questions made me feel like a live chicken thrown into a pot of boiling water.

"You'll ruin your life if you go on like this." His serious tone made him sound exactly like other teachers. It was the first time I had heard him speaking like that. I began to sing "The Internationale" in English.

Arise, ye workers from your slumber,
Arise, ye prisoners of want.
For reason in revolt now thunders,
and at last ends the age of cant!

"Stop, please," Second Prize Wang said impatiently. But when he saw me singing with my eyes closed, he smiled. "All right. No one will let you have a heroic martyrdom. It's been ages since there was an execution at the East Hill Graveyard. Now, seriously, what do you really want? Maybe I can help you."

I sealed my lips and turned my head away.

The hospital ward was icy white. My mind was blank, and there was a dispiriting coldness inside of me. The plaster cast on my leg made me look like a gravely ill old man.

"Do you think I'm a thief?" I asked abruptly.

"No," he replied. "I don't."

"Mother said I'm a thief and she can't face people now because of me."

"I don't think you are a thief. I think you will still become a gentleman."

Perhaps that word—*gentleman*—was just too much to take. Sadness overwhelmed me. I suddenly grabbed on to Second Prize Wang and began to cry. He didn't say anything. He just patted my shoulder and let me cry my heart out.

I ask myself even to this day: Why did I refuse to reveal what I was after—that I wanted to steal the dictionary? Would revealing this have been more shameful than being a burglar? No matter how hard I think about it, I cannot find a satisfactory answer. I once tried to borrow the dictionary but was turned down. Perhaps that single rejection was enough to last me a lifetime.

II

Second Prize Wang was still standing beside my bed when Father walked into the ward.

Father was in his army uniform. The collar flashes and the insignia on his cap caught the light in that white room. He was not at all embarrassed to be dressed like that, and even acted naturally, as if he were a member of the People's Liberation Army down to his bones, as if he had been born like that.

He did not look at me. Instead, he went over to Second Prize Wang. "As Love Liu's father, I am deeply ashamed and would like to apologize to you." He then bowed low.

What Father did shocked me. Second Prize Wang backed off a few steps. He even blushed. "It's not that serious. I'm not blaming him—quite the opposite. As you probably know, I'm very fond of this boy. Whatever he was doing in my room, whatever he wanted, I would have given him."

I was moved by what Second Prize Wang said, but Father was poker-faced. I could see his cold eyes behind his thick glasses.

"Mr. Wang, could you excuse us? I would like to be alone with my son."

Second Prize Wang nodded repeatedly, but as he reached the door he turned back and said to Father, "You are rarely in Ürümchi these days. If you have the time, I would like to talk with you."

Father was surprised. "You and me? Talk about what?"

"I would like to talk about your son."

Father looked reluctant. He paused. "I—I don't have time."

Second Prize Wang did not expect Father to act just like Mother. He fled the hospital room as if he were the thief, not me.

III

"Your mother hit you?" Father caressed the red mark on my face.

I nodded.

"She shouldn't have hit you." As soon as he said that, he burst into tears.

I did not expect him to cry. I thought he would be tough. I watched him, not knowing what to do. At the same time, I felt guilty for my crime.

He wiped away his tears, then pulled out a filthy handkerchief and blew his nose. He burst into tears again, as if my crime made him as miserable as I was.

I did not know how to comfort him, so I just watched. Father sobbed endlessly, like a woman. He seemed completely without shame, even more so than I was for having attempted to steal.

I was worried my father would beat me. My leg was in a plaster cast. I wouldn't be able to run away. Lying in a hospital bed, I'd be defenseless. But Father did not have the slightest intention of beating me. He just kept sobbing.

At the time I thought he cried because of me. Only later did I realize he was crying for himself. He had completed the design for the hydrogen bomb research complex and was no longer needed at the base. His mission was over, and he had to leave the military. When someone's services are no longer needed, we use ancient sayings like "the bow and arrows are put away when there are no more birds to shoot" or "cook the hound when the hares have been run down."

Father coming home meant he was like the hound, as good as cooked.

IV

"Why did you go into his room?" Now Father was asking me this question.

I kept my mouth shut and again tried to get away with being silent.

"What's in his room that's so irresistible to you?"

It was a simple question, but it hit a nerve that made me want to cry. I felt a tide rise in my heart, and then waves of longing crashed over me.

What about his room was so irresistible? How was it that no one understood? Didn't they realize there was something beautiful in that room, something profound? I'd had it with grown-ups. Their lives were wasted. Living the way they were had made fathers exhausted and dumb, and mothers hysterical and oblivious. And it had made English teachers lose their dedication and give in to mothers. I'm done for, I thought to myself.

"Why did you go into his room?" Father raised his voice a notch. I noticed the whites of my father's eyes looked much larger than his pupils. Father blinked, then blinked hard again, and at that moment Mother walked into the ward.

She looked exhausted, as if *she* and not Father had been the one to travel far and wide to get here. The dull gray jacket she was wearing did not conceal her slender figure. Mother was beautiful, even in those hard times. She stood there like a statue or like one of those tall white poplar trees lining Xinjiang's roads, withstanding the hardships of nature.

It now occurs to me that the reason I hated my mother was not because she was so strict but because she never answered my questions. I was bandaged and bedridden, and yet the first thing she said was, "Now that your father has returned, tell us: Why did you break into your teacher's room?" Father also looked at me.

I was silent and could not bring myself to look into their eyes.

"Does he have pornography? Is that it?" Her question was like a bullet shot into my heart.

Father could not quite understand Mother's question, but he was rattled by the word *pornography.* He stared at Mother but kept quiet.

"Say something!" Mother shouted at me.

I suddenly raised my head. I looked at Father, then at Mother. "Why don't you just kill me," I blurted out.

My parents were dumbfounded and immediately looked at each other. Then everything went dark. The room became hazy, and then whiteness took over. A flock of white birds fluttered before my eyes, and my leg began to ache. In my daze I noticed that Mother had a lunch box in her hands—she had brought me food. She knew I had to eat. But she didn't know why I had gone into Second Prize Wang's room.

V

I returned to class three months later. Sunrise Huang sat next to me.

"Does your leg still hurt?" she quietly asked.

I did not respond.

"We have some Yunnan White Medicinal at home." She reached behind her and gently tugged at my hand, which was resting on the back of my seat. My heart filled to overflowing. I hadn't known a girl's touch could be so captivating. I wanted to hold her hand tightly, but in the end I chickened out.

Sunrise Huang did not look at me. She was staring straight ahead as usual, her face giving off a rosy glow. Before that moment I had never felt so close to a girl, so close that you could feel her breath, which was as fresh and sweet as honey. And as for her Yunnan White Medicinal, whatever it was, it had to be good. Unlike the usual bitter Chinese herbal medicines, I was sure it would be sweet.

Sunrise Huang's long hair, gathered in a bun, reminded me of the flowers that bloomed on the Ili steppes in northern Xinjiang, where herds of sheep passed to drink at the banks of the Ili River, and where the air was pristine. Her hand was right next to mine, and with the slightest of movements I could have grasped it, but I hesitated a hundred times. I've never been decisive, and because of this many opportunities have slipped away from me. I was anxious. I feared tears might well up in my eyes at any moment.

The light of the late afternoon sun gave the classroom a warm golden hue. There was a youthful exuberance around me, and everyone in the room was happy—except for me.

VI

On the way home that evening, Sunrise Huang walked ahead of me. I lagged behind because I was afraid to look at her after what had happened earlier in the afternoon. But Sunrise Huang acted as if nothing had happened, walking along gaily and even singing to herself. Suddenly she stopped and turned around.

"Why are you walking so slowly?"

I did not answer.

"I've been waiting for you to catch up so I could tell you something."

I watched her in anticipation.

"But now I can't remember what I wanted to say."

We looked at each other without speaking. "Ah, I remember." She broke the silence. "I wanted to say that ever since our families swapped units, I still haven't gotten used to it, and I go the wrong way all the time. I always turn left after the entrance instead of going up the stairs."

"Does your mother still feel the place is haunted?"

Sunrise Huang thought for a moment. "No, but she once said to someone that she's a jinx to the men in her life. Do you know what that means?"

I shook my head.

"It means she keeps on killing them. If she had ten husbands, ten would die."

"Will you be a jinx to your husband?" I asked, not knowing where I got the courage.

She giggled. "That depends on whether I take after my mother or my father. Who knows?" she answered cheerily. "Maybe whoever wants to be with me will die."

She cackled and ran off, still laughing. That was creepy.

When I was a child I often saw ghostly flames flickering in the cemetery. The night Second Prize Wang carried me to the hospital on his back, I caught a glimpse of a ghost furiously fanning those blue flames. Later, people said it was the ghost of Sunrise Huang's father, and that he fanned the flames because he could not accept his fate. What could he not accept? He was already dead, wasn't he? What was there not to accept? Although Second Prize Wang said he was not an atheist, my parents proclaimed they did not believe in god, only in science and the thoughts of Chairman Mao. I must have inherited their beliefs and become a youthful atheist because I thought that if Sunrise Huang's father refused to accept his fate, he should have cursed, fought, and taken action when he was alive.

Sunrise Huang had run off, leaving me to walk alone. It was getting dark. The word *jinx* horrified me, especially coming from the lips of Sunrise Huang, who had earlier in the day offered me medicine from Yunnan. I thought about what happened to her father, the Nationalist general, and then to her mother's lover, the Communist, and I got goose bumps. I started to run.

My parents were talking about something when I opened the door. As soon as they saw me they stopped. Recently, they'd been like that, as if I were the opposition—I always felt I was being left out.

I couldn't stand the atmosphere at home. The moment I walked in, an idea came to mind: I will run away from home. Just like a Uyghur, I'll roam about on a donkey with only a bundle of clothes and follow the Ürümchi River right into the Tianshan ranges, and I'll never look back. I won't say a word to my damn parents. Maybe I'll ride a donkey to Peking like that old Uyghur Kurban Turum and meet Chairman Mao. I heard that after he shook hands with Chairman Mao, Uncle Kurban never washed his hands again. If I could make my way to Peking like him, I would never wash my hands again, either.

Both of my parents were staring at me like interrogators. I lowered my head, fearing I might have done something wrong.

"Why have you been coming home so late?"

"What have you been up to?"

"Did you go back to your English teacher's room?"

"Why don't you have the slightest inclination to work hard for your future?"

"Why are you so different from other children?"

They always bombarded me with questions like that. If the bohemian colonies had existed in those days, I would have run away from home to hang out with the rock stars I adored.

Without waiting for them to ask again, I said, "I didn't go to the English teacher's room today."

My parents exchanged glances. "Then why are you home so late?" Mother demanded.

"Sunrise Huang said she had some Yunnan White Medicinal, and she said her mother was a jinx to her husbands."

My parents exchanged glances again.

"So you went to her house again?" Mother asked.

I said nothing.

Mother stared at me for a long moment, then sighed. "Go wash your hands. Let's eat."

That night I dreamed of Ahjitai. She spoke to me, but I was too shy to look at her. She said many things and even recited Chairman Mao's poems in Uyghur.

VII

The next day was bright and sunny. The snowcapped peaks of the Tianshan Mountains stood out against the bright blue sky.

I set out very early and wandered moodily around the grounds of the Hunan Cemetery. It was almost lunchtime when I came across Garbage Li. I wanted to avoid him, but he rushed over to the tree I was perched in and clambered up it in no time. He sat right next to me and gave me a big smile.

I knew Garbage Li liked Sunrise Huang; she was his first love. He pursued her with a persistence that is rare today and was always trying to get information about her out of me.

"I know where you can see Ahjitai!" he declared out of the blue.

My heart fluttered. I had not seen her in ages.

"She goes to the public bathhouse every Sunday at noon. Go behind the boiler room, climb over the stack of coal, and you can see her through the second window. She'll be completely naked. You'll see everything."

What he said set my whole body on fire. I felt very thirsty all of a sudden. From his smile I knew he was fully aware of the titillating effect his words had on me.

"It must be all steamy in there," I challenged. "There's no way you can see clearly."

He answered smugly: "Steam is like clouds—it swirls about. As soon as it clears up, Ahjitai's backside will be as clear as daylight. I'm telling only you; don't tell anyone else. I've seen it all many times."

I nodded, then began to climb down the tree.

"Sunrise Huang has been ignoring me lately," Garbage Li said, tugging my arm. "Can you find out for me what's up? Last week I caught her a rabbit, which seemed to make her very happy. I can't sleep because I think about her all the time."

I broke into laughter. "I'll ask her," I replied, trying again to make my way down the tree.

He tugged my arm again. "Do you masturbate?"

I blushed and feigned incomprehension. "What do you mean?"

He grinned. "I'll teach you one of these days."

I landed on the ground forcefully. "Who needs you for that?"

I ran off toward the boiler room behind the canteen and the bathhouse.

VIII

It was noon Peking time, but no one was in the canteen because mealtime was not for another two hours. I mention Peking time because in those days Ürümchi used Xinjiang time. Wang En-mao was persecuted for this. He was accused of establishing an independent kingdom. What's that you say? Who was Wang En-mao? He was the guy in charge of Xinjiang. He was eventually sent away, but we kept on using his Xinjiang time. Because of Xinjiang's location, the sun comes up later than in Peking. The sun comes up in Peking at five o'clock, but we'd have to wait until seven o'clock to see it. When the sun has already set behind the hills in Peking, we still have red clouds in the western sky.

As I ran toward the boiler room, a popular song kept rattling around in my head:

People compare Chairman Mao's writings to the sun,
I say the sun cannot compare, just cannot compare.
The sun rises and sets behind the mountains,
Chairman Mao's thoughts are eternally radiant,
Ah, yah hu hey, forever radiant, forever radiant.

There were quite a few people at the entrance to the bathhouse. It was the women's washday. In Ürümchi, bathhouses were for both men and women, but they were assigned different days. Men washed on Saturdays and women on Sundays. Women. Women. Apart from the words of the song, all I could think of was women. What are women? I don't know. They are kittens. Or puppies. Rabbits. Flowers. Grass. A river. Women are tears. Women are the sun in the sky. Women are the thoughts of Mao Ze-dong. . . .

The people at the entrance to the bathhouse were all women. They held their enamel basins, and many young girls used handkerchiefs to tie their hair in buns. Women really are clean, I thought. They even go to the bathhouse with their own enamel basins. And their towels are so fresh, as if with the scent of sunlight on them.

The women did not notice me. They were busy brushing their hair. Their faces were rosy from the steam. It must be great to be a woman. After they had bathed, they enjoyed the view of the Tianshan Mountains and the white clouds and were not in the least bit hurried. At the time I was not able, as I am now, to look at myself objectively: a boy who snuck into someone's dormitory to steal something, then ran off behind the boiler room to steal a look at women. You tell me, what is he? He must be a juvenile delinquent.

As I reached the rear of the boiler room, everything became quiet. There was another old elm tree with a thick trunk. Next to it, in a pile, were large lumps of coal from the Dahong Gully. I stepped up onto the coal and leaned toward the windows.

The boiler room was made of red brick, and its windows were high and small. To the right, under the second window, were two large lumps of coal. I became acutely aware of my heartbeat. I hesitated, thinking what I was doing was criminal. If I got caught, Mother would say that was the end of my political life. Dying is nothing compared with ending your political life.

I looked at that window and knew that if anyone discovered me, either inside or outside the boiler room, I'd be done for. Despite those fears I still clambered up. The lumps of coal were tightly stacked and didn't wobble in the least. I slowly brought my face up to the window. Through the glass I could see lots of steam floating around the bathhouse. I realized I was looking down onto the very place where Ahjitai loved to linger, where the beautiful Ahjitai would luxuriate in hot water. I nearly swooned at the thought, and when I recovered I could clearly see a woman with long hair and a white body. The image assaulted my face like a strong wind. It was Ahjitai. It really was Ahjitai. I first saw her back, her long legs, her fair hair, her shapely waist, and her smooth, round bottom. Was it really Ahjitai? My breathing became quick and shallow. Out of anxiety or fear, I don't know which, my eyes welled up with tears, which soon ran down my face. Then a miracle occurred: Ahjitai turned around. Were those a woman's breasts? I thought of the breast pump at the cooperative store.

Ahjitai's eyes sparkled as she enjoyed the pleasures of bathing. I looked at her closely, taking her in from head to toe. At first I shivered, then I began to feel hot. As she scrubbed below her belly button with a washcloth, her breasts appeared to quiver. They were pure white, like the mushrooms found in the wilds of the Tianshan Mountains. I could hardly breathe. My legs became wobbly, and I started to lose my footing on the lump of coal. It felt slippery, like a block of ice, and I fell to the ground.

As I scrambled to my feet, all I could think of was running away. I had to get away.

I thought I'd accomplished what was most important in my life: I'd seen Ahjitai naked. If I were to die today, I'd have no regrets.

I began to run. Nothing else mattered except running, running like a madman. I couldn't tell if the light I saw was Ahjitai or the sun. Bright light seemed to shoot out from her in all directions. She hovered above me no matter how fast I ran. When I took one step, so would she. I could not escape her face—or her eyebrows, her round shoulders, her quivering breasts.

I have no memory of how I left the boiler room and the bathhouse, of how I must've bounded through the pigpen and the canteen on my way toward the school. I didn't see anyone along the way. All I could see was Ahjitai's smiling face floating in the air. Suddenly someone grabbed me.

"Good afternoon," a voice called out in English.

I froze on the spot, as if being awakened from sleepwalking, and replied instinctively in English, "Good afternoon."

I looked up to see my English teacher. Second Prize Wang was well turned out as always, and his bright eyes revealed a hint of a smile. There was nothing in his face to suggest he intended to interrogate me. But still my face became hot.

He studied me for a while. "Where are you going?" he finally asked in English.

My mind churned slowly. Still blank-eyed, I answered in English, "I don't know."

IX

When I got home, Mother was washing Father's army uniform.

Washing clothes in those days was an ordeal. Mother had to rub Father's uniform on a scrubbing board. His uniform was important to him. It was proof that he was no longer damned, that his luck had turned. It was proof that his superiors valued him and that he had used his talent to serve his country. Father would never give a thought to whether the hydrogen bomb was intended to kill people. The opportunity to work again was all that mattered to him. He was a complete pragmatist, and pragmatists have no fear. They aren't even afraid of ghosts; why would they worry about little things like whether their clothes were dirty? Once Father put on his uniform, he didn't want to take it off, even when it was covered with greasy stains, which turned the water in the washbasin black.

Mother did not betray a hint of resentment while washing Father's clothes, which proved just how much she loved him. She was smiling and even hummed a song from the Soviet Union. Her humming was barely audible, but it alarmed Father. "Careful!" he exhorted. "You don't want to let anyone hear that!"

Mother cast an affectionate glance at Father. There was a lascivious glint in her eyes, no doubt left over from the sweet exchanges of the previous night. Just then the sun lit up Mother's youthful face like a spotlight would. "The sunshine is perfect," she said. "We can hang your clothes outside to dry."

"Is that safe?" Father fretted.

She shook her head and continued humming.

"You'd better stop that," Father warned.

But Mother couldn't suppress her urge to sing. A husband and wife, both given the opportunity to make use of their talents in a time like that—what could be better? Like the proverb says, "Everybody has something they were born to do"—and you'd better be ready when the opportunity comes along.

Mother's joyful mood was contagious, and soon Father's mood lightened, too. He joined her in humming, supplying a bass line to Mother's melody.

I thought they were a little bit strange upstairs, but I knew better than to say anything.

X

Mother attached a rope to a tree and hung Father's clothes on it. She told me to stand guard. Like a high jumper, she took great strides on her way back to our unit. We lived on the ground floor, so it was easier to get to our apartment now that we'd exchanged units with Sunrise Huang. And getting outside into the light was easier, too. I was even closer to nature.

Father's clothes fluttered in the wind like a flag announcing good luck.

I sat on the doorstep and soon became bored. I stared blankly at the sky.

Sunrise Huang came by. She looked at me and then at the uniform.

"You father looks great in uniform."

"Didn't your father also wear a uniform?"

"His was a Nationalist army uniform. Awful."

"Their officers' hats with the visors look great—they're in the American style."

"Really?" She cheered up.

"Of course," I replied.

"Well, come upstairs to my place. We've got a great photo of my father in uniform."

I followed her upstairs. She clambered up onto a large suitcase and retrieved a photo out of a small box on top. It was a picture of her father in a general's full dress uniform.

"Which looks better, a Communist army uniform or a Nationalist one?" she asked me.

"You tell me."

"No, you tell me."

We both burst out in giggles.

"You're reactionary," she said.

"No, you are," I shot back.

I was in a good mood as I left Sunrise Huang's unit. But then I discovered that Father's uniform was gone. I broke out into a cold sweat.

XI

I will never forget Father's reaction when he heard his uniform was missing.

He bounded out of the apartment, stomped around the tree like a lunatic, and searched frantically in every direction. The wall near our building was very high because there was a different work unit on the other side. Like a kung fu master, he sprang up onto the wall to see if someone had tossed his uniform over it.

Then he jumped down.

At the same time, Mother began to interrogate passersby, looking for leads.

My mind was in a haze. Watching my parents rushing around, I felt like a bystander.

Hidden behind his glasses, Father's eyes were like a bottomless lake, glinting with fear and despair.

In the end, Father bellowed in desperation at Mother, "I told you not to hang it outside!" He roared like the Ürümchi River.

Mother spoke with equal despair. "I told Love Liu to keep watch," she whined. "I had no idea he'd wander away."

Both my parents glared at me, as if I were their sworn enemy.

Father strode over to me scowling. "Not even your grandfather's death hurt me this much," he barked.

As he spoke he slapped my face with all his might.

The force of the blow spun me around like a compass.

Mother rushed up and restrained him before he could hit me again. "Not that hard," she implored.

But Father clearly wanted to hit me again.

My ears were ringing, and behind the ringing I heard Father's howl of desperation again. "Not even your grandfather's death hurt me this much!"

XII

That evening I ran away.

In those days all you needed was a few yuan in your pocket and you could run away from home.

By dusk I was hungry. I was strolling by the Horse Market near the Hundred Flowers Village. Next to the large mosque there was a Hui Muslim restaurant. Cooked goat's feet were on display in the window. You outsiders don't like to eat this sort of thing because of the smell, but they really are delicious. When I was small—that is to say, before my days of wanting to wear cologne and act like a gentleman—my friends and I would often gorge ourselves at the Horse Market.

If my memory serves me correctly, goat's feet cost just five fen each back then. I stared at the food like a starving donkey. The old restaurateur wore a white cap and had a long white beard. He looked at me sympathetically, as if he knew I was a hungry little runaway.

I pulled out a fifty-fen note and bought ten goat's feet, then sat in a corner and began to gobble them down. They were so tasty I could not help moaning with pleasure as I ate. I nearly buried my face in the mountain of bones.

I was getting full, and as I drifted off in thought, the door opened and a woman walked in. She wore high leather boots and a large shawl. The last rays of the sunset lit up her skin. When she turned, my heart jumped. It was Ahjitai. Yes, it really was Ahjitai.

She ordered a bowl of soup. As she sat down to drink some tea, I accidentally knocked over a bottle of vinegar.

That was when she turned around and saw me.

Our eyes met. She recognized me and immediately smiled, lighting up the whole restaurant and the darkest afternoon of my life.

XIII

"You didn't come with your mother?" she asked, walking toward me.

I put down the goat's foot I was gnawing on and looked at her, too nervous to say anything. Ahjitai's presence made me ashamed of my raucous gobbling. I suddenly realized how unsophisticated I was, and that I didn't deserve to speak English.

Ahjitai didn't seem to notice my distress. She sat down next to me. "You really like goat's feet, don't you?"

I nodded hesitantly.

"I like them, too," she said with a smile. "But your English teacher doesn't. I brought him here once. He tried one but spat it out."

I began to blush, ashamed of my gluttony.

"Second Prize Wang is not from Xinjiang," she continued. "He's different from us."

I nodded.

But I felt bad. I didn't want to be from Xinjiang or from Ürümchi. I wanted to be from Shanghai or Peking, or at least from Xi'an. But I was from Xinjiang, I thought, and what's a delicacy to me is inedible to Second Prize Wang.

"May I have one?" she asked.

Nodding and smiling, I pushed the plate over to her, delighted to know she wanted to eat something of mine.

"When you smile you have dimples, just like a girl." She giggled.

She ate the goat's foot elegantly, barely moving her lips and certainly not emitting the awful noises I made when I ate. I wanted to curse myself for being such a pig, but I couldn't do that in front of Ahjitai because she was half Muslim, and it would be impolite to curse in front of her.

I did not dare look at Ahjitai, so I lowered my head.

When her noodle soup came she asked for an extra bowl and gave me a large portion. "Eat it. I can see you're hungry. You must be famished."

I began to eat, as politely as I could at first, but before long I was making noise like a steamroller. My face was burning.

Ahjitai watched me without the slightest sign of disapproval. Many years later, whenever I recalled her expression, I could see appreciation in it.

The most beautiful woman in Ürümchi was sitting with me, sipping soup and eating my goat's feet, and she was looking at me with her beautiful eyes.

I broke out in a sweat. I was ashamed of having stolen a look at her.

She pulled out a white handkerchief to wipe my brow.

I refused to take it.

She smiled. "But you're sweating."

"My face is filthy," I protested.

"Why are you here alone? Why don't you go home?" she asked, casually extending her arm to wipe my forehead.

My eyes reddened, but I would not let myself cry. I was determined not to be a crybaby.

A woman's attentiveness is a wonderful thing. You must savor it if you are lucky enough to experience it.

We started to drink tea. The brick tea in those days was much stronger than the tea they have in Xinjiang now. It was as dark as coffee. The small teapots we used in Xinjiang were beautifully made. More tea came. I drank quietly and glanced at Ahjitai from time to time.

She looked serious. What was she thinking about?

I looked down and stared at the tiles beneath my feet. It occurred to me that it would soon be dark. Clouds shadowed my heart.

"Are you going home?" she asked.

I shook my head.

"Well, in that case, come to my dormitory for a while."

I instantly became deliriously happy, and the dark clouds were swept away.

We walked from the Horse Market to the North Gate. Ahjitai was a magnet for people's eyes, and people looked at me, too, especially boys my age. Jealousy was written all over their faces, and some even yelled out. Ahjitai walked fast. People stared at her because she was beautiful, so she always walked fast. I tried my best to keep up with her, but by the time we reached Tartar City Street I was sweating profusely.

"Does it bother you when people watch you?" she asked.

I did not know how to answer.

"It bothers me," she continued. "I wish I didn't look like this."

I remained silent.

In the twilight Ahjitai's hair looked even more golden. Her skin was snowy white—no Han Chinese had skin like that. Only Ahjitai did. I had not seen any American movies—just Albanian and Russian films—but it was clear to me that there was no one as beautiful as Ahjitai. Not even the wife of Lenin's assistant Vasily in the Russian propaganda film *Lenin in 1918* could compare, nor could Lenin's wife. After I grew up I saw beautiful women from all over the world. They all had skin as white as Ahjitai's, and golden hair. But what Ahjitai said forever haunts me, affecting my taste in women:

"I wish I didn't look like this."

XIV

The sunlight was fading when we arrived at the Hunan Cemetery, but it was not yet dark, so we walked in without much hesitation. No one else was there. It was quiet except for the rustling of leaves in the old trees. I thought I also heard skylarks singing. The narrow path unfolded as we walked, its end receding in the distance.

"I'll sing you a song. A Uyghur song," Ahjitai said.

She started to sing before I could respond.

In the Tarim
Not a soul
Just bleak desert sands
I left home for far-off lands
From lovers' eyes tears flow
Oh, Tarim
From lovers' eyes tears flow

Ahjitai sang in tune. Her voice was warm and mournful, and it seemed to linger in the old elm trees.

"My father taught me this song. He's buried in Kashgar, in southern Xinjiang."

Her mood descended into melancholy. She stared off into the distance.

We walked in silence. As we headed toward the exit of the Hunan Cemetery, I couldn't hold back any longer.

"What's a lover?"

Ahjitai blushed but said nothing.

The image of her blushing face is a constant reminder of how incredible she was. Just the word *lover* would make her blush. It must have had enormous power over people in the years of my youth.

"Do you want me to teach you that song?"

"Can you teach me in Uyghur?"

Smiling, she nodded and began to sing.

As I walked beside her, learning the song line by line, I discovered I really was a genius at languages. Not only was my English pronunciation good, my Uyghur pronunciation was accurate, too. Ahjitai was excited. "No wonder your English teacher likes you."

Before long I was able to sing the whole song. As we were about to come out of the Hunan Cemetery, the singing in the woods had become a duet.

A woman's voice.

A boy's voice.

We came to a point in the elm grove where the path narrowed, forcing our bodies closer together. My heart began to race, and I had butterflies in my stomach as I deliberately drew myself even closer to her. I could feel her warmth, a feminine warmth I'd never experienced before. I couldn't help brushing my hand against hers.

Ahjitai seemed to be aware of something but said nothing. She just continued singing.

I was shocked by my audacity. My whole body stiffened, and my heart pounded wildly. You really are a terrible child to start doing things like that at such a young age, I scolded myself.

Ahjitai could tell there was something different about me. She smiled. Her smile was like the winter sun, warming my face with its light.

Just as I was debating whether to touch her hand again, we walked out of the Hunan Cemetery.

I could see Ahjitai's beautiful hand from the corner of my eye and wished the path was just a little longer so I'd have another chance to brush against it.

Ahjitai stopped singing, but her voice lingered in the elm grove of the Hunan Cemetery and somehow embedded itself into my head and my heart.

Ahjitai's dormitory was on the eastern side of the cemetery, not far from where I lived. It was in a row of wood-framed brick buildings. There were thick columns at the entrance made of pine from the Tianshan Mountains. Her building was built years ago but still gave off a strong pine scent. I heard that the Nationalist army colonels garrisoned in Ürümchi used to live there, but that was long ago, and the building was now quite run-down.

We'd reached her door, and I was anxious, full of curiosity about her room, wondering what could be inside. Would there be perfume or other intriguing things? Would it be posh? *Posh* was a popular word at the time because Sunrise Huang had announced in class that my parents' house was posh since we had a bearskin. That aroused the curiosity of the girls in the class, and they all wanted to come over, but Mother would not allow it. She did not want visitors, she said, because she loathed visiting other people's homes, so I missed out on getting to see inside other people's homes. What does Ahjitai have at her place? I wondered.

She opened the door and went to switch on the light. I stepped in after her and felt giddy with excitement, as if I were stepping into a palace.

The light came on, momentarily startling me, but then I froze in shock: There was the English dictionary.

It was the same one—Second Prize Wang's. It looked like it had been thrown on the bed like a sweater or a sock.

It was the dictionary I couldn't find the night I broke into Second Prize Wang's dormitory. I felt sad, and a bit angry. Why did I break my leg? Because of that dictionary. Why did my parents hate me? Why did I want to run away from home? Because of that dictionary. But don't think I hated it. On the contrary, I felt only affection for it, so much so that I forgot about Ahjitai—that she was the most beautiful woman in the world and that I was in her room. It was as if I were alone with a glittering treasure chest.

I walked over to it and flipped it open. The word *masturbate* appeared again before my eyes.

I don't know why, but I felt like crying. If I hadn't noticed Ahjitai's puzzled expression, I might have burst into tears.

"What did you find in the dictionary?" she asked.

My eyes spoke "masturbate," but I said nothing. What did I see in the dictionary? That was a good question.

I held the dictionary close to my chest, stroking it as if it were a favorite pet I had lost.

Ahjitai let out a little laugh. I looked up at her and again noticed how beautiful she was.

As I emerged from my reverie, I realized I was in Ahjitai's room and that Ahjitai was standing next to me. I could feel her breath on my neck.

Ahjitai was still smiling, but a sudden knock on the door abruptly changed her mood. There was another knock. And then another.

I saw that Ahjitai was much more scared than I was. Her pure white face turned ghostly, and her body grew rigid.

I hugged the dictionary even closer to my chest, but I didn't know what to say. The moon outside the window, alone in the vast sky, caught my eye.

The knocking became more urgent.

Ahjitai cast a glance at me, then calmed herself and adjusted her hair, as if she were Jiang Jie, the legendary female revolutionary martyr, heading to the execution ground. She then went to open the door.

The man at the door was tall and wore glasses with thick lenses just like my father's. He smiled at Ahjitai—a smile as pure as the snow lotus flowers on the Tianshan Mountains. He looks familiar, I thought. Where have I seen him before?

As he walked into the room he noticed me. "Whose child is that?" he asked.

"Director Fan, this is one of my former students," replied Ahjitai.

"A student!" he said with a laugh. "Why does he look older than his teacher?"

He laughed again—I guess he thought he was being funny. His laugh was deep, as if all the good fortune in the world were his.

When Ahjitai greeted Director Fan, I remembered who he was—the man who had once slapped my father across the face. He was currently in charge of our entire compound. I was angry at myself for not recognizing him and secretly berated myself: How can you forget such a person?

Director Fan walked over to me and tried to take the dictionary from my hands, but I clutched it tighter.

He was surprised and pulled harder. "Doesn't this child know how to smile?"

Then he yanked the dictionary from my grip, like a tyrant retrieving his sword. “I don’t often come across this dictionary,” he commented while flipping through it. “I saw it once in the library when I was at Tsinghua University.”

Despite being nervous, Ahjitai put on an ingratiating smile.

Director Fan randomly turned to a page and read out some English. “Do you know what that means?” he quizzed.

Ahjitai shook her head, smiling.

“It’s from a poem by the British poet Shelley—‘If Winter comes, can Spring be far behind?’ ”

“Director Fan is so knowledgeable,” she flatteringly responded.

Director Fan began to laugh. He looked so charming with his white teeth and matching white shirt and his lean chin. Also, he could recite beautiful poetry in English. How could a person like that slap my father, even if Father did leave off an ear on Chairman Mao’s portrait? I was so angry I felt like blood would spurt from my eyes.

“Young man, go home now,” Director Fan suddenly said to me. “I have things to discuss with your teacher.”

I turned to Ahjitai, hoping she would say, “Let him stay.” But I was disappointed. She cast a quick glance at me and then looked away.

Remembering the feeling of the dictionary in my arms, I did not really want to leave. But I stood up like an obedient child anyway.

Ahjitai turned to me. “Go home, and don’t run away again,” she said with contrived cheer. “Your parents will worry about you.”

I found myself standing outside in the moonlight. My heart sank when the door slammed shut.

I went over to the window at the back of the house to see if I could peek inside. The curtain was not drawn, perhaps because Director Fan was in such a hurry, or perhaps it simply did not occur to Ahjitai.

Director Fan was about to hug Ahjitai.

She tried to avoid him.

I saw Director Fan mouth something.

Ahjitai pushed him away.

He then jumped on her again.

I saw him grab Ahjitai tightly, and her hair became disheveled.

I suddenly got an idea. I jumped down from the window, ran to the front, and started to bang on the door. It went quiet inside. I pounded on the door with all my might. When I heard someone coming to the door, I dashed off to the rear courtyard and hid behind an old elm.

The door opened, and I saw Ahjitai, her face pale, standing in the moonlight like a plaster-cast sculpture. Director Fan stood behind her.

"Come back inside," Director Fan ordered.

Ahjitai looked reluctant. "Please go," she implored.

"Don't talk in the doorway," said Director Fan. "It'd be bad if someone hears."

Ahjitai looked as helpless and confused as a lost little girl. At the time I did not understand why she seemed so terrified of Director Fan. If she refused to go back in or kicked him out, I thought, he wouldn't dare kill her, would he?

I never understood how women could dillydally in a situation like this. They are always hesitant when they want to reject someone. That was exactly what was going on here. Director Fan is such an evil man. He slapped my father, and he could beat up anyone in our compound if he wanted to. Ahjitai should not give in to someone like him, even if it meant becoming a martyr. I recalled the night she slapped Second Prize Wang. She was so decisive, like a true heroine. But with Director Fan she was behaving like a different woman.

To my surprise, Ahjitai obediently went back inside.

I crawled up to the door and listened. “Director Fan, please don’t,” I heard Ahjitai beg, sobbing. “You are a leader I respect. Don’t.”

“Be a good girl, now.”

Again I began to pound on the door with all my might.

The room went silent.

I continued pounding.

Someone approached the door, and I scampered off to hide behind the tree again.

This time Director Fan opened the door. “Son of a bitch,” he fumed, seeing no one. He had no idea who he was up against.

All of a sudden he pulled out a gun. His face turned ugly. Standing in the moonlight, he looked like a paper cutout.

I became scared, unsure of what I had done. Could I really protect Ahjitai? What if Director Fan were to find me and kill me?

Director Fan put his gun away, glared back at Ahjitai, and stormed off toward the administration building.

Ahjitai stood bewildered in the doorway, seemingly unsure whether to laugh or cry. I could see fear all over her face.

Director Fan soon disappeared into the Hunan Cemetery. Wasn’t he scared of ghosts? He was probably an atheist like my parents. He didn’t even slow down when he entered the cemetery. That proved he feared nothing. Was it because he had a gun? Guns could kill people, but could they kill ghosts?

Ahjitai finally went back inside and closed the door.

My heart swelled—I’d saved Ahjitai!

I went to her door and raised my hand a few times to knock but was too scared to follow through. I looked up at the moon. A kind of emptiness crept into my heart. I didn’t know if Ahjitai would open the door for me. Then I heard her sobbing.

It was heart wrenching. I had always thought of her as happy and never expected to hear her sobbing like this.

Then I heard my mother howling my name like a wolf.

Father was calling me, too. From the sound of his voice I could tell he regretted hitting me.

Their voices came from the Hunan Cemetery.

My parents suddenly seemed as helpless as Ahjitai. I remembered Father smiling at Director Fan after being slapped. His army uniform was the only symbol of status he possessed, his shield against being beaten, the proof of his contribution to the nation—and I had lost it. I remembered seeing photographs of Father wearing Western-style suits. Some were taken in Shanghai, some in Peking, some in Moscow. He used to love being photographed in a suit, but he now considered his army uniform to be more precious than anything in the world. He was right to have hit me, I said to myself.

I ran into the Hunan Cemetery and followed their voices. When I got close, I watched them in silence, feeling pity for them. But then I sensed something frightening about the word *family* and even the concept of parents. Like a wild animal, I hid in the dark and watched for a while, then quietly snuck out of the cemetery.

XV

It was the middle of the night when I arrived back at the Horse Market.

I knew there was a row of dilapidated houses at the southwest corner. Built long ago by General Ma Zhong-ying as a temporary barracks to house his troops in Ürümchi, the ramshackle sheds and adobe houses were now a haven for the homeless who had found their way to Xinjiang. These people—known as "drifters"—were not former soldiers of General Wang Zhen's Second Army Corps, nor were they educated people like my parents who had been dispatched by their work units to assist with the construction of Xinjiang. They had begged for food the entire way here. Kids like me thought of *drifter* as a swearword that meant the same as thief, bastard, thug, or robber. And now, I thought to myself, I couldn't go home even though I had a home. What am I if not a drifter?

I walked by the decrepit structures and discovered they were all occupied. Cheers and laughter drifted out into the street from the candlelit sheds. It had been a long time since I'd heard so many people laughing together. You would never hear hearty laughter like that in the compound where we lived. Especially in our apartment—my parents lived in fear. Yet whenever our neighbors raised their voices, my parents would stand behind the door and listen in. They appeared to be doing all the right things and claimed to have no interest in other people's affairs, but they took great pleasure in eavesdropping.

I continued to walk, shivering in the chilly autumn air. Then I noticed a rickety door hanging open. There was no candlelight or the sound of anyone inside, so I walked in. It was dark and I stepped on something soft. I heard a cry, and someone clambered up.

I froze.

The person I stepped on got up, struck a match, and looked at me closely under the flickering light. He was relieved when he realized I was just a child. Then he lit a candle. A thin man in his thirties came clearly into view. "Why don't you go home, sonny? What are you doing here?"

I could tell I didn't need to be scared of him. "I don't have a home. Can I sleep here tonight?"

"You can sleep over there." He gestured to a wooden board by the wall and tossed over a ratty cotton quilt. Then he lit a Mapacho cigarette. It was so strong I began to cough. He laughed and put out the cigarette. "What's your name?" he asked.

"I'm Love Liu."

"People here call me Zhang."

XVI

My time with Zhang is a blur. It was a little more than a month from when I met him until his death. It was the entire duration of my days as a runaway, and for a long time I was ashamed of that experience. All I can recall now are the highlights: a boy from a background like mine going out begging with Zhang and even stealing leather from a factory.

It was cloudy the day I went with Zhang to steal leather. It started off well, but we were spotted clambering over a wall. Zhang was already on top of the wall and tried to pull me up, but the people chasing us grabbed my leg and pulled me back down. Zhang had to run off without me. The people held me for a day and even hit me, but I didn't sell Zhang out. They whipped me ruthlessly with a leather belt, leaving welts on my head and neck. In the evening they finally let me go. Zhang was waiting for me behind an old elm near the factory gate. I was deeply touched and almost burst into tears. He hugged me. Seeing the welts on my neck, he asked, "Did they hit you?"

I nodded.

"And still you didn't sell me out?"

I nodded again.

"The pigs' feet I stole yesterday are all yours," he said, still hugging me.

We returned to our lair at the Horse Market, and he boiled some water. "What a great kid—didn't sell out his friend."

We talked late into the night, the room lit by candlelight. I told him a lot about me, and about Second Prize Wang. I sang "Moon River" for him. The beauty of English lit up this corner of the slum in an instant, as if the words of the song spilled out like a string of pearls onto the floor of a splendid palace:

Moon River, wider than a mile,
I'm crossing you in style some day.
Oh, dream maker, you heart breaker,
wherever you're going I'm going your way.
Two drifters off to see the world.
There's such a lot of world to see.
We're after the same rainbow's end
waiting 'round the bend,
my huckleberry friend,
Moon River and me.

Zhang was fascinated by my singing. "So young, and you can sing English songs. You'll be like Premier Zhou, if not Chairman Mao, one day. I have a relative who's a soldier in Peking. He's a company captain. I'm told he's often in meetings with Premier Zhou and Madame Mao and Ji Deng-kui. Next time I go home I'll tell him to help you out."

At the time I believed it, thinking that influential people could exist in a shack like his, just like what I was told about Marxists coming out of a remote mountain gully.

That's right, I also wanted to talk about Zhang's death.

Zhang was an early riser. He'd gone out in the morning but come back excited because he'd seen some pigeons at the No. 7 Middle School. "They can't fly because they've been hit by buckshot. They've been there all night. Pigeon is delicious. You're too thin and need to fatten up a bit. I'll get you some pigeon meat." And so I went off with him to catch pigeons.

The pigeons were resting on the chimney high above the boiler room behind the school.

Zhang told me to wait below while he climbed up the iron ladder. He slowed as he reached the top to avoid startling the pigeons. As he moved closer to his prey, I almost burst with excitement at the prospect of eating a pigeon.

When he finally reached the pigeons, he stretched out his hand. They didn't look like they were going to fly away. Then I heard a deafening sound from behind. Someone was shooting at the pigeons. Startled, Zhang lost his grip and fell from the top of the chimney stack. He landed next to me with a thud. Soon a crowd gathered. I heard mutterings of "He's dead! He's dead!" I could not bring myself to look at Zhang, but what he'd said the night before echoed in my ears: "So young, and you can sing English songs. You'll be like Premier Zhou, if not Chairman Mao, one day."

Zhang's death made me want to end my time as a drifter. I did not go home immediately but waited for Sunrise Huang on her way home from school. It was dusk. Walking by herself, she sang along with the music coming from the compound loudspeakers:

Glorious light radiates on Peking's golden hills
Chairman Mao, that golden sun
What a warm light, what a loving sight,
It makes serfs' hearts shine bright.

It felt like a homecoming when I heard this popular song about liberated Tibetan serfs, and though I looked filthy, my heart felt pure. I ran toward Sunrise Huang, my steps in sync with the melody of the song.

My sudden appearance startled her, and at first she didn't recognize me. I had not cut my hair or washed my face in over a month. She laughed when she finally figured out it was me. "So you're still alive. You were almost expelled from school, but luckily for you the principal intervened. Your parents have been worried sick. They scour the Hunan Cemetery every day after work. It was like you had dug yourself a hole and disappeared into it."

"Has Second Prize Wang asked about me?"

She nodded. "He asks me every day whether you've come back. He once canceled class and organized everybody to look for you."

"Have you started new lessons?"

"Of course we have." Then she lowered her voice. "Now don't tell anyone," she confided, "but Second Prize Wang has taught me a lot of English poems. The most beautiful one is by Yeats." She recited it in English. The musicality of it was comforting and brought me back from hell to the world of the living.

I didn't go home right away because I was afraid Father would beat me. It was getting dark, and I trudged around the Hunan Cemetery like an old man. As my mind flooded with memories, I thought how strange it was that a teenager could be so nostalgic, as if he already had a long life to look back on.

The moon came out, and the silhouettes of the trees swirled around me. Just as I was thinking about whether to go home, I heard my parents calling my name.

Like Zhu Zi-qing, who wrote a famous essay about his father, I saw my father from behind. It was heartwarming, but I felt like crying at the same time. Mother stood by his side. They looked like two children, drawing strength from each other.

Slowly, stealthily, I walked toward them, almost floating, like a flickering blue flame. When I appeared next to them, they quickly turned around in fright. Father stepped back two paces, his mouth wide open in horror. Mother held his hand. When they realized I was not a ghost, Father's expression turned to joy. He was back to wearing an outfit of gray fabric, the fabric worn by ordinary people. I deeply regretted not keeping careful watch over his uniform.

Mother reached out to me and hugged me tightly to her chest. That night, as I lay in bed, I thought I felt someone gently stroking my face. At first I thought it was Sunrise Huang, and then Ahjitai. Gradually I realized that one hand was Father's and the other

Mother's. In my dreams I knew they loved me. But I dreamed more of Ahjitai, of how I had helped her that night and of what she had looked like in the bathhouse.

My parents returned to their room. I was half asleep, but I vaguely knew what was happening around me—it was raining, and the pitter-patter of the rain made me feel hollow inside. An expanse of white suddenly overtook me, as snowflakes danced in the air. I became confused. Then I heard Uyghur folk songs mingled with Chinese ones, sometimes mournful, sometimes shrill. But a line of poetry was what stood out, the one Director Fan read out to Ahjitai:

"If Winter comes, can Spring be far behind?"

FOURTEEN

I

Bajiahu. Why is this place called Bajiahu, which means "Eight Households"?

Some say the name comes from the eight mansions built by Genghis Khan's eight younger brothers, or maybe it was his eight grandsons. I knew very little about history, but I found this story implausible. Bajiahu—what an unfortunate name. Peasants from the Hui Muslim minority must have come up with it. Xinjiang is a multi-ethnic region. If you want to figure out who the native inhabitants of a place were, or who named it, you need to listen closely to its pronunciation. If you read out Bajiahu, mimicking the accents of the Hui people who live in Ürümchi, Qinghai, or Ningxia, you'll know what I mean.

Unfortunately, there are no more mosques in Bajiahu. I heard there used to be a large one, but it was burned down during a war early last century. On its site was now a bed of green alfalfa, like a lake of rippling water spreading all the way to the foot of the mountain. The mountain also had a unique name, but I can no longer recall it. What I do remember is a Uyghur folk song about Bajiahu:

> *Baby boys sleep holding their baby sticks,*
> *Baby girls on the grassland watch baby boys. . . .*

The song's flowing melody has a strong flavor of the Urtiin duu, a traditional Mongolian "long song." But this just overcomplicates the story of Bajiahu's past.

No matter which ethnic group you believe was the first to inhabit Bajiahu, though, the language of its folk songs would soon mingle with another language—the English of Second Prize Wang.

II

Summer arrived, and it was an eventful one.

You may have never spent a summer in Ürümchi, where summer is glorious, deserving of its own poem—and in classical Chinese no less, since modern Chinese seems inadequate to my memory of it.

There was a dairy farm in Bajiahu where we used to work. We worked hard every day and were drenched in sweat. There were two types of work: cutting alfalfa with a sickle, and making mud bricks to build cowsheds. I cannot recall much about the peasant who taught us how to use a sickle. All I can remember is that Second Prize Wang came to Bajiahu with our class.

Why did he come with us for the hard labor instead of staying at school to teach? Was it some kind of punishment? Who knows?—it has been so long—but it didn't make a lot of sense. In any case, he was there.

When it was just the two of us, Second Prize Wang became more relaxed. He was even a bit reckless. Standing in the middle of a lush alfalfa field, he would say to me: "You need to have more of a 'Viennese repose' when you recite a beautiful essay. You should aim to achieve an 'artistic state' and finally a 'peaceful mind,' which is a unique 'serenity' that results from 'resignation.'"

Nowadays, many people talk like Second Prize Wang did. They're people who've come back from the United States or Europe. Their

Chinese is rusty, so they mix in English words here and there to remind us that they cannot speak much Chinese anymore. Indeed, there are times when English is more precise than Chinese, better for expressing complex ideas. Whenever I hear someone sprinkling English into his Chinese, I think of Second Prize Wang standing at the foot of the Tianshan Mountains, telling me, "You need to have more of a 'Viennese repose' when you recite a beautiful essay." It was clear when he spoke that he was passionately in love with English. He would recite paragraph after paragraph, even though much of what he said I could not understand. After each performance he would say to me, "I want to thank you for giving me the opportunity to perform, for letting me speak these words to you." And one day he even concluded with a deep bow.

Now is the time, I said to myself, and again made the most important request in my life: "Can you lend me the dictionary?"

He looked pointedly at me, as if judging whether I was a crook. Finally, he agreed. "One week," he said.

The dictionary was huge, and that night I stayed up very late reading it. I got up early the next morning before sunrise and went outside to recite. I wished I could memorize the whole book.

Sunrise Huang came out to the field that morning. She was wearing a floral-printed shirt and looked just like I imagined an English girl would look. From a distance she greeted me in English. "Morning." I greeted her back. It was surreal—like we were speaking English onstage in a play. She walked toward me cheerfully, and my heart filled with sunlight. "Sunshine," I said, and she smiled her radiant smile.

That was when she saw the dictionary in my hands. In an instant her delicate face turned ashen, and the sky clouded over at the same time. I looked at her and actually felt guilty, as if I'd stolen the dictionary and she'd caught me.

Sunrise Huang tried to snatch the dictionary away. I stepped back instinctively and clutched the book even tighter. She pressed one step forward, but instead of retreating farther, I put on a tough face. I was not acting at all like a gentleman.

The sky brightened again. Sunrise Huang's face flushed with rage, but you could easily mistake her expression for happiness.

"Time to go. We have to start work right after breakfast," I said to change the subject. She did not move. I knew what she was thinking.

"Why you?" She pouted. "Second Prize Wang has never lent me the dictionary."

I did not want to hear her out, so I turned around slowly and was about to head back to our dormitory when I heard Sunrise Huang shout at my back, "Wait!"

I jerked to a halt. "Your mother and my mother have both banned him from having contact with us. Why would he lend it to you?" She fired off her question before I had time to turn around. I thought she was being ridiculous, so I didn't respond and resumed walking. But I was a bit nervous, as I imagined hatred-soaked bullets shooting me down from behind.

Sunrise Huang darted toward me like the wind. She could run as fast as a monkey—to use an English saying. Then she sprinted away.

That was a memorable morning. For Sunrise Huang, the fact that Second Prize Wang lent the dictionary to me was evidence that he did not love her. She discovered that, in the mind of Second Prize Wang, whom she adored, she could not measure up to me—a boy who pretended to be educated and who wore eyeglasses with clear lenses just to make himself look sophisticated.

Sunrise Huang fell apart. She considered confronting Second Prize Wang, but her pride held her back. She looked devastated all day while we were cutting the alfalfa, just like when her father died.

That evening we bathed in the dormitory, which wasn't a habit for us until our English teacher told us, "You must bathe every day to keep your body clean."

Steam billowed around our bodies, and I peeked over to look at Second Prize Wang while splashing water on myself. With his eyes closed, he was enjoying sponging himself with a hot towel. He wore a pair of black underpants with an elastic waistband; they must have come from Shanghai, since you would not be able to find underpants of such quality in Ürümchi.

No one else was as self-conscious as Second Prize Wang. We were all naked, and we playfully nudged one another as we bathed, filling the mud-brick house with laughter. Many years later I saw a similar scene in a migrant workers' dormitory on a construction site in Peking, and I thought it looked filthy. But my memory of us bathing at the dairy farm is a fond one.

Sunrise Huang stormed into the room while we were having fun. She did not knock; she just marched straight into the naked crowd like a sleepwalker.

We were stunned. Some of the boys even screamed like frightened women.

Sunrise Huang did not seem to notice our naked bodies. She went straight up to Second Prize Wang and glared at him. Her lips trembled.

Second Prize Wang was calm. He reached for a blue-striped toweling blanket—maybe this is what's called a bath towel nowadays, but back then it was rare, a sign of sophistication. I feel as if I'm making it sound like everything about Second Prize Wang was exceptional, even his giant penis.

Second Prize Wang wrapped the towel around his body and asked

Sunrise Huang what was wrong, whether something had happened in the girls' dormitory.

Sunrise Huang locked her eyes on his. "I want to borrow the English dictionary, too!" she demanded.

Second Prize Wang now understood. "First of all, you should knock on the door before entering the men's dormitory. It's important," he said to her. "Second, I can't lend you the dictionary right now."

"But why did you lend it to Love Liu?" She was almost shouting.

"That's my business. I'll explain it to you later."

Tears burst from her eyes and streamed down her face. Sunrise Huang could not face Second Prize Wang's rejection. She left the room stupefied. Second Prize Wang sat on his bunk, the towel still wrapped around his body.

That evening, he asked me to go out for a walk. We strolled on the grassy field. It was a bright evening, and before us we could see the field rolled out to the horizon like a mottled carpet.

"Her mother came to school and spoke to me. She even slapped me." In a remorseful tone, he talked as if he were criticizing himself in a meeting. He paused for a moment. "Two mothers have slapped me. All because I like their children and like to speak with them in English."

He sounded calm, like he was telling someone else's story.

"I saw my mother slap you."

He looked startled.

"I saw it all from the tree," I added proudly.

He could not figure out what tree would allow people to see into his room.

Watching his puzzled face, I thought: Grown-ups are another species. They live in a completely different world from us.

I almost burst out laughing but did not know what there was to laugh about.

He did not seem to notice my smirk. "I can't have any contact with her. I'll be suspected again if I lend her the dictionary. I'm scared," he said, knitting his eyebrows.

The word *scared* rocked me. My English teacher actually told me he was scared. Sophistication and elegance and so many other things I longed for came with English, a language he knew so well. Yet behind the glory came the sigh of an adult: I'm scared.

Those words made me shiver. I glanced up to see if he was upset. Although his face was downcast, he appeared to be calm.

"Then why did you lend it to me?"

He turned to me for a moment, then looked up at the moon. "You should thank God for that. You're just a boy, not a girl, and God knows that. God knows everything."

"Is there really a God?"

Second Prize Wang hesitated. "My grandfather thought so, and my father thought so, too," he finally replied. "If you promise not to tell anyone, I'd also say yes, there definitely is a God."

I was speechless. In that atheist-dominated world, someone in the dark actually told me, "There definitely is a God."

We walked slowly. From the distance came the sound of someone singing a Uyghur folk song blended with the tinkling of donkey-cart bells. I could understand some of the lyrics because I'd studied Uyghur, thinking it would give me access to Ahjitai, to her beautiful face and neck. I'd heard her singing the same song.

Riding a horse over a hill,
I came to Ili
Where I met the beautiful Amanguli. . . .

We listened. For some reason I liked the sound of "Ili." It felt foreign, like English. I remember in those days, skylarks would follow the warm spring wind coming from Ili.

"Did you know your grandfather?" I asked abruptly.

"Of course."

"Did he speak English?"

"He spoke to me in English when I was very small."

"Did he meet God?"

Second Prize Wang paused and thought about my question. "It's hard to say."

"I've never met my grandfather. Father said he died right after the liberation of China in 1949. He hanged himself," I told him. "I overheard Father telling Mother," I confessed.

"Do you wish you'd met your grandfather?"

I nodded. "Does God know about all of this?" I asked.

"Yes."

At that moment, the crimson sky was fading to darkness. The singing was still wafting toward us. Though the song sounded Islamic, I thought about the God Second Prize Wang believed in.

III

We were on our way back to the dormitory. From the distance we saw a girl lingering in front of our door. Second Prize Wang sped up. I followed him.

It was Sunrise Huang. Her freshly washed hair was tied back with a handkerchief. Her face looked pale under the moonlight, but her eyes were sparkling.

She marched straight toward us when she saw us coming. I was a little nervous, as I did not know what she wanted. She stopped in front of Second Prize Wang and held him with her eyes. The two of them were like lampposts facing each other on a street at night. Their eyes locked.

"I'm joining the People's Militia," Sunrise Huang said, breaking the silence.

Second Prize Wang seemed a bit surprised but did not say anything.

"The head of the farm has already approved. So has our principal. I'm starting tomorrow," she announced.

"Now we still can study for half a day while spending the other half laboring," said Second Prize Wang, carefully wording his response, much as he did in his English classes. "Members of the militia have to give up their studies completely. They have to participate in patrolling, drilling, and shooting practice every day. In other words, once they take up guns, they are different from you ordinary student . . . revolutionaries."

"This is as it should be. We revolutionaries are different from you ordinary people," she corrected him.

I found this amusing. "Don't you still want to study English?" I chimed in.

She turned to me and smiled. Dimples appeared on her delicate face.

"In my next life," she replied, walking away.

Second Prize Wang froze on the spot, following Sunrise Huang's receding figure with his eyes until she disappeared into the girls' dormitory. He then turned to me but did not say a word.

I stood next to him, also speechless. The air grew heavy, as though there were a funeral in Bajiahu. A warm wind came from afar.

V

On many afternoons since that day, just when we were exhausted from pulling up weeds in the fields, Sunrise Huang and Garbage Li would whiz past us on the backs of galloping horses, leaving behind the clatter of hooves and the sound of Sunrise Huang's laughter and exaggerated shrieking.

Second Prize Wang would always look up and watch them. "What are you looking at?" I would ask. What I really meant was: She goes by every day; why do you still bother to look?

"I'm looking at Sunrise Huang and her gun," he would reply.

Sunrise Huang and Garbage Li were already in the distance. There was still dust in the air.

One day, after watching them pass, he asked me abruptly: "Would you carry a gun and ride a horse like that?"

"No."

He looked at me curiously. "Why not?" he pressed on. "Don't they look impressive?"

"I don't like guns," I answered.

Second Prize Wang's eyes sparkled. He seemed pleased with my answer.

Our friendship grew stronger. Everyone could tell there was a bond between us.

V

One night we sat on the giant wooden wheel outside the dormitory after everyone else had gone to sleep. I was telling Second Prize Wang what I'd seen in the bathhouse, and about Ahjitai being naked. He stared at me with wide eyes.

"I couldn't see clearly at first because of the steam. Gradually it cleared. She wasn't wearing anything. She was completely naked. Her back was red from the hot water. Her hair was wet. I didn't expect to see her. Before I went, I thought Garbage Li was lying. I thought he was just teasing me. And I didn't really want to go. I didn't know I would actually end up going. It's quiet by the boiler room. Nobody goes there. And now that it's summer, even people who work in the boiler room don't go there. . . ."

Bathing in the moonlight, I felt a mixture of guilt and excitement.

Second Prize Wang just listened in silence. His eyes encouraged me to keep talking. Then I stopped.

"You're lying," he challenged. "You said the window is high and small. But you are short. There's no way you could've reached it."

"I stacked a few chunks of coal under the window."

"Coal? That's impossible. How can you stack up chunks of coal in such a short time?"

"They were there already when I arrived. I don't know who put them there."

"You just said you did. So you *are* making this up. You should be a writer when you grow up."

"I didn't make it up. I did see her. There was steam inside. . . ."

"Right. You're lying again. The window was small, and there was steam. Plus, it was dark inside and bright outside. How could you possibly have seen her?"

"I did see her. Ahjitai is white. She's whiter than other women, whiter than my mother, whiter than Sunrise Huang."

"She—she really is white?"

He seemed to be thunderstruck by what I had just said. "Is she really white?"

"As white as the snowy mountains."

"Liar. What's the color of a snowy mountain? What's the color of her skin? They are different things with completely different textures."

I was excited and ignored his questions. "I saw her breasts when she turned around. They're like snowy mountains," I gushed.

Second Prize Wang grabbed my arm. "Did she turn around? What did you see?"

I shook off his hand. "I got scared. I thought she might see me. So I jumped down and ran away."

"Did she really turn around? Why did she turn? You really didn't see anything, did you?" He would not give up.

"I was terrified. I didn't see a thing," I bleated, unsure myself of what I'd really seen.

Under the moonlight, his eyes stared blankly. "It's summer now," he said, repeating what I had said earlier.

We were silent for a long moment.

The confession brought me satisfaction. Peeping at Ahjitai in the bathhouse was probably the worst crime I'd committed in my youth. My heart still races when I think of it. But that night, when I told my English teacher what I'd done, I felt a peace of mind unlike any I'd experienced.

Second Prize Wang's eyes went blank again. He gazed at the moon and stopped talking.

I felt sorry for him. "When I was in your room I saw the photos you took of Ahjitai. You took them in the West Park next to Yuewei Cottage. The lake was sparkling. . . . I liked the backlit photos the best. Why don't you give them to her?"

Second Prize Wang did not face me. He looked embarrassed and hesitated for a moment. "She doesn't want them."

"Now that I've told you about peeping at Ahjitai in the bathhouse, will you think I'm a bad child and never talk to me again?"

He shook his head, still looking at the moon.

"Can I borrow the dictionary for another week? I want to write down more words," I entreated.

He studied me for a while and was about to say something when we heard a gunshot from the direction of the boiler room. On a quiet night like that, it shook the earth. The gunshot was followed by a girl's wailing. I quivered. I was sure the voice belonged to Sunrise Huang.

VI

If I close my eyes, I can see Sunrise Huang. She is skipping down the path to the bathhouse outside the Hunan Cemetery. When she passes the boiler room, her cheeks glow red, reflecting the burning coal. Her hair is still wet. In the next moment she is carrying a gun, bouncing about on the Bajiahu grassland. Even though the gun seems too heavy for her, she puts on a jolly face as if she is carrying it effortlessly. Sunrise Huang was so stubborn. On the night Second Prize Wang and I first talked about God, she insisted on becoming a member of the People's Militia with Garbage Li.

God versus the People's Militia. Can I talk about them in the same breath? Would that be a good title for an essay or a piece of music? It sounds silly, and not funny at all.

Did the head of the dairy farm and our principal approve her request because they liked her? I don't know. Maybe she was able to join simply because our nation needed more people in the militia at the time.

The period when Sunrise Huang and Garbage Li were members of the militia was probably the happiest of their lives. While the rest of us were laboring and sweating under the sun, they strolled past us on patrol, chatting and laughing, rifles slung on their backs. With the sun shining on them, they beamed with youthfulness and high spirits.

Garbage Li was brilliant at sports. He set the record for one hundred meters at 11.9 seconds; to this day it remains the school record. My best time was fifteen seconds. He learned to ride a horse soon after jumping on one's back for the first time. His jump was as agile as Mayumi's in the Japanese movie *Manhunt* that we saw many years later, in which Mayumi rode a horse and rescued her lover. Garbage Li could also shoot. We often heard reports of his high scores in target-shooting competitions. He scored even better than the farmers, most of whom were originally soldiers of the 359th Brigade. They came with Commander Wang Zhen and were the same brigade that was famous for successfully converting wasteland in the Communist base at Yanan into productive farmland during the blockades by the Japanese and Nationalist armies. They had used guns in combat. For Garbage Li to achieve better scores than these soldiers in shooting competitions was a great honor for our school.

After hearing the news, Second Prize Wang took some time to process it before saying, "Perhaps Li Jian-ming will become a general one day."

Li Jian-ming was Garbage Li's real name. Second Prize Wang never called him Garbage Li. We could remember Garbage Li's real name only when Second Prize Wang called him by it.

But back to the gunshot: I hear it whenever I close my eyes and picture Sunrise Huang.

That night, Sunrise Huang and Garbage Li were sitting in the boiler room, waiting for the water to boil. Sunrise Huang had told Garbage Li that she wanted to bathe and had asked him to carry the hot water from the boiler room because she was scared of the dark. So Garbage Li went to the boiler room with her, toting his rifle.

When they were in the boiler room, the water's bubbling sparked an argument. Sunrise Huang thought the bubbling meant the water had reached its boiling point, but Garbage Li thought he knew better. "Bubbling water is not boiling, boiling water won't make a sound," he said, reciting a common saying.

"Do you think you know everything just because your father works in the maintenance unit?" Sunrise Huang challenged.

"I *do* know everything," Garbage Li countered.

Sunrise Huang picked up the rifle that Garbage Li had propped against the wall and pointed it at him. "I'll shoot you if you keep being so cocky," she warned.

"Go ahead. There aren't any bullets in it," he retorted. But Garbage

Li forgot he'd taken some bullets from home the day before and loaded them into the rifle. A friend of his father's, who worked in the Wulabo Military Supplies Warehouse, had brought the bullets to his home.

Sunrise Huang pointed the gun at him. Garbage Li stepped forward, pressed his face to the muzzle, and moved from side to side. "Pull the trigger. Do it," he teased.

"Are you sure there aren't bullets inside?" asked Sunrise Huang.

"Just do it," Garbage Li urged.

"I'm really going to do it," Sunrise Huang warned.

"So do it, pull the trigger. We Communists are not afraid of death!" Garbage Li declared, mimicking Communist martyrs in revolutionary movies.

Sunrise Huang pulled the trigger. A deafening sound came from the boiler room.

Part of Garbage Li's face was blown off.

Sunrise Huang was horrified. She squatted beside Garbage Li's corpse and wailed. Her hair was disheveled, and her skirt flopped like a nightgown. With her pale neck and skinny legs, she seemed to be floating in the hazy light, the way clouds and the White Pagoda are reflected in the lake in Peking's Beihai Park. When I saw Sunrise Huang that night, I knew she'd finally gone insane.

VII

I cannot help feeling guilty whenever I think about Garbage Li. I always looked down on him and talked about how his father worked in the maintenance unit and my father was a chief engineer.

The death of Garbage Li brought us back to school from Bajiahu's dairy farm and turned Sunrise Huang from a schoolgirl into a prisoner.

Three months later, Mrs. Huang was sick and asked me to visit

Sunrise Huang on her behalf. She told me she'd arranged a permit for me. On my way to Liudaowan Detention House, I felt I had so much to say to her.

Sunrise Huang was mostly silent during my visit. At first she did not raise her head or even glance at the hair clip her mother had asked me to bring her.

I noticed her hair had turned blonder, like the hair of a Russian girl. Her skin also seemed lighter. These changes made me think for the first time about how she was a girl and there was a gender difference between us. She did not notice my expression. She did not even want to know why her mother had asked me to visit her, but she did eventually put on the hair clip, which made her hair seem shinier.

As soon as I saw her I thought she would cry. But she did not. I could not understand where this young girl had found her strength. After I grew up, I heard the story of Zhang Zhi-xin: She was a Communist Party member who refused to change her critical views on the idolization of Chairman Mao and the party's ultraleft policies, even after being jailed and tortured. To prevent her from shouting slogans on her way to the execution ground, her jailers cut her vocal cords. I later also read poems that paid tribute to her and thought the poets were making a fuss about nothing. Didn't they know? That's just the way women are.

Sunrise Huang and I stood there, facing each other. I thought we just weren't meant to talk on this visit, even though I could tell from her expressive eyes that she was no longer insane. But as I was about to leave she abruptly said: "I heard you're the son of your mother and our principal. Is that true?"

The sunlight shining on her face through the window made her glow like a nymph.

FIFTEEN

I

Second Prize Wang was like a missionary in those days, only his religion was English. He was always calm and willing to teach anyone interested in learning English. Using the only dictionary he had, he'd start with the alphabet and the International Phonetic Alphabet, then move on to vocabulary and sentence forms, then to grammar and articles. He could not compare with the missionaries who came to China in the nineteenth and twentieth centuries, who managed to spread the word of God in China and were widely admired. But what could Second Prize Wang do? He was so insignificant; there was almost nothing in his control.

For a while in our school, we had what we called an "English corner." It was like a church for the worship of English. Sometimes the "corner" was in Second Prize Wang's dormitory, sometimes in our classroom, and sometimes in front of the graves at the Hunan Cemetery. But the corner kept getting smaller, and in the end only Second Prize Wang and I took refuge in it. To us, every conversation in the English corner was a church gathering or a language practice session. Maybe that was all he could offer: a two-person English corner.

"Am I the son of my mother and the principal? You're a grown-up: Do you think it's true?" I once asked.

"I don't believe it," he replied in English.

"Do you think I should ask my mother?"

"Please use English," he reminded me.

"Do you think I should ask my mother?" I repeated in English.

"No, you shouldn't."

"I followed my mother once. I know they had that sort of relationship," I reported.

"Don't talk to me about these things."

"But I have no one else to talk to. There's no one else I can ask. I've been studying myself in the mirror to see if I look like my father. The more I look in the mirror, the more I think I don't look like my father. But I don't want to look like the principal, either."

"You shouldn't think too much about these things. You must learn to wait."

"Wait until when?"

"Wait until you can no longer hurt your mother with this question. Remember, no matter what the circumstances are, you must never hurt your mother."

II

We had conversations in English every day.

"Is Sunrise Huang mad?" I asked him.

"No, she's not. She's an intelligent girl."

"Does it make you sad to see how she is now?"

"Not just sad. It also makes me think a lot."

"Sunrise Huang often stared at you from behind. Did you know that?"

"Yes, I knew."

"But why did you seldom look at her?"

"Because I'm a teacher and she's a student, a female student."

"If we were not in China but in the United States, would you look at her?"

"No. You students are too young."

"Will you marry her when she grows up?"

"I'll be an old man when she grows up."

III

"Ürümchi's a big place with tall buildings. In English it could be described as a 'city,' right?" I asked Second Prize Wang.

"It can only be called a 'town,' " he replied.

I was annoyed. There's no doubt about it, I thought, Second Prize Wang is from Shanghai. As a true outsider, he's just so different from an unsophisticated Ürümchi boy like me.

"You should visit Shanghai one day, or even go to New York, Paris, or London," he added.

"Have you been to New York, Paris, or London before?"

His eyes clouded, and he lowered his face. "I could have gone there," he said.

"Have you been there or not?" I pressed on.

"No."

"I don't need to go anywhere." I smirked. "Ürümchi can be called a 'city' regardless."

"Remember, you must not tie yourself to Ürümchi when you grow up. You must see the world. The Tianshan Mountains are blocking your view."

I resent people who are critical of the Tianshan Mountains, so I reacted defensively. "I don't have money."

"So just roam about."

"I'll be shot dead if I go as far as our border with the Soviet Union. Why don't you go roaming about?"

"In the future," he answered in English. "But I'll be old by then."

I was taken aback by the word *old:* What did it mean? Did it mean "dying"? Garbage Li died before he became old. I looked up at

Second Prize Wang and noticed a white hair. Did that mean he was old? I wondered. Of course, thirty-something is quite old. I used to think that thirty years was long enough and that I'd have no regrets if I died by thirty—I could even kill myself. But I am forty years old now, and still dragging out my ignoble existence.

"You have a white hair," I told Second Prize Wang.

He looked at me and blushed. For the first time, his noble appearance, his English, and his knowledge of Western culture were overshadowed by his growing old. I felt sorry for him.

"There's not much hope for my generation. But one day, if you stand on a street corner in Europe or the United States, you must remember what I said to you," said Second Prize Wang.

"What did you say to me?" I asked, puzzled.

His eyes became blank. Then he smiled faintly and turned to the mirror. "By the way, bring that dictionary back to me," he said while examining his white hair.

IV

When we returned from Bajiahu, Second Prize Wang was again stripped of his right to teach.

The gunshot incident had nothing to do with him, but he was blamed for it, thanks to our principal. The principal claimed that he had asked Second Prize Wang to stand in for him on the day of the incident, since he had to go to a meeting. There was no way Second Prize Wang could defend himself because everything the principal said was true—yes, there was a meeting, and yes, Second Prize Wang was in charge that day—except he was not responsible for militia activities. Second Prize Wang shut himself up in the dormitory every day and waited for the school's verdict. He'd told me he would gladly accept a severe punishment if it would bring back Garbage Li and give an intelligent girl like Sunrise Huang another chance to study

English—even if the punishment meant his own death. But I said to him, "Then who's gonna teach us English?" Second Prize Wang studied me closely, as though he had just found me. "I didn't think of that," he finally said.

We undertook our English-corner discussions religiously after that, in all sorts of places. It was about repeating sounds, situations, and sentences in English. It was also about me growing up.

SIXTEEN

I.

It was Sunday again. Another women's wash day at the bathhouse. I dithered about whether to spy on Ahjitai. Would she bathe today? I missed her.

I'd have no regrets if I got caught spying on Ahjitai, I thought. But what a waste if she weren't there and I got caught spying on other women.

I juggled the thought over and over again in my head. Finally, I decided I'd follow her.

I went to Ahjitai's dormitory. My plan was to wait for her to come out. If she went to the bathhouse, then I'd peek at her through the window at the back. This was no doubt a sensible plan.

Her door opened while I was watching from behind a tree.

I saw Ahjitai shove out a refined-looking man. It was Director Fan, the most powerful man in our compound. Ahjitai was fuming. I had never seen her so angry. She hurled a whole roast chicken at him.

Director Fan picked up the chicken. His face betrayed no emotion. Without saying a word, he disappeared into the Hunan Cemetery. It was a sunny day.

I wanted to salute Ahjitai: She had thrown out two of the most sought-after things in those days—a roast chicken and Director Fan.

Ahjitai went back inside and shut the door.

I snuck off to her back window. Ahjitai was leaning on the table, sobbing. I felt like crying, too.

Abruptly Ahjitai stood up. She walked to a corner of the room and picked up a large silver basin. She was going to the bathhouse! My heart began to race.

II

I went to the back of the boiler room. The two hunks of coal were still by the window. I felt relieved.

The bathhouse was as steamy as last time, and I heard water splashing. When my eyes got used to the dim light, I saw Ahjitai's hair. Then her back came into view. She was as white as the last time I'd seen her.

As my thoughts of Ahjitai were spinning around in my head, I felt a pair of eyes on me. The steam slowly cleared away, and I saw Ahjitai looking at me.

She looked at me calmly, as if she were standing at the lectern. She did not seem to be embarrassed of her nakedness.

Time seemed suspended as we gazed at each other like that. All I could see were her eyes; everything else had disappeared.

As I came out of my reverie, I realized that I was not in my bed dreaming but peering through the window behind the bathhouse. The eyes I gazed at were really Ahjitai's, not a woman's from my imagination. Thunderstruck, I jumped down and immediately ran off.

It was only August, but autumn had already arrived in Ürümchi. Yellow leaves fluttered in the air and glimmered in the sun, making me dizzy.

It was my birthday. I turned seventeen that day.

III

I wandered around for a long time before ending up at Second Prize Wang's place. I saw some white foam on his face as he studied himself in the mirror. He was shaving.

I was short of breath and tried to calm myself.

"Why is your face so red?" he asked.

"I was just at the bathhouse and saw Ahjitai."

He continued shaving.

"I saw Director Fan being thrown out of her room," I added.

His hand slipped, and he cut his face. Blood puddled on his cheek, turning the white foam red.

"I saw her naked body from the front today."

He rinsed his face, not looking at me.

"She's white, as white as snow," I continued to report.

Second Prize Wang became hysterical. "I can't stand children like you who tell lies. She was taking a bath. Why would she turn around?" he shouted. "Also, why did you follow her, then come here to tell me about Director Fan leaving her room? What exactly do you want? Spying on people is a most disgusting thing, don't you realize?"

He shouted the last three words. That was the first time I saw the scary side of Second Prize Wang.

I was shocked. Why was he so worked up?

"Get out! Out!" he shouted.

I glanced at him apprehensively, then walked heavily out of his room.

IV

I was alone, wandering the streets of Ürümchi, a place built by my parents' generation, a place that in English can only be called a "town." The sun was shining, but I felt gloomy. Then I got to the

Nationalities Theater. Looking up at this magnificent structure designed by my father, I felt better, proud of Ürümchi. I thought Second Prize Wang had gotten it wrong this time. Ürümchi *was* a "city." When I walked past the theater I saw the Tianshan Mountains. At that moment, Sunrise Huang, Garbage Li, and Second Prize Wang, with his single white hair, all flashed through my mind.

My memory of that day is vivid—for it was on that day, for the first time in my life, that I felt I was aging.

V

Someone called out to me from behind. I stopped. I knew it was Second Prize Wang. He came up and put his arm around my shoulders.

"I thought you'd never talk to me again," I said.

"I'm lonely. You're important to me. I don't want to lose your friendship."

My heart twitched, but I held back my tears. "How did you know where I was?" I asked.

"I followed you," said Second Prize Wang. "I'm sorry." He gave me a gentlemanly bow.

We strolled along the Ürümchi River. The water turned greenish in autumn. Falling leaves were swept away by the raging current. It was noisy. I started skipping stones. Second Prize Wang joined me.

"Did you really see Ahjitai completely naked?" he asked out of nowhere.

"Yes, I did."

"You saw everything?"

He blushed the instant he whispered the question. I had never seen his face turn red so fast. It looked scarlet in the midday sun and stayed flushed for a long time. His voice trembled, as though he knew he was despicable.

I could see his embarrassment and yearning. That was the only time I ever felt pity for him. Under the poplar trees by the river, he seemed frail. The cut on his face was strangely noticeable.

"I saw everything," I replied.

The second I said that he squatted down as if he had lost the strength to hold himself upright. He would have collapsed and been unable to get up if he weren't a gentleman. He held his head in his hands and trembled as if he were severely ill. He held that posture for a long time and didn't look up.

I was not surprised by his reaction. I knew I was capable of having sinister thoughts. When Karl Marx was seventeen, he wrote an essay about how he'd decided to devote his life to the interests of humanity. At the same age I could understand Second Prize Wang's devotion to Ahjitai.

For some reason I began to describe Ahjitai's body in lurid detail. I had an active imagination, and having seen her body with my own eyes, I was able to describe her in terms as lively as the Ürümchi River.

Second Prize Wang stared at the ground the whole time. He didn't dare look up at me. Exhausted from talking, I lay down on the grass and dozed off. By the time I woke up it was dusk. Like the Chinese poet Li Bai a thousand years ago, waking from another of his liquor-fueled dreams, I yawned, stood up, and walked home. I felt I was ready to collapse. Why was it so exhausting to describe Ahjitai's naked body?

VI

Ever since that day, I worried constantly that Second Prize Wang would ask me to return his dictionary.

Mother used to nag me for not returning borrowed items, saying it was a serious shortcoming of mine. I'd failed to steal the dictionary, and now I was plotting to keep it. Was I using my descriptions of Ahjitai's body as a way to make Second Prize Wang forget about the dictionary? Or was I just trying to give him what he couldn't have, since Ahjitai would never belong to him?

It was Saturday, a day I'll never forget. Early that morning my parents had had an argument. Then Mother started to tidy up the house. I could tell from her grousing that she was really upset. Grumbling about how fate had treated her unfairly and how resentful she felt toward her husband and child, she sounded like any other woman in her shoes. I was lying on my bed reading the dictionary when Mother came in and started to clean my room. Her every movement made me shiver. Then she spotted my eyeglasses on the bed. "Are these yours?" she asked me, holding them up.

I nodded.

"Are you nearsighted?"

I didn't answer.

She put on the spectacles. "Are they prescription or clear glass?"

I remained mute.

"Why do you have these?" she barked.

Her voice caught Father's attention, and he came in from the other room. "Who let you buy these?" he boomed. "Who gave you permission?" he demanded, raising his voice.

They were being insufferable, but I did not bother to explain. I was not at all afraid of them. In fact, I despised people who bellowed like that.

Father stepped closer. "You've got to explain yourself," he ordered. "What's going on in your head? Why are you being so self-obsessed?"

As if to provoke them, I yawned loudly, picked up the dictionary, and started flipping through it.

Father dove at me, attempting to snatch away the dictionary.

I ducked, and Father's head hit the headboard. "Ow!" he squealed. I couldn't help laughing.

Even more enraged, Father grabbed the dictionary and tried to wrest it away from me. I clung to it as hard as I could.

"Who taught you these vain habits?" he demanded.

"Vain? I'm just copying you!"

Hearing me say that, Father went berserk. Yanking with all of his might, he finally took hold of the book. He then began violently tearing the pages.

It took me a moment to realize what he was doing. I charged at him and snatched the book back. Some pages fell out. I felt a pain in my heart and squatted down on the floor, holding the dictionary in my arms as if it were a wounded animal.

"What're you doing? The dictionary's not his!" Mother called out.

Father glared at me without saying a word. I could hear him puffing like an executioner, exhausted after finishing his job. Eventually he caught his breath. When he saw how upset I was, a hint of regret flashed in his eyes, but then he held his head up and marched out of my room. Mother followed him. Since that moment I realized that no one can hurt you more than your family. And it's always done in the name of love.

I stared at the dictionary and gathered up the torn pages. Waves of panic washed away my sadness and even my hatred toward Father. The only thing I could think about was how to face Second Prize Wang.

That night I couldn't sleep. Mother snuck into my room and attempted to take the dictionary from me, but I sprang up and clutched it to my chest.

Mother screamed as though she had seen a ghost rise from a coffin. I glared at her in the dark, fearing the dictionary would suffer more abuse. Mother took a moment to compose herself. "I just wanted to help you glue the pages back."

I didn't say a word. I just waited until she left the room in disappointment. I turned over and put the dictionary under my stomach, vowing to sleep on my stomach for the rest of my life.

I tried to avoid seeing Second Prize Wang, but I couldn't help myself and went back to his dormitory a week later.

Second Prize Wang was as eager to see me and seemed to have forgotten about the dictionary. No matter what we were talking about, he kept trying to steer the conversation to Ahjitai, so, like a cunning conspirator, I talked to him over and over about Ahjitai's naked body, except that what I said was a little different each time, as I spiced things up with my imagination. They say that to express yourself well, you have to start practicing early, so I practiced by describing Ahjitai's naked body again and again.

"I'll take you to see Ahjitai, but you have to let me borrow the dictionary for one more month," I proposed to Second Prize Wang.

He hesitated for a long moment. "No. I have my principles, and I never trade them for anything," he finally said to me.

"Then I'll go by myself."

Just as I was about to shut his door, he rushed over to me and said, "What you are going to do is against the law."

I ignored him and continued out the door. When I reached the school's main gate, I discovered that Second Prize Wang was following me. His walk was not gentlemanly at all. In fact, he seemed a little crippled, like a class enemy in the revolutionary movies I used to watch in those days.

VII

Second Prize Wang quickly caught up with me. We had almost arrived at the boiler room. He grabbed my hand like a child, looking helpless and even a little embarrassed. Our eyes would meet from time to time, and I could see the desire hidden deep within him. Women's voices splashed around with the water. Second Prize Wang's eyes lit up. How should I describe them? Well, his eyes were like those of the Red Guards on Tiananmen Square in 1966 when they finally glimpsed Chairman Mao in the distance—something they had waited years to see.

Second Prize Wang marched ahead of me. He looked so eager, like that time he performed parts of *Hamlet* in English for me—everything around him dropped away, and he stood as if on a stage.

I was surprised by how anxious he seemed. I warned him to slow down and be quiet because I sensed something was wrong—the chunks of coal that were once stacked beneath the window had disappeared.

He didn't seem to hear me and rushed to the second window. When he realized how high it was and that there was nothing for him to step on, his eyes dimmed. The look of helplessness and embarrassment again clouded his face.

"There used to be chunks of coal here. Someone must have taken them away."

"You didn't lie to me, did you?"

"Ahjitai *is* in there. This is where I saw her."

Our eyes locked. I could tell he didn't believe me.

"Ahjitai is in there for sure."

Second Prize Wang seemed completely at a loss. Sure, he knew all about London, Paris, the United States, and Russia, but he had no common sense. He started to spin like a top we used to play with in the snowfields.

"Why don't we do this? You squat down and let me step up on your shoulders so I can see if Ahjitai is in there," I suggested.

He was excited. My quick thinking impressed him. "And then you'll let me step on *your* shoulders?"

I nodded.

He squatted down.

I felt like reaching for the clouds as Second Prize Wang slowly stood up. I didn't realize standing on someone's shoulders could make me so tall. Everything seemed to be moving in slow motion. I finally grabbed the window ledge and managed to prop myself up on it with my elbow.

Steam, thick steam. Was it James Watt who invented the steam engine? Why didn't his steam engine vacuum away the steam in the bathhouse? Steam brought glory to James Watt, but it brought us frustration. I could not see a thing because of it.

"Do you see her?"

I was busy searching for her and didn't respond. Then the lights went on in the bathhouse, and the steam began to clear away. I saw two women sharing a showerhead. Yes, there she was! It was Ahjitai! She was standing underneath the nozzle, and the other woman waited off to the side. I almost whooped with excitement but quickly collected myself and whispered urgently: "Mr. Wang, I can see her . . . I can see her, Mr. Wang!"

I could tell he was anxious, but as an only child I was selfish and didn't want to get down. I wanted one more glimpse of Ahjitai's body, even though Second Prize Wang was quaking with anticipation. Time was ticking by, but I stayed up there, waiting to catch a frontal view. A few more minutes passed, and then I reluctantly jumped down from his shoulders, feeling disappointed.

It was my turn to squat down and let Second Prize Wang step up on my shoulders. I had no idea he'd be as heavy as a mountain. I started to tremble but kept trying to stand upright. He ascended slowly, like the morning sun, and then without warning my legs gave way.

Second Prize Wang wasn't prepared for this. He was focused on the window, not what he was standing on. He plummeted to the ground.

Seeing Second Prize Wang covered in dust and struggling to get up, I felt guilty. "Let's try again," I encouraged him.

But he was hesitant. "Are you okay? Am I too heavy for you?"

"Come on, don't waste time or she might leave," I urged.

He jerked himself up. Again I squatted, and he stepped up onto my shoulders. As he was about to climb up, I felt my legs giving way. "No, no, no, I'm losing it, I'm losing it," I cried.

He jumped down.

I looked up and saw his anxious eyes.

"Let's try it again," I offered.

He was reluctant, but I squatted down anyway.

Again he stepped onto my back. I felt an agonizing pain in my shoulders—his leather shoes were chafing my skin. I whispered to myself: Had we planned this, I would've asked him to wear canvas shoes. I tried to stand up. "Don't move," he ordered. He then jumped and grabbed on to the windowsill. The thrust from his jump threw me to the ground.

Lying there, I saw an expanse of blue sky above me. Its vastness made me giddy. I shut my eyes for a moment, then opened them, then shut them, then opened them as if it were a game. Second Prize Wang clung to the window ledge, pulling himself up as if he were doing chin-ups. He was covered with dust, and sweat streamed down his face.

Second Prize Wang slowly lifted himself higher and higher. His head was already above the windowsill, then his shoulders. I applauded him in my head and marveled at his strength. He was such a strong man. As he was about to get to the best viewing point, I whispered, "Can you see her?" He puffed without saying anything. "Look to the left," I suggested. He did another chin-up but then turned to me, short of breath, and said, "I don't want to watch anymore. I . . . I am a . . ." He didn't seem to have the strength to finish what he wanted to say. He screwed up his face from the effort, and in a voice of extreme distress he said, "I shouldn't watch, right? I . . ."

Then someone yelled, "Get the pervert!" A group of eight militia members rushed at us. Second Prize Wang froze like a robot, his hands still clinging to the windowsill.

The head of the militia pulled at him roughly. "Don't wanna come down, do ya?"

Like a stuffed sack, Second Prize Wang hit the ground with a flop. Lying on the ground, his face covered in sweat, he stared blankly at the sky for a moment, then slowly closed his heavy eyelids.

IX

Father took me to a room in the administrative building. It was already seven o'clock. Through the window I could see Second Prize Wang's face bathed in the evening sunlight. The ordeal seemed not to have left any trace on him. He was clean shaven, and his jet black hair was meticulously combed. Even the single white hair I'd spotted earlier looked unusually well placed. Two men stood behind him, holding guns. A man from the security unit sat in front of him. Second Prize Wang cast a glance at me the moment I stepped in. A hint of a smile flashed across his face. It was too subtle for the other people to notice, but I knew he was happy to see me.

The principal sat on the left side of the room. He gave me a strange look when Father and I sat down to his right. I felt uneasy. I glanced over at Father, then turned to the principal to compare the two. The principal was a good-looking man, nicely dressed and with a majestic bearing. Father was habitually hunched over, and without his army uniform he could no longer impress anyone. I felt sorry for him and regretted not guarding his uniform. Had he come in uniform, I thought, he would have felt better, even without the insignias on his cap and collar. At least in front of the principal he would not look so suspicious, like a downright class enemy.

The principal stood up abruptly and glared at Second Prize Wang. He then stepped forward and slapped Second Prize Wang's face. "As a teacher, how dare you abet a child in such an activity!"

Second Prize Wang did not argue. He did not look at me, either. He just lowered his head like a criminal.

Director Fan entered the room at that point. He greeted everyone, and we all stood. Director Fan looked Second Prize Wang up and down before he exchanged a glance with the principal. He then turned to the man from the security unit. "Did he confess?"

The man nodded.

"It's all the English teacher's fault. It has nothing to do with the child," the principal chimed in.

Looking at the principal, Father beamed with gratitude.

"This is a terrible incident, just terrible," Director Fan announced. "It has caused serious damage to our society and must be dealt with severely." He scowled at Second Prize Wang. "What else do you have to say?"

"As a teacher, I—I instigated my student. I broke the law and willingly accept punishment under the law."

"Law? Punishment? Who do you think you are?" Director Fan smirked. "What era is this? Who are you to invoke such lofty concepts?"

Looking at Second Prize Wang, I was tormented with guilt when I heard him say, "As a teacher, I—I instigated my student." It wasn't true. I was the one who had dragged *him* to the bathhouse. I'd been there before. Lots of boys did that sort of thing. *I* dragged him there. *I* proposed the deal: In exchange for the dictionary, I would take him to see Ahjitai. Why was it now *his* fault?

I broke into a sweat. My guilt made me want to cry. I wanted to confess: *I* am the one who instigated this terrible incident. *I* am the one who is morally degenerate. *I* am the one who should be severely punished. I turned to Second Prize Wang. He did not look at me but appeared calm. I then turned to Father, who locked me in a threatening stare. From the corner of my eye I noticed the principal was also nervously looking my way, probably sensing that something was going on in my head.

Suddenly I shouted, "He didn't see a thing. Nothing! It was me—"

Father charged at me, kicking me hard before I could finish my sentence. I fell to the floor. "You were led by your teacher to do such a disgusting thing. You neglected to reform your thoughts and took up all that bourgeois stuff," Father barked, as if he were leading a political denunciation rally. "I'm gonna kill you!" He then started to strangle me.

I was horrified by Father's outburst and didn't know what to say. Father stared at me with his bloodshot eyes. I was confused because I could see tears welling up in his eyes. I became silent amid the suspicion, horror, and anxiety.

The principal came over and pulled Father aside. "Mr. Liu, you shouldn't do that. It's not the child's fault. A child is like a blank canvas on which the most beautiful images can be painted. It's all up to us adults and teachers. On the surface it appears he may have caused the problem, but the root cause is you. You may take him home now, but you must give him proper guidance from now on. I will also ensure his close supervision at school."

Father was fulsome in his gratitude. "Thank you very much, Mr. Principal. Thank you very much, Director Fan."

The principal then turned to Director Fan. "Shall we let these two go now?"

Director Fan was yawning at that very moment. He nodded his head with his mouth wide open.

Father walked in front of me and held my hand. Just as I was about to leave the room, I glanced over at Second Prize Wang, hoping he would look at me, but he did not turn his head. Father pulled me away violently, then turned around and carefully shut the door.

The corridor was dark. There was not a glimmer of sunlight. My mind was blank as we walked.

I have no idea how I spent the next few days. All I can remember is feeling semiconscious. I was ashamed for not openly telling the truth. Again and again I struggled and confessed in my head. I was like a tuberculosis patient waking up with night sweats.

X

A week later a public sentencing rally for Second Prize Wang was held in the East Wind Cinema.

The audience shouted slogans when a trussed Second Prize Wang was escorted onto the stage. All the students in our school stood up to get a better view of him while chanting "Down with hooligan elements!" It was a festive scene.

The denunciation of Second Prize Wang went on forever.

Finally it was my turn. The principal escorted me onto the stage and gave me a script to read. It was a thick stack of paper crammed with details of how Second Prize Wang poisoned me with his bourgeois influence.

The principal patted my shoulder and stepped down from the stage. Now it was just the two of us onstage, Second Prize Wang and me. Everything around us seemed to disappear, and there was silence, nothing but silence, as if we were in Hamlet's castle. I had dreamed so many times about being center stage, I thought. Now I was here, but for an entirely different reason.

Our eyes met. He looked calm. I was Prince Hamlet, and he was the king.

A smile appeared on his face. Second Prize Wang gestured for me to start. He seemed to glow onstage, as if all the lights were on him.

I felt giddy, like I was back in the fields at Bajiahu. The sun lit up the snow-covered mountain, and I saw Garbage Li and Sunrise Huang race past us on horseback. Then that night's gunshot went off again in my head, startling me out of my dark reverie.

All of a sudden I threw that stack of paper up in the air. Sheets of paper fell around me like snowflakes.

Everyone, including Second Prize Wang, was shocked. The theater fell silent before erupting in madness.

In the midst of the tumult, I dashed backstage, stormed out the side door, and ran like a maniac toward the Hunan Cemetery.

When evening came I was hungry—intensely hungry. I was ashamed of myself for feeling hungry when I thought of what Second Prize Wang was going through. I climbed up into an old elm, stared up at the stars, and waited for my parents to call my name. Instead of going back voluntarily, I wanted them to beg me to come home.

But my parents did not come out to look for me. They were more patient than I was, it seemed, and this must've been their punishment for me, since they'd surely eaten their dinner already.

XI

I expected my parents to thrash me when I got home, but neither of them showed any sign of wanting to do that. They didn't even ask anything.

Instead, they dished up some stewed pork and rice they'd bought from the canteen and said they'd kept it especially for me.

I sat down and started to gobble it up. They sat next to me and watched me eat. I knew that was their way of showing their love. I was their son. I was growing up and would be stronger than Father. I was their future and their hope.

After watching me for a while, Father lit up a cigarette and took a drag. He seemed to loosen up a little. "You still have to do a self-criticism at school. You must do some soul-searching, and you must do it properly," he said softly. "That Second Prize Wang." He smirked and shook his head. "The verdict was announced today. He's been sentenced to ten years."

I suddenly lost my appetite. I stared at my food, unable to eat. I sat in silence for a long time, then raised my head to speak to Father.

"I'm terribly ashamed of myself."

Father said nothing. Mother was silent, too. I paused and fixed my eyes on Father, expecting him to look back at me, but he didn't look up. With his brow knitted, he looked like Rodin's sculpture of the Thinker.

"And I think you're shameless," I blurted out.

Father went berserk, lunging forward and slapping me.

I kicked him hard in the guts, and my poor father crumpled to the ground. I stood frozen to the spot while my mother wailed.

Refusing Mother's help, Father struggled to get up. Mother studied his face, worried he might be injured. He was more enraged than I'd ever seen him. He charged toward me and howled: "This is rebellion! We're finished!"

I felt no regret for what I had just done. I was ready to retaliate in an instant as I watched him jumping about. He dragged me to the door, opened it, shoved me outside, and slammed the door shut.

I never felt as cold as I did that night.

XII

I didn't go anywhere. I just sat on the concrete step outside the front door.

Late that night, Mother came out to usher me back inside. "Come on inside. Go to bed."

I shook my head as an adult would.

Mother began to cry. "Son, do you have any idea how difficult life is for your mother these days?"

I glanced at her. In the light from the corridor she appeared frail, like someone with hepatitis.

"Father did what he did for you, his only son. He can't take any more heartbreak."

"I was the one who dragged my English teacher there. Really. He didn't want to go—I dragged him there."

Mother rushed over to me and tried to muffle my mouth.

"He could have looked inside," I persisted, "but he chose not to. He . . ."

Fearful the neighbors would overhear, Mother used all her might to try to drag me inside, but I wouldn't budge. Her clothing tickled as it rubbed against my skin. She looked at me tearfully.

I gave in and followed her inside. How would I face Father? I wondered.

But Father did not come out from his room.

I undressed and went straight to bed.

Silence fell over the house. Then Father's crying pierced the silence. It was like the howling of a wolf.

SEVENTEEN

I

The sky over Ürümchi was deathly pale the day another hydrogen bomb was detonated.

We had no idea the H-bomb was responsible for what we saw. The treetops looked backlit, and the houses seemed brighter than usual. The distant mountains blended into the mist, and Bogda Peak was just a gray pall. I looked up at the sun and knew something was very wrong. Everything around us was as hazy as overexposed film.

The white sky was suffocating, and I could barely open my eyes because of the blinding light. I desperately wanted to find a place where I could hide when suddenly I thought of the air-raid shelter. It was Mother's design, and I was sure her love and the darkness would protect my eyes.

I dashed to the air-raid shelter, as if seeking refuge from a storm, and charged in like a ray of sunlight.

II

As I raced down the steps I felt I was being submerged beneath the ocean. I couldn't see a thing, and I had difficulty breathing. I was familiar with this feeling from my many previous trips to the air-raid shelter, but it was now more intense.

At last I found my way to the massive main hall. It was like a modern hotel lobby, which by the standards of the time was quite luxurious. The floors and the four walls were clad with stone tiles quarried deep in the Tianshan Mountains. Interior design was unheard of for most Chinese, but our air-raid shelter was graced with it. Like the ten major projects in Peking, or the Peking hotel, Mother's air-raid shelter was Ürümchi's own showpiece.

I saw a light and heard the sound of sweeping.

I waited for my eyes to adjust and, to my surprise, saw that the person sweeping was Ahjitai. I blushed, but it was dark and I knew Ahjitai would not notice.

With her head down she continued sweeping, apparently ignoring me.

Just as I was about to retreat, she stopped me. "Why are you here?"

I paused, then said, "No reason."

"Why would you choose to come here?" She chuckled. "It's like a tomb."

"Well, why are you here?"

"To sweep the floor," she replied. Then she added, "There are things kids just don't understand."

"What don't I understand? I know everything."

She tittered. "What do you know?"

"You threw Director Fan out of your room, and he's getting you back, right? He's punishing you, right?"

She didn't look at me and started sweeping more vigorously.

I began to explore the hall. Everything was new to me—it really was an impressive place. I felt proud of Mother. She was dedicated. She took seriously any task assigned to her. Otherwise, how was it possible for such a landmark structure to exist in Ürümchi?

III

When Ahjitai had finished sweeping, she grabbed a towel to wipe her face.

Embarrassed, I sat on a step with my head down. But she walked over to me and asked in a whisper, "Did Mr. Wang drag you to the bathhouse?"

"No," I replied hesitantly. "No, *I* dragged him there. It's all my fault. I'm guilty."

"You're only a kid. What are you guilty of? You're just scared."

"I am guilty."

I'd been hearing those words ever since I was a child. First my father said it, and then lots of other people—*I am guilty*. I never expected to hear those words come out of my mouth with such sincerity.

After I said it I began to cry. The whole air-raid shelter echoed with the sound of my crying. Cool and dim, the shelter felt eerie. The sound of my sobbing frightened me and sent shivers down my spine. My hair stood on end. I almost forgot about Ahjitai. Horrified by what I'd done, all I wanted to do was cry.

Ahjitai passed me the towel she'd been using. I looked up at her. My eyes were blurred with tears. I took the towel but was overcome with guilt. I felt so sorry for Second Prize Wang. I knew it was my fault. The regret I felt for him was even greater than what I felt for Father.

Suddenly the ground started to shake. My crying came to a halt.

Ahjitai was terrified. She stood rigid, as if frozen. I rushed over, grabbed her hand, and dragged her toward the exit. She followed me with heavy steps, stupefied. I pulled her up the stairs, and she started to run with me. We scampered up the long staircase. Then there was a deafening sound as the main gate collapsed inward. Rocks and gravel shot toward us. Instinctively I turned to push Ahjitai out of harm's way. In that same moment the lights went out. Darkness swallowed us. We stumbled back down the steps and once again found ourselves in the large meeting hall. Another loud noise came from the direction of the entrance, and more rocks and debris tumbled into the main hall. We ran to a corner for safety. Another violent tremor began, and Ahjitai squeezed my hand as hard as she could. In our military training we were taught to head for the smallest room during an earthquake. We retreated to a long corridor on the northern side of the hall. I could feel Ahjitai shaking. "We'll be fine," I reassured her. "Relax."

Another loud noise came from the main entrance, and half of the main hall collapsed. Ahjitai screamed.

I was glad we'd sought refuge in the tunnel. My hand was still hurting because Ahjitai would not let go of it. But I was proud of that. We sat down on some straw matting.

After another round of aftershocks, everything went quiet. Death seemed just around the corner: The exit was blocked, and there was no way out.

Ahjitai, however, grew calm. She stopped her panicking and loosened her grip on my hand.

Gradually our eyes adjusted to the darkness enough for us to be able to see each other. Ahjitai's eyes were bright. Their soft glow was soothing, and I calmed down, too.

Ahjitai stood up and found several candles in a recess in the wall. She lit one with a match, and suddenly the tunnel was illuminated.

Our eyes met, and she giggled. "We'll be fine. Relax," she said, mimicking my voice.

My face flushed with embarrassment. I regretted having said something that Ahjitai could mock.

"You are really brave."

My face was now on fire. Even though the light was dim, I think she could tell how red it was.

She seemed to be saying something, but I couldn't hear. I just stared at her. I was in seventh heaven for the chance to look at her so closely.

She stopped speaking and just looked at me. I lowered my head. Silence and darkness enveloped us again. Despair crept up on me like a rolling fog. I felt terrible and started repeating in a steady drone, "We're dead, we're dead." I shook my head, but my despair came back even stronger, as if an orchestra conductor gestured for a crescendo. I hated my mother for designing this air-raid shelter.

I hated my father, too: He had helped her by designing the H-bomb research center. The earthquake was their fault. Couldn't my parents have anticipated that their son and Ahjitai would be buried alive here?

I was so young, but I was about to die.

Ahjitai was so beautiful, and she, too, would soon die.

Ahjitai was quiet. I raised my head to look at her, but her mind was elsewhere. I reached out for her hand. It was ice cold.

"What's wrong?" I asked.

She said nothing.

I wished I could hold her hand until I died, but I pulled my hand back after a while so as not to upset her. She, however, extended her hand to hold mine.

"Are you scared?" I asked. "Your hands are cold."

She shook her head. "I'm not really scared. I've thought about death a lot. I just never expected it would be like this."

Her words were upsetting. I held her hand even tighter, and then pressed it to my chest.

After a while I looked up at her. She was looking at me, too. There was something noble in her eyes, yet there was also understanding.

Afraid she would disappear, I pressed her hand firmly to my heart. I repeatedly said to myself, This is Ahjitai's hand.

All through childhood I had dreamed of holding Ahjitai's hand like this. Death hung over us, yet I was overcome with joy. I choked up from the thrill of experiencing this miracle in the last moments of my life.

After who knows how long, Ahjitai tried to pull her hand away.

I resisted and did not let go.

She smiled. "It's tiring."

"I'm not tired."

"*I'm* tired," she responded.

But still I held her hand.

Ahjitai waited awhile, then firmly pulled her hand back.

A passion I had not previously experienced welled up in my heart. "I want to stay like that. I don't want to be separated from you."

"You really are still just a kid." She sighed.

That felt like being stabbed. "I'm not a child," I said loudly.

Ahjitai almost laughed. "I'm afraid of dying, too, but there's nothing we can do. It's fate."

I grabbed her hand again.

This time she did not pull it back. She just looked at me quietly.

"I want to hold your hand until I die," I said.

She gently stroked my hair with her free hand and sighed.

Time passed rapidly. Her hand gave me infinite courage.

After a while she whispered, "Why did you spy on me in the bathhouse so often?"

Now I really couldn't raise my head.

"Could you see me clearly?" she continued.

I nodded. She said, "I knew every time you were there peeking at me."

I loosened my grip on her hand. It might have been dark, but I'm sure she saw me blush.

"What's the matter?" she asked.

There was nothing I could say.

IV

We had been buried underground for a dozen or so hours. We were running out of candles—just one stump remained—and air.

Ahjitai stared at the candlelight. "How old are you?"

"Seventeen."

"You've never touched a woman?"

"Never."

She sighed. Placing my hand over her heart, she asked, "Can you feel my heartbeat?"

I nodded. "Your heart is beating faster than most people's."

"Feel your own heart—it's beating even faster."

She was right. My heart was almost jumping out of my chest.

"Do you want to look at me up close?"

"Yes," I eventually said.

She began to remove her clothes.

I was shocked and nervously pondered whether I should continue staring.

She rested her coat neatly on the straw mat, then lay her sweater down as well. She didn't look at me. She concentrated on what she was doing, as if it were some kind of ceremony. That gave me the courage to watch her.

She casually glanced at me when she was about to take off her shirt. There was not a hint of shyness or passion in her eyes. My heart raced wildly again, and I felt dizzy the moment I saw her naked body. She held me close to her, and we lay side by side on top of her clothes. I nervously caressed her skin. I'd never felt anything so smooth and tender. All of a sudden, I started to tremble uncontrollably. I felt waves of pleasure between my legs, and my body was soaked. Slowly, I was submerged in a tiredness I'd never before experienced.

I remember Ahjitai smiled and held me even tighter. Then I closed my eyes.

VII

A few days later it was the men's turn at the bathhouse. Water splashed. Silhouettes moved in and out of the billowing steam. Symbols of manhood swayed like branches in the wind. I could think only of Ahjitai. When hot water splashed on me, it reminded me of the heat of her body. Again and again I thought to myself, Ahjitai, where are you?

All of a sudden the sound of music floated into the bathhouse. It was solemn funerary music, and it formed a backdrop as integral to that moment as the Tianshan Mountains are to Ürümchi or stones are to a riverbed.

Suddenly, the principal dashed naked around the bathhouse. He burst into every cubicle and shouted, "Chairman Mao is dead! Chairman Mao is dead!" He sounded at once excited and weak, and his thing flopped about.

"Chairman—Mao—is—dead."

VIII

I felt like a plant just soaked in sweet dew and growing taller with every step I took, as if I had just come out of the bathhouse feeling refreshed. Someone was going to be executed in Ürümchi. I had heard about it a few days earlier.

The anticipation was becoming unbearable. Chairman Mao was dead, and something ruthless had to be done to prevent our enemies from wriggling out of their dark hiding places. I grew up watching "strike hard" campaigns against crime, and the big ones always excited me.

Executions were festive occasions when I was a seventeen-year-old in Ürümchi. Apart from the eight revolutionary model Peking

Operas, we had nothing exciting to watch, although years later I heard that some people in Peking had access to screenings of foreign films. People tried every way imaginable to sneak in. Because foreign VIPs were welcome at screenings, some tall and fair-skinned Chinese would get hold of suits and make ties out of handkerchiefs and try to slip in. Kids in Peking had it so much better than we did.

But nothing was more entertaining for us than an execution. The Russian director Vsevolod Meyerhold said he liked to watch people quarreling, but we liked to watch people get executed. Where does our cruelty come from? Did it fall from the sky? Were we just born that way? To borrow Chairman Mao's words, It's not hard to watch just one execution in a lifetime, but watching nothing but executions is really challenging.

The leaves of the ash trees lining the streets of Ürümchi were golden yellow that day, and the elm trees had begun to wither. Crowds of people gathered to witness the open trucks transporting criminals from the west of the city to the East Hill Graveyard.

Executions were necessary to maintain social stability, and they brought us kids enormous joy. At the age of eight, when I was first allowed to go outside on my own, I would wait on this street for condemned criminals to be trucked past. They would stand on open trucks, their heads shaved and their faces flushed as if from having eaten too much mutton broth the night before. Criminals sentenced to lesser terms would accompany the condemned on the trucks. It was for educational purposes—they were there for their own good.

I squeezed into the crowd, staring into the distance while munching on sunflower seeds and spitting out the husks. The convoy of trucks was late, just like the buses and trains in those days. I threw a glance to the east after my eyes tired of looking west. Out of the blue, the first lines of an essay I wrote in primary school came to my mind: Today the Tianshan Mountains are towering. They are standing in the east like the Jade Emperor, ruler of heaven.

At that moment the crowd cheered. The convoy appeared like the rising sun.

IX

Sunrise Huang and Second Prize Wang were standing on the same truck.

I've not been able to figure out why this was. They were locked up in different places: Sunrise Huang in the juvenile delinquent facility, and Second Prize Wang in the No. 2 Prison at Qidaowan. But today they were together.

Sunrise Huang's face looked tiny from the distance, but I knew it was hers. Her hair was flying about in the wind, and her thin frame seemed smaller than usual because she was standing next to a tall Uyghur man. Second Prize Wang stood on the other side of the Uyghur man.

As the convoy approached I could see them more clearly.

Second Prize Wang was clean shaven as always, but the hair on his head was shaved off, too. His face was ashen, and he seemed to be covered in dust.

Sunrise Huang's face glowed. She held her head high, and when she spotted me she raised her head even higher.

The crowd roared when they saw her, a pretty young girl, standing on the truck. Everyone was gesticulating and commenting, and Ürümchi's festive mood built to a climax.

At first nobody noticed the singing, not even me. Then I heard a voice wafting like smoke in the air: *Arise ye workers from your slumbers.*

The words were English, and I could tell it was Sunrise Huang singing. Her voice was full of courage and passion. The seventeen-year-old stood there like a revolutionary heroine, singing full-throated in another language, unafraid of the gloomy path ahead. She really was insane.

The open truck was now her stage. Her voice was loud and clear, like the clarion call of the trumpet. She sang in perfect English, full of pride.

The spectators howled with laughter. In my childhood, nothing was more fun than watching bullets rip through human flesh and seeing scarlet blood spurting out.

But that day was no fun. I did not expect to see the two of them on the truck.

Second Prize Wang's face lit up when he heard Sunrise Huang singing. Like a breeze, her singing blew the gray dust off his face. Second Prize Wang turned toward her and held her in his gaze as if it were the first time he'd seen her, as if he had never been her teacher, as if she had never been his class representative.

Sunrise Huang was not looking at Second Prize Wang. It was almost like she didn't recognize him or didn't know he'd taught her the song. She sang fortissimo, as if it were the most famous passage in an opera and she wanted to interpret it beautifully for the whole world to hear.

Just then rays of sunlight shot out from behind the clouds, and my eyes met Second Prize Wang's.

I saw tears well up in his eyes and stream down his face.

The convoy accelerated toward the East Hill Graveyard, and the cheering crowd ran after it. East—that's where the sun rises, and where Ürümchi's executions are carried out.

The Tianshan Mountains formed an unusually radiant backdrop to Second Prize Wang's crying. When I saw him sobbing and his heaving shoulders, it was the first time I really understood sadness.

His tears ran down his face like a river, like our Ürümchi River. In early summer the snow melts, and the water flows through meadows, forests, deserts, and the Gobi, forming an oasis in Ürümchi.

I have never tasted water from the Yellow River or the Yangtze. As a native of Ürümchi, I grew up drinking Second Prize Wang's tears.

EIGHTEEN

I

The autumn of 1978 was the unluckiest time in my life. I failed the university entrance exam.

A lot of students passed that exam, especially in my class. Almost half of my classmates got into a university, but not me. Even so, I continued to carry myself proudly, pretending to be a gentleman. The children and parents in our compound sneered at me: He wears spectacles (and with clear lenses, no less), dresses up prim and proper, and smells of cologne. He walks around every day with a book under his arm like an intellectual. When everyone else finished studying, he kept at it, but he couldn't even pass the university entrance exam. Obviously his brain is stuffed with rotten bourgeois rubbish, and there's no room left for knowledge.

My parents were extremely disappointed in me. They graduated from Tsinghua University and were among the few Tsinghua alumni in Ürümchi. Having once studied in the Soviet Union, Father was an exemplar of the Ürümchi intelligentsia. The way they saw it, apart from dressing outrageously and making a spectacle of himself, their only son cared nothing about keeping up the family name. He didn't even get into a university—neither an engineering school nor a college of the arts.

As their son, however, I thought, Why do I have to pass an exam to go to a university? It's not like I want to kill someone or steal things or become a member of the Gang of Four. All I wanted was to study. Why would they prevent me from going just because I didn't pass the exam? No one can take away someone's right to learn.

When I told my parents this, they stared at me in shock, convinced they were witnessing an evolutionary regression, a threat to the survival of humanity. The Cultural Revolution had really messed everything up and their child must be sick, they thought.

In fact, they took me to the hospital, but the doctors couldn't find anything wrong. As I was walking down the narrow path from the mortuary and heading to the North Gate, I saw Sunrise Huang coming toward me. She had a school emblem pinned to her clothes. I was surprised because I had not heard that she passed the university entrance exam. Sunrise Huang saw me and gave me a radiant smile. "I've been meaning to look you up," she said, "but I haven't had time." I nodded and threw another quick glance at the school emblem.

"When did you pass the exam?" I asked.

"In the first batch."

"You're not sick anymore?" I asked.

"You're the one who's sick," she joked.

And then her mother, who was walking behind her, caught up. Her face turned suspicious as soon as she saw me. "Hurry up," she urged her daughter. "We don't want to be late."

Sunrise Huang didn't say anything else to me as she walked toward the hospital.

"Can I write to you?" I appealed to her back.

"Use English," she replied, "so I can practice."

The Tianshan Mountains were still with me, and Bogda Peak was like my shadow. I even learned the word *firmament*—the ever-present blue dome of heaven. I desperately wanted to go to Peking or Shanghai, but without passing the university entrance exam I knew

I'd be stuck in Ürümchi for the rest of my life. Where did I go wrong? What they said was right: When everyone else stopped studying, I'd kept at it. Whom was I studying with? Second Prize Wang.

Whenever I felt lonely I thought of Second Prize Wang. He had been locked up in jail for more than a year, but I never went to visit him. I looked at a map once to see where his labor camp was located, and only then did I discover that two of the world's greatest deserts stood between us: the Taklamakan Desert and the Gurbantunggut Desert.

Would the sun dry out Second Prize Wang and turn him into another southern Xinjiang mummy?

II

Mother aged. The once fine wrinkles at the corners of her eyes became as thick as the bark of an elm tree and crept over her face. But she was as elegant as ever. Her background, her academic record, and especially her marriage to Father all made her visibly proud.

In the morning, as the sun shone down on the parking lot, people would see her in a tailored suit, stepping out of a car with a hardhat in her hand. As the chief of the technical department, she was always the one to accompany officials from the bureau's head office to inspect progress at construction sites.

The car would wait in the lot, a patient chauffeur in attendance. People were as polite to her as they would be to the first lady. She was, after all, a stylish woman in a position of authority.

Mother carried herself with elegance. No one else was as friendly, forgiving, and graceful. Her tall, slender figure stood out like a poplar tree after a storm.

She was no longer terrified of being called a "technical authority."

Father was one, and now she was one, too.

I just didn't get it. How could she be considered a "technical authority"? Her most important design was the air-raid shelter that had almost buried me.

But mother became a full-fledged technical authority.

My parents occasionally took out the phonograph to listen to Glazunov. They'd turn up the volume, and the sound of violins would float out the windows, filling the compound and even all of Ürümchi. The music enhanced their intellectual aura.

"This couple—Liu Cheng-zong and Qin Xuan-qi—is such a mystery, they are so different from ordinary folk," people would gossip.

Completely different.

One weekend, Father was about to leave for America and Europe. "There will soon be a huge project in Ürümchi," he announced excitedly and somewhat mysteriously.

After Father left, Mother went to her room to water her flowers. She loved flowers. She'd been surrounded by them growing up, but for many years there were no flowers in her life. Whenever she told me this story, she'd get choked up.

Someone knocked on the door. Mother glanced toward it but continued watering her flowers.

I opened the door and was surprised to see the principal. He stood in the doorway with a humble smile on his face. Under his arm he held a package wrapped in newspaper. His clothing was tattered and filthy. Compared with how he'd looked in the mid-1970s, he could have been mistaken for a different person.

When he recognized me, he froze for a moment. We hadn't seen each other in at least two years. I'd heard he'd been sent to labor at Moonlight Salt Lake because he'd been branded one of the "three types of people" who were punished after the Cultural Revolution.

He was a confederate of his Tsinghua classmate Director Fan and the cosignatory of a letter they'd written to Madame Mao, one of the Gang of Four. All of this came to light after Madame Mao's arrest.

"I need to see your mother." I let him in. He went straight to her bedroom. Mother jerked up like a frightened chicken when she saw him.

The principal had love written all over his face. "I'm off to Maralbishi in southern Xinjiang to work on the Xiaohaizi reservoir." He then handed the package to Mother, explaining, "These are my diaries—they date back to my years at Tsinghua University. You are in them—you know that. They're my most valuable possession. I don't have any relatives, so I want to leave them with you."

From the corner of her eye, Mother spotted me standing behind the principal. "Love Liu, close the door," she ordered.

I had to obey, but I put my ear against the door.

"You shouldn't have come here," she said. "I don't want this stuff."

"I don't think I can last for long in southern Xinjiang. It's tough there, and I won't survive. I want you to keep them."

Mother said nothing.

"May I ask you one last question?"

Mother remained silent.

"Is Love Liu my child?"

My brain exploded when I heard that.

"No."

"But other people say that . . ."

"I'm a woman. I know."

"I hope this is one time in your life you are not lying."

"I have never lied in my life."

"Farewell, then."

The bedroom door suddenly opened, and the principal stumbled out of the room. Mother did not see him off. He went to the front door and opened it himself. I followed him, not knowing why. As I was closing the door he turned to look at me. I saw tears in his eyes.

Mother resumed watering her flowers after the principal left.

Later I furtively read one of the principal's diaries. It was full of words of love and passion, all of them for my mother. He said he had only ever loved once, and that his love was for Mother. He liked to quote the same poem as Director Fan: "If Winter comes, can Spring be far behind?" I was moved by the grace of his words when I suddenly realized how similar the principal and Director Fan were—that's why together they were able to write such a great letter to Madame Mao. They were once talented youths, but would they survive the current political climate?

Three days later the principal committed suicide behind the boiler room where Second Prize Wang and I had spied on Ahjitai. The principal wore bright khaki trousers and a sunny white shirt. He had nothing with him other than an Ürümchi ration coupon for five catties worth of rice. What was he doing with a ration coupon in 1978?

I could see sadness hidden deep in Mother's eyes the day she learned of the principal's death. "Am I related to the principal?" I asked her.

"Why would you ask such a thing?" she replied, shaking her head.

"People have been gossiping about it behind my back ever since I was a child. Even Sunrise Huang mentioned it."

"They're talking nonsense."

I did not question her any further. Many years later, after DNA testing became available, I had it confirmed: My DNA matched Liu Cheng-zong's. Mother had not been lying.

III

Father did not look old. "See, I don't have a single white hair," he often bragged.

"Chief Liu is incredible," people would also say. "He doesn't have any white hair."

Father seemed reborn ever since the National Science Conference in 1978, when the Chinese government announced its modernization drive. His eyes glistened with tears when he heard Guo Moro, the president of the Academy of Science, quote a poem written a thousand years ago by the Tang dynasty poet Bo Ju-yi. He embraced Mother right in front of me, shamelessly displaying their passionate nature as intellectuals. He would never forget having to stand up on scaffolding to paint portraits of Chairman Mao, nor would he ever forget being slapped. Those memories motivated him to make up for what he had lost. What really surprised me was how he loved to sing a popular song of the time with the line, "In twenty years, we shall meet again."

Looking at Father's jet black hair, I wondered, half in fear, half in sorrow, where he would be and whom he would meet in twenty years.

The large construction project Father hinted at was in fact a new Nationalities Grand Theater. He was fascinated by the classical architecture he'd seen on his trip to Europe. He took lots of photos of Amsterdam, Paris, and Heidelberg. The women in Ürümchi had begun wearing batwing sleeve tops, and everyone dreamed of modernization—the slogan of the day was the Four Modernizations—but Father was drunk on classical architecture. "I despise the new Paris, but I am very fond of the old Paris," he said, fondling the photographs he brought back from his trip. "I feel the same dislike for the new Peking, but I love the old Peking. There's nothing new, or old in that sense, here in Ürümchi. The architectural style I set in the nineteen fifties has been more or less preserved."

He was talking to Mother.

Those were the happiest days of their lives. They could stand proud again. They had boundless energy and were needed everywhere. "We intellectuals have only one desire—to serve the motherland," they would blurt out every chance they could.

Father would often linger outside the Nationalities Theater near the city's south gate. No one was more self-congratulatory. He believed the future development of the whole city would be a continuation of his work: a dome, a spire, marble columns, sculptures, all the minority architectural styles, and a pastel yellow theme reminiscent of old Paris . . . all these elements would blend to create a unique place, different from any other city in China, or anywhere else in the world.

My parents often went for walks in the evenings and would insist on dragging me with them. I was usually quiet while they'd prattle on endlessly. One evening Father abruptly stopped talking. Up ahead he saw Director Fan in a wheelchair. He wore a blue Mao jacket and looked directly at Father through his white-framed eyeglasses. Director Fan had jumped off a building around the time the principal committed suicide, but he'd survived.

Father slowly walked toward him.

Director Fan's face betrayed no sign of nervousness as Father approached. He expertly maneuvered his wheelchair to face Father.

Their eyes locked, but no words were exchanged.

The three of us walked past Director Fan. He turned his wheelchair and stared at us as we walked away.

"Virtue has its own reward," Father intoned, "and vice its own punishment."

"He didn't die even after jumping off the fourth floor," I blurted out. "His resilience is incredible."

"What do you mean 'resilience'?" Mother snapped. "No wonder you didn't get into a university. You can't even differentiate between a derogatory term and a complimentary one."

"Didn't I often say in those dark days, 'If Winter comes, can Spring be far behind?' " said Father.

"Director Fan once recited that line to Ahjitai," I blabbed.

What I said instantly changed their mood and made them painfully aware that their son was an idiot.

As soon as Ahjitai's name rolled off my tongue, I felt a cramp in my heart and a profound sadness started to spread inside me. I could no longer hear anything my parents said. I shouted to the mountain, "Ahjitai, where are you?"

The mountain replied, "She just left."

I cried out to the ocean, "Ahjitai, where are you?"

"She just left."

It was as if there were only one long sound in the whole world: Ah-ji-tai-where-are-you?

IV

It took Father three months to complete his design. During that time he was like a composer immersed in his score. Father beamed with pride when he finished. Just like when he first put on his army uniform years earlier, he had his nose in the air and a swagger in his step. But no one besides me seemed to notice.

Father's superiors reviewed his plan and rejected the whole thing out of hand. "Wrong. It's completely wrong. Ürümchi doesn't need a medieval castle, it needs a modern theater," they decreed. They made it clear what they wanted: a modern design.

Father disagreed. "Ürümchi needs an integrated style, and that requires respect for its history," he insisted.

"What history? Ürümchi's just a small town," they countered. "Your style is old Soviet stuff. It's dark inside even in daylight, and the outside looks bulky. Plus, it would cost too much to build." For Father that was another slap in the face.

"Tears flooded down his cheeks the second Chief Liu walked out of the conference room," recalled Father's student Song Yue. "He refused to get in the car and insisted on walking, so I had to walk with him. The whole way he cried out loud: 'From the thirties through the forties, and from the fifties to the present, Ürümchi has had a consistent style—the style of the Nationalities Theater. Ürümchi has history, it has a history. . . .'"

"Liu Cheng-zong has gone mad," Song Yue concluded.

When he returned home that day, Father grew quiet. Instead of working on a new design as his superiors instructed, he decided to compromise by making some changes to his original design. He rarely spoke to Mother because this time she did not agree with him.

To make matters worse, Mother as good as stabbed him with what she said: She agreed with everyone else that Ürümchi should march toward modernization, that modernization ought to be the common goal of intellectuals in Ürümchi. They had waited too long for change and now must embrace it.

Father didn't respond. He just fiddled with the phonograph and listened to his hoary old Glazunov records alone. The violin sounded dusty. His room filled with music, yet it also filled with the hint of autumn.

A few months later Father submitted a revised design. With hardly a glance, his superiors angrily pronounced: "We must promote younger talent. Your student Song Yue will be the new chief architect. Your post is rescinded. Go home and await further instructions."

Alone at home, Father did not waste a second. He immediately went back to design mode, redrafting every page of his designs by hand, line by line. It was before the days of computers, and he refused any assistance.

Mother cried when she saw Father in this strangely manic state. She bought him a new desk, a huge draftsman's desk, and Father worked on it day and night. His hyperactivity frightened me. When he worked, nothing else mattered. He couldn't hear anything going on around him.

One day I bought an Andy Williams tape that included "Moon River." As the sound of the song filled my room, Father came in. He listened for a while and then said, "I used to sing that song ages ago." Then he began to sing the bass harmony, in English, not in Russian, and interpreted each line for me as he sang.

Moon River, wider than a mile,
I'm crossing you in style some day.
Oh, dream maker, you heart breaker,
wherever you're going I'm going your way.
Two drifters off to see the world.
There's such a lot of world to see.
We're after the same rainbow's end
waiting 'round the bend,
my huckleberry friend,
Moon River and me.

I'd never seen Father so charming. His English was perfect, without the slightest trace of a Russian accent. He acted as if art were the highest purpose in life, as if he were another Second Prize Wang explaining things I needed to know when I needed them the most.

" 'Moon River' is from the movie *Breakfast at Tiffany's.* The female lead, Audrey Hepburn, was our favorite actress—your mother's and mine. She sang 'Moon River,' and it won the Oscar for best song. It's a beautiful love story, that film."

Hearing Father say this was like seeing the last glimmers of the setting sun. His face was flushed with excitement—typical of people with high blood pressure—and he muttered to himself: "Two drifters is an interesting concept—sometimes you and I are like the two drifters in Mark Twain's novel *Huckleberry Finn.* Huckleberry Finn left home and was raised by a rich family, but he couldn't stand the restrictions of a civilized life and ran away. He poled a raft down the river with a black man named Jim. They had all sorts of experiences—good and bad—on their journey and formed a deep friendship."

"Huckleberry is Huckleberry Finn from Mark Twain's novel?" I gasped. This knowledge of Father's amazed me because it had nothing to do with architecture.

Father nodded without looking at me.

For some reason I didn't want to hear Father pour out his feelings anymore. I was somehow hurt to discover he could sing English songs. We were silent for a long time. Like coals that had burned out and turned to ash, Father seemed to be fading away. "I miss my English teacher. I miss Second Prize Wang," I whined.

Father returned to his desk without saying anything. After a while he called me over. I stood beside him as he continued to work on his designs. There was silence.

Suddenly Father looked up. "I wronged your English teacher."

"Father, when you'd beat me and I'd just stare back at you, did it make you even more angry? I know most kids just cry like it really hurts and they won't get beaten as hard."

Father smiled and began to hum "Moon River."

"Why didn't you sing me even one song in English when I really needed to hear it?"

Father was at a loss, as if I had shouted at him. Tears began to pool in his eyes. "Your father is a pragmatist. I always did what I thought was best for you."

Father died, but not at his large new desk. He died in the new Jiangong Hospital's cardiac ward. The day he completed his new designs, Father posted all of his drafts on the wall. It was a lot of effort for him. He stood there admiring his own work. Within ten minutes he suffered a heart attack.

Father died after two days in intensive care. Mother was at his side in his final moments. He died like a child in her arms.

Father's last wish was for my tape of "Moon River" to be played at his memorial service at Yan-er-wo near the tombs of revolutionary martyrs. As the hall reverberated with the sound of English, I realized it was Father's final apology to Second Prize Wang. Although Second Prize Wang could not be there because he was still serving his sentence in Maralbishi County, I was sure he could hear Father's apology.

Twenty years later I returned to Ürümchi from Peking. It was winter. I walked past the Nationalities Grand Theater. Clad in white ceramic tiles, it looked like a gigantic public bathroom. There are now buildings like that all over China. But when I went to see the Nationalities Theater, I was awestruck. It was as if Father were resurrected before my eyes: The elegant fifty-year-old structure seemed to be infused with his soul. The dome, the granite pillars, the sculptures, the lines, the marble staircase, the round windows . . . everything reminded me of Father. Once considered outdated, it now looked modern. Perhaps it's inappropriate for me to say this because he was my father, but I hope that everyone who visits Ürümchi will compare the two buildings and tell me what they think.

V

I once dreamed of being a diplomat. I mentioned this to Second Prize Wang.

"People should have ideals," he said cheerfully, "just like a room should have windows."

But the fact is I did not get into a university and only just managed to complete vocational college in Ürümchi. I was assigned to teach English at my alma mater, the school where Second Prize Wang had once worked. Whenever my old classmates would return to Ürümchi from all corners of the country, the sight of them wearing their university emblems pained me terribly. I often thought to myself that of all the children in Ürümchi, I most deserved to go to a university. I should be in Peking or Shanghai or Canton, but I got stuck at the bottom of the Tianshan Mountains and became Second Prize Wang's successor.

I dressed fastidiously and wore cologne like Second Prize Wang, and I enjoyed giving the young girls private lessons. I felt that singing songs in English to those intelligent girls was the most beautiful thing in my life. The biggest difference between me and Second Prize Wang was that I didn't give a damn if people said my morals were suspect. I'll say it out loud for everyone to hear: What I like most is to spend time with intelligent young female students.

Despite being a mere English teacher, I was rather proud of myself in my midtwenties when I'd walk the streets of Ürümchi. I was surrounded by English, and that endowed me with a temperament that most people lacked.

Two years passed quickly, and I was just as lonely as I'd been as a child, still feeling like an outsider. I was obsessive about becoming a gentleman. I polished my shoes compulsively and wore a crisp white shirt every day. I had become nearsighted from reading so many English books. I bought a pair of thick black-framed glasses through whose lenses I ventured to the United States and Europe and to the eighteenth, nineteenth, and twentieth centuries.

One autumn afternoon, after tending to my father's grave, I was walking across the West Bridge when the sight of someone made my heart leap. I sped up. The man also recognized me, and we were both short of breath from excitement.

Second Prize Wang stopped first and smiled at me.

I stood before him, feeling nervous and shy.

He looked me up and down in silence.

I wanted to ask him if he had been released early for good behavior and if he had been held in Maralbishi County just before he was released, but I couldn't utter a word.

Second Prize Wang still wore a well-pressed dark wool suit like the one he had years ago, and his shoes were as shiny as I'd remembered. He had more white hair now, but his face was still closely shaved.

Although his clothes were no longer in style and his shoes were old-fashioned, his eyes were still bright and full of passion.

From the distance, the Tianshan Mountains witnessed our reunion. Wind stirred the leaves in the treetops, and clouds moved across the sky. I could hear the Ürümchi River, which seemed to grow louder as we stood there with our eyes locked.

Second Prize Wang studied what I was wearing and looked at my permed hair for a while. Finally, he broke the silence.

"Have you graduated yet?"

"I didn't get into a university."

He seemed surprised but said nothing.

Tears welled up in my eyes and spilled down my face, but I did not wipe them away.

Every year, melting snow from the Tianshan Mountains runs through forests, gullies, foothills, and meadows, traversing Wulabo Gorge and Yan-er-wo, past my father's grave, then on to Ürümchi and under my feet, carrying a sound like a melody played on that battered old phonograph. I wanted to bawl my heart out. I wanted my wailing to shake Ürümchi and to reach as far as Peking so people there would hear it, too.

Second Prize Wang watched me in silence for a while, then patted me on the shoulder. I saw the same kind and forgiving smile that I remembered.

"I live in the dormitory at the Ergong Agricultural Machinery Plant's School," he said, then walked on.

I turned to watch him go.

He stopped and turned around. "By the way, bring that dictionary back to me."

AFTERWORD

English is based on my experiences growing up during the Cultural Revolution. For someone of my generation from China to recount stories of the Cultural Revolution is as common as someone from Germany recounting stories of World War II. But when *English* was first published, in China, we did not dare describe it as a novel about the Cultural Revolution. Instead, we just said it was about growing up. My fear of talking about what I have written reminds me of my childhood, when I had to study English in secret, as if I were a criminal.

As I drafted an outline for the book, my heart began to fill with cruelty. Violence pervaded my childhood. I watched adults fight—their ability to devise new forms of violence was incredible. They would pour bubbling hot tar onto a person's face or bludgeon someone's stomach with a cudgel while he was sprawled on the ground, begging for mercy. I watched as burly Red Guards killed a female teacher and paraded her body around the school grounds in the same way that as children we would pull sleds over fields of snow. They exposed her drained, slack face to the bright sunlight and finally tossed her body onto a pile of trash next to the toilets, forbidding anyone to collect her corpse. Nowadays, whenever someone waxes nostalgic about the Red Guards, I recall what they looked like when they killed someone.

When I was a child, my family lived next to a pigpen. I could hear the pigs' squeals as they were slaughtered. In those days suicides were common, and when people would hang themselves their tongues would stick out. In supermarkets many years later, I couldn't be sure if I was looking at porcine tongues or human tongues.

When I was in elementary school, struggle meetings were held against our teachers. With the lights turned off, we six-year-olds would rush up to the front of the classroom to kick our teachers in the guts as hard as we could.

Later, when beating people was prohibited, we took to torturing animals. We once threw a cat from the top of a building, but it didn't die. The older children told us cats have nine lives, so we poured stolen gasoline over the cat, lit it, and watched it light up the dark night.

The Russian theater director Vsevolod Meyerhold said that if you couldn't find him in the rehearsal room, look outside to see if anyone was arguing. He liked to observe arguments, he said, because that's when you see someone's character most clearly. Meyerhold was eventually killed, and his wife was stabbed more than forty times. Was Meyerhold's tragic demise the price he paid for loving to watch people fight?

At age twelve I began to play the flute. I eventually learned to play Bach, Tchaikovsky, Borodin, and many others. Even now, when I hear pieces I have played, like Mozart's concertos in C and D major, I am overcome with nostalgia. Yet in my novels and essays I have been embarrassed to refer to the Western composers I am so familiar with. In my twenties I could talk freely about Czeslaw Milosz or Henry Miller but would be too ashamed to mention Mozart, for fear of being ridiculed for taking a minority position. But it was Mozart's music, more than anything else, that captured my sadness.

This is the spirit in which I wrote *English.* I chose not to overstate the cruelty of the era because it has already been recounted ad nauseum. The faces of the perpetrators and of those who suffered have been described with such passion, as if China's tragedy stemmed entirely from good people being too good and bad people being too bad. I find such descriptions revolting. And yet the melancholy lyricism of Mozart cannot fully capture the turbulence of that time.

Seeing the innocence of today's teenagers (who in my time would already have learned to kill), I can't help noticing how jaded and cynical I've become over the years. In thinking back on my childhood while writing *English,* I was drawn more to the moments of tenderness and forgiveness than to the violence and cruelty. I would often pause in my writing not just to wait for new details to come to mind but, more important, to give myself time to imagine whether someone like me, who has few illusions about the world, would find beauty in such moments.

I am grateful to my agent, Joanne Wang; my editor, John Siciliano; and my translators, Martin Merz and Jane Weizhen Pan, for giving my novel new life in English.

—Wang Gang
Beijing
June 2008